GIRL, UNDER OATH

JOHN ELLSWORTH

BOOKS

By John Ellsworth

Michael Gresham Legal Thrillers

The Lawyer
The Defendant's Father
The Law Partners
Carlos the Ant
Sakharov the Bear
Annie's Verdict
Dead Lawyer on Aisle 11
30 Days of Justis
The Fifth Justice
Girl, Under Oath
Lawyers in Gray

For Jon and Adriane and Deb

Vinci Books

vinci-books.com

Published by Vinci Books Ltd in 2025

1

Copyright © John Ellsworth 2021

The author has asserted their moral right to be identified as the author of this work in accordance with the Copyright, Designs and Patents Act 1988. This work is a work of fiction. Names, characters, places and incidents are the product of the author's imagination or are used fictitiously. Any resemblance to actual persons, living or dead, places and incidents is entirely coincidental.

All rights reserved. No part of this publication may be copied, reproduced, distributed, stored in any retrieval system, or transmitted in any form or by any means, including photocopying, recording, or other electronic or mechanical methods, nor used as a source for any form of machine learning including AI datasets, without the prior written permission of the publisher.

The publisher and the author have made every effort to obtain permissions for any third party material used in this book and to comply with copyright law. Any queries in this respect should be brought to the attention of the publisher and any omissions will be corrected in future editions.

A CIP catalogue record for this book is available from the British Library.

Paperback ISBN: 9781036704629

Printed and bound in Great Britain by Clays Ltd, Elcograf S.p.A.

Prologue

I watch the witness raise her hand. I hear the old familiar oath:

Do you solemnly swear the evidence you are about to give is the truth, the whole truth, and nothing but the truth so help you, God?

Do you know why they raise the right hand? Because, long, long ago, they cut the thumbs off liars. So…when you went to court, you raised your right hand to prove you were not a liar. At least, this is what the Jesuits taught me in law school.

My name is Michael Gresham, and I have toiled inside these Chicago courtrooms thirty years and counting. I have seen it all. Drunk judges, stoned lawyers, speeding witnesses, senile bailiffs, sleeping spectators. You name it, I've seen it up close and firsthand. And much more than that.

But the strangest story I've heard from the witness stand is the one you're about to hear from me. The story of a woman accused of poisoning her husband. He had died "under mysterious circumstances." That's what the police say when they haven't a clue what happened. Anyway, Jennifer's Joe died under mysterious circumstances, and then the State of Illinois, in all its power and majesty, indicted Jennifer and put her on trial. Two weeks later, guess what? Guess what the jury did?

Let me back up. I should probably take this from the beginning. Let you form your own judgments. I'll try to tell you about her in such a way I don't force my opinion on you. Because, believe me, I have one.

So look at your own hands. All ten fingers there? Funny thing, me, too.

But here's one thing I know about every last one of the ten thousand witnesses I have heard testify in a court of law.

They all lied.

That, ladies and gentlemen, is one big basketful of thumbs.

Chapter One

JENNIFER

Joe was dying, and he pulled me close.

"One last thing, Jennifer," he whispered to me. His tiny voice scraped and rasped. But it was Joe, nonetheless.

"What's the one last thing?" I asked. Tears formed in my eyes, waiting to let loose only after he had taken his last breath, which would be any second. Joe hated tears, so I was waiting, but it was a struggle, for I loved the man with every cell and fiber in my body. After fifteen years together, I could feel my very flesh tearing loose as he slipped away.

"One last thing. Give her a million dollars of the... insurance money."

My ears alerted. "Give up the insurance money?"

He inhaled a shallow, thready breath. "Pleeeeease," he exhaled.

"Give *who* one-million dollars?" I called into his bad ear. I didn't know anyone who should get one million dollars from Joe's life insurance. I was the sole beneficiary of the insurance policy. Had always been the sole and only beneficiary since we took out the policy when Joe was thirty. Now he was forty-five, and I was to take my two-million dollar fund and give someone—what the—? "Give *who* half?"

"Elise." He spoke. "Elise gets half."

Then he died.

Two weeks later, the detectives showed up at my house, wanting to talk.

Elise was the week after.

Chapter Two

MICHAEL

The first time I saw Jennifer Ipswich was at the Evanston Racket Club. Her blond hair was wet and streaming water as she climbed out of the Olympic pool. Here she came, walking right at me, one finger freeing water from her ear, the noonday sun dancing on her mouth as she made ready to smile. She approached me and stuck out the hand with the ear finger. She smiled. "You're Michael Gresham?"

I said, "I am."

Her smile broadened. "My name is Jennifer, and I guess I need a lawyer. Everyone says you're the one to get. When can I see you?"

"Who's everyone?"

She turned and pointed at a clutch of women at the next cabana, drinking iced tea and talking. "They say so. They know you."

"See a lawyer about what?" I didn't know that my specialty was what she would need.

"Can it wait until we're at your office? Poolside hardly seems the place."

She had me there. In that brief moment, I tried to place the name or the face—*some* thing, since she acted like we had known each other since forever. "Have we ever met?"

"Nope. I'm a doctor, pediatrician. Unless you have a kid between naught and thirteen, we've never met." She dropped her hands and giggled. A knee raised, and she bent forward, amused at herself. TV commercial smile, refrigerator white teeth, maybe the mom who just fed her kids some wonder vitamins. Healthy, fawn-colored skin, faultless in its bath of SPF 40—except for tiny white flecks encircling her face, maybe small scars. Then she was turning and looking for her brood, Henny Penny, the mother hen.

I was dumbstruck.

She was beautiful, obviously intelligent with the MD behind her name, and no indication of anything remiss. Next time, I would learn to look at the shadows, listen for the echo, and feel the emotional fingerprints. But for once, I didn't have a follow-on line to offer: "Please, call my office" or "Drop by Monday" or any of the usual, noncommittal lines that keep people at arm's length. Everything about her said she deserved more than that; she deserved to have me pluck a calendar out of the July sunlight and make her an appointment then and there.

Then I heard myself saying, "How about Tuesday morning, seven o'clock, my office?"

"Seven it is," she said. "Whether I'm done with my rounds or

not, I'll be in your office. And thank you, Michael Gresham."

"And thank you, Doctor—Doctor—"

"Jennifer. Everyone calls me Doctor Jennifer. Jennifer is good because we're friends now. Ta."

She turned back to the pool and dove in, entered

without a splash, and then executed a crawl to the far end where she stood, shook her head, and glanced around as if expecting the world to bend to her. And why wouldn't it? It always had.

I returned to my novel.

Jennifer came to my office and hired me because she had been indicted for the murder of her husband. She was unclear on why she had been charged. She was in great distress over the charges—and who wouldn't have been? This was an entirely different woman than the smiling, confident woman at poolside. So I set about determining whether I was the lawyer she needed. As I poked and prodded into her past, it came out that she was once diagnosed as bipolar.

"Was it an accurate diagnosis?" I asked.

"Okay, here's what it was. I was living with my boyfriend, David, in San Diego. We were both accepted at UCSD medicine. This was a year before I married Joe. Anyway, David Goldman was Jewish, and his mother wanted to know more about me than he ever wanted to know. He was happy with willing flesh, but she wanted more. She wanted pedigrees, bank accounts, religions, Evanston contacts, mutual acquaintances—the stuff that matters, she said. Whatever that meant. Anyway, he had become upset. He said I was cycling."

"Cycling?" I asked her for clarification.

"Hmm...yes. Mood changes cycling. He had supported himself through undergrad as a psych tech, which lent him a certain credibility. 'You're rapid cycling,' he told me one Saturday. He had said it offhandedly while watching the

Cubs and dishing someone's batting average. I was bored with baseball—who isn't?—and started striking his xylophone with my fingernail. The noise pissed him off. He was shooting me dirty looks and trying to watch the game at the same time.

"He grumbled and jumped up and clicked off the game. Off to his bedroom, he stomped. It was something besides baseball, so I followed him in there. I remember nothing more except I wanted to go on a picnic. It didn't have to be a big deal. Just get out in the grass with a tuna fish sandwich and iced tea. But there he was on our bed, his hands behind his head, staring at the ceiling. 'You're cycling,' he said to me again. 'You need to see someone.' So, he made an appointment with a psychiatrist he knew, and I went to see him.

"'Be here fifteen minutes early to do the paperwork,' the receptionist informed me. When I got there, she handed me a clipboard and pen. 'Please fill this out and sign at the X.' I did the usual boxes and a couple of explanations, like a plantar wart for the skin doctor and heart palpitations for the cardiologist. Then I really got into it and started writing on the back of the doctor's intake forms. All of our boyfriend-girlfriend problems came flowing out in black ink. I filled eight pages with observations about my sex life with David. I got pretty lurid, lots of details, even the kinky stuff we did—the cameras and battery-powered stuff. You might think I was testing the doctor. I wasn't. My feelings were all true. Then I turned it in at the desk and sat down. Ten minutes later, I was being ushered into the doctor's office.

"The shrink had read my notes before I even entered his office because no sooner had I seated myself than he said, 'You're bipolar.' It took all I had not to crack up. 'Really?' I said. 'Why do you say that?' He waved my paperwork at me and shook his head. 'Have you read what you wrote?' I told him I certainly had read it. I had reviewed and even initialed it. 'None of what you wrote surprises me or upsets me. I'm not talking about the content. I'm talking about the quantity of what you wrote. Eight pages?'

"He started me on Depakote. It's a common drug for bipolar. Lithium for people with money. I took that religiously for a few months, put on eight pounds, and immediately dropped out."

I asked, "How did that feel?"

She shrugged. "I didn't feel a thing. Which upset David, so he kicked me out. That same day, I found a job as a barista in a drive-through coffee hut. Low-cut peasant blouses, handing out coffee to San Diegans bound for work at defense contractors. It was a kick in the self-confidence-butt to be leered at by sleepy software engineers who hadn't had their first caffeine kick yet. I stayed in San Diego, waiting for medical school to begin, couch surfing for a few days until I found the right place for the next four years. It even came with a stray cat, two blocks from the sand in Ocean Beach."

As a lawyer, it was a lot to take in: the bipolar and Depakote, the sexual athleticism, medical school. Sitting there in my office and looking across the desk at her, there was much more I needed to know about Joe's death, but I knew I was going to have to go slowly with her. I asked her, "So, did the diagnosis take? Have you gone back on the Depakote?"

Her face exploded in a wide grin, and she exclaimed, "Of course not! I haven't taken it, and I haven't experienced rapid cycling, as my old boyfriend put it. I've been very stable. I graduated from medical school, endured four years of pediatric residency, produced two children for my husband, Joe, every day managed 200 out-of-control patients between 0 and 13, invested in mutual funds and lakefront condos, and have kept order at home. Nobody has been more stable than me."

"Got it."

It sounded stable. I knew I couldn't have pulled off all that.

Of course, who was I to judge? I was the lawyer who accepted her at face value.

So, I jumped in and took her case and her money. As she was writing a check for the retainer, she said, almost offhandedly, "There's one other thing I'll need your help with, too."

"What's that?"

"My husband, Joe, evidently had a woman in Paris. She wants money."

"Of course."

"So, will you take it on when she sues me?"

"I don't know about that. I don't do much domestic work."

"It shouldn't be that complicated. I'm the real wife. She's in Paris, France. Please say yes."

"I'll look into it. We can talk later, let's say if she brings legal proceedings or hires a lawyer."

She ripped the check from her checkbook. "Fair enough."

Chapter Three

JENNIFER

My name is Jennifer Ipswich. I'm five-seven, blond by secret sauce, slightly overweight, slight overbite that Invisaligns are curing even now at thirty-something-but-not-forty, and a big day for me anymore is a new Crockpot. We have two kids: Abel, who's nine and thinks Legos are much more than demons to be stepped upon in bare feet in the dark, and Sarah, who at eleven is already several grades ahead of me.

Joe and I had our medical practice, *Ipswich and Ipswich, Physicians and Surgeons*. I'm the first-named because, even though I'm younger than Joe, I got out of med school ahead of him because he served in the Gulf War, and I did not. I stayed in med school while our class went on without him. All the police and DAs and lawyers want to know how Joe and I first met.

Here's the condensed version. Many years ago, I walked into the Paris Ritz bar to find Vincent D'Orion, emeritus bartender, polishing the stemware in preparation for the evening crowd. At that time, I was spending a year in

France, zooming around on my Vespa, searching for my future.

We spent a long, slow June afternoon, lo those many years ago, commiserating over wine coolers—him on the business side of the bar and me on the other, when—I don't know, around four o'clock —the place was suddenly overrun with seventy-year-olds who'd just debussed in the hotel's no-parking zone and were streaming into the bar looking to get out of the heat and ease the parch.

Without a word, Vincent tossed me an apron that said RITZ above the pocket; he indicated I should pitch in. Imagine me, a sort-of-into-college student sitting out her sophomore year, serving drinks to folks old enough to be my grandparents but filled with the same wanderlust that had kept me twisting the throttle on my scooter.

I hopped tables the rest of the night. Next day, I returned, waitressed again, and the next, loving every minute of that exciting, wonderful old haunt that once accommodated Ernest Hemingway and Charlie Chaplin.

That first night around ten, I'm guessing it was, I was still serving and getting just a little ready for a cigarette break when a soldier wearing desert fatigues suddenly reached and touched my elbow as I was taking drink orders one table away. "Miss, can I ask you a question?"

I tilted my head at him.

"What's your name?" he asked all innocence, like a tourist asking directions to the Louvre.

"My name is Jennifer. And you're with the woman who just went to the powder room."

"I'm with Natalie? Nope, just a friend. Why don't you put your number on my tab and let me double it with your tip?"

I couldn't keep from smiling. "Nice try, soldier."

"Joe. Just Joe. I was sent here by the US Army to meet you and sweep you off your feet. We've just got to meet and talk. What time do you get off?"

"No, thanks. I'm not looking, and you're not my type even if I were. I don't like guns, and I don't like soldiers."

"I don't do guns. I'm a medical assistant. No guns, only STDs."

"So long, Joe. I've got customers waiting."

"Remember tab, telephone number. I'll only call once, and you can hang up, or we can talk and go from there. It's fate."

"It's not fate, Joe. It's a bar, and you're lonely."

An hour later, he signaled they were leaving, and he needed his tab to settle up. Helplessly—yes, helplessly—I watched as my hand scrawled my name and number at the bottom of his bar tab. Maybe, like Joe, I was lonely, too. Perhaps he looked a little like Bruce Willis in that year's *Pulp Fiction*. It turns out I had a low-level crush on Bruce, and Joe could've been his double.

Later that night, he called after I got off work. I was bone-tired, alone in my hotel room, listening to an all-night FM station broadcasting Lena Horne.

Joe sounded bright and sober, not unlike a friendly travel agent. "So, listen, Jennifer, we need to meet. Are you busy right now?"

"I'm exhausted and climbing into bed as we speak. Make it snappy, Joe."

"Natalie's an army asset. She's a civilian code-breaker, an expert in Arabic. She wanted to see the Ritz, so I brought her by. No boyfriend-girlfriend stuff. Purely friends. We need to meet, you and I."

"Where is she now?"

"In her room. On her own dime. At least I think she is.

She might also be out for a night on the town, for all I know."

"Why the heavy pursuit, Joe?"

"I've dreamed your face before. I think we knew each other before."

"Right. Okay, nightie-night, Joe. Thanks for calling."

"All right. You remind me of pictures of my mother at your age."

"That's sick. I don't date men who think I'm their mother. Your turn."

"All right. You're gorgeous, and I'm lonely. I have to get back to Kuwait in two days, and I wanted to meet someone for a roll in the hay. So, hang up on me and tell me to go screw myself."

"Joe, you're cute, very Bruce Willis-y, but I'm not like that. Not interested."

"You working tomorrow?"

"Yes."

"Can we have a drink on your break?"

"You don't quit, do you?"

"Not with you. What about it? One drink?"

"Who's paying?"

So, there we were. Sure enough, the next night, we did have that drink and several more drinks after I got off work at the Ritz.

I also violated one of my own rules. It turned out I *was* that kind of girl, especially once I got to know him and fell in love on the third drink.

All right, then, this was the same story I told to my lawyer, Michael Gresham, to the first detective who paid me a call, to the district attorney, and the jail psychiatrist.

I doubted if so much as a word of it changed, person to person.

Chapter Four

MICHAEL

Jennifer was horrified she was going to be convicted of murder for Joe's death. Of course, she was horrified; I would've been, too. I never understood how my clients get through it. So, she called me on the phone and told me she was between patients and needed to talk. It was always like that. They needed to hear my voice. It was all right; that's what they paid me for, to be there for them when they couldn't be there for themselves.

"Am I free to talk openly with you?" she asked me.

"Of course," I told her. "As your attorney, please tell me everything. What's up?"

"Well, it turns out that Joe had taken on another family in Paris."

"Another family? Who is she?" I asked.

"As he was dying, he told me to give half of the insurance money to somebody named Elise. I've been going back through his records and snooping around his things. It has begun to dawn on me how blind I was. I should've seen right through him."

"And if you had seen right through him, what would you have seen?"

"Joe had another wife. I guess you could call her a wife. He had married this woman in Paris and been shacked up with her for I don't know how long. This is the woman he was talking about when he was dying. I'm waiting every day for her to come calling. I know she's going to want part of what Joe owned, and it's going to be a mess. I go to work every day with my heart in my throat, filled with worry. I don't know what I'm going to tell my staff when she comes calling. I don't even know what I need to tell her when she does. Do I just avoid her altogether and refuse to talk to her, Michael?"

"I don't think I'd do that. I think I would talk to her and find out what she has on her mind. Maybe it's something as simple as the insurance money. Maybe, given a little time and distance from your anger at Joe for this, you'll feel like sharing with her. For me, I always encourage my clients to buy their way out of situations if possible. Over the long run, it's always much, much cheaper than getting involved in lawsuits. Lawsuits tend to drain bank accounts, and, in the end, only the lawyers are better off. So yes, I would encourage you to talk to her and see what she has on her mind."

"I hate her already. I want nothing but bad things for her. Anybody who would sneak around with another woman's husband deserves nothing but bad. And even worse, what if he has children with her? That's possible, you know. Joseph always wanted to have children around. I think it made him feel virile or something. I don't know what I would do if it turns out he has a child in Paris. I would die. Or someone else would die."

"Please, let's not get into talking about others dying.

That makes me very uncomfortable when my clients say stuff like that. I should advise you up-front that lawyers must come forward and tell the police and the court when a client is getting ready to commit a crime. Especially a crime of violence. So when you tell me that someone deserves to die, it scares the living crap out of me. My first thought is always to ask whether or not you're serious and whether or not I need to take steps."

"I don't know that I'm serious. But I *am* very angry. Joe has hurt me beyond repair. I'm going to do everything I can not to run him down in front of our kids. But inside, I'm going to be hating him for this mess he left me with."

"Well, let's leave it at this, that you're going to talk to her and hear her out. At that point, you and I will talk, and we'll come up with a plan. That's always best. Is there anything else you need to share with me?"

"Not really, and, no, I don't really want to see somebody dead. But if it happened, I wouldn't lose any sleep over it."

We hung up then, ending our conversation.

When I looked back through my file, I realized I didn't make any notes of the conversation, which was too damn bad, given what was coming down the track. I always made notes in an attempt to protect myself.

But this time, I violated my own rule and didn't paper the hell out of her file.

My mistake.

Chapter Five

JENNIFER

Elise Ipswich came to my medical office, just like I had told Michael she would. I was on break from seeing patients—it was stomach flu day for the little ones. There I sat, hidden behind the pile of paperwork on my desk and inhaling an apple. The receptionist buzzed and told me Elise Ipswich had appeared without an appointment. She was insisting upon seeing me without delay. She was, said Misty, the receptionist, "Dressed to the nines. Also, she says she's come from Paris, France, Doctor Ipswich."

I told Misty, "Stall her five minutes." My fingers flew on my keyboard. I pulled up Joe's Visa card statement year-to-date. I sorted by Paris. My gaze raced down the Visa card statements for the last six months of his life. One thing became clear quite fast: the Ritz was his favorite eatery. My mind was flying now. Aha! Every last one of the damned charges on his Visa was for two meals. Never just one. Elise was more real than real. And you know what the worst part was? He hadn't made any attempt to cover up his binary dinners. Always two diners, never just Joe. The charges didn't come right out and name her, but they didn't have to. I knew my Joe, and his Elise knew me as well. He never could eat alone. Or sleep alone. Or watch TV alone. The woman out there in my waiting room had made it a double. And now she had come to collect on his bar tab.

My part of the medical practice was pediatrics. Joe's was infectious diseases, and he spent quite a bit of time overseas with a focus on French-American medicine. For years, Joe had spent two weeks each month in Paris at his foreign practice. The French patients loved him. I couldn't ever go because the kids needed me home and, besides, I hated jet lag, I didn't do well with abrupt changes, and Joe thrived on the ten or eleven hours of uninterrupted work time he got flying from Chicago to Paris and home two weeks later.

I buzzed my receptionist. "Show Elise in."

I steeled myself and wished I were six inches taller in my chair.

She swept grandly into my office and settled, without being asked, into a patient chair, folding her hands on her knees and meeting my gaze. Two silver combs held her hair back in waves from her face, her neck was Audrey Hepburn, and her smile was all Michelangelo. It was too much. My gaze dropped to her ring finger. Sure enough, engagement and wedding rings purchased at Les Beaux Diamants de Charvel, one block north of the Ritz on Place Vendôme. I would know that princess cut anywhere because it was the exact same set as mine.

It was then I knew.

We had lost *our* husband.

"I'm here for my one-half," Elise said coolly in a thick French accent, placing her hand on the surface of my desk as if staking a claim.

"Your half? Excuse me?"

"Our husband. He said you would gladly give me one-half when you learned about our daughter and her medical needs."

My heart froze in my chest. What was this? Daughter? As in *Joe's* daughter? With medical needs yet?

"I don't know what you're talking about, Miss. Joe and I have been married since my early twenties. He wasn't married before me, and I know we were never divorced."

"No, but he was married under French law—*Miss*. To me." She held out her hand as if to shake. "I'm Elise."

I took her hand and shook it. Anything else wouldn't be like me. I was happy, gregarious, outgoing, and a people person. I extended my hand to shake even though I knew it was all downhill from there.

I plunged ahead. "Well, he might have been married to you under French law, though I doubt it was legal, but his U.S. assets belong to me. If you're here for money, you'll leave an unhappy widow. I know American and Illinois law and none of it consists of exceptions for victims of a bigamist." When I said the words, I realized, with a start, that my feelings toward Joe had shifted tectonically. I was actually starting to dislike him intensely. Bastard, leaving me with this mess to clean up!

"Our daughter needs daily injections, a medication that runs one-thousand euros a week. Joe always laid in a good supply whenever he was home. But we've about run out, a month after his death."

"That sounds terrible. Do you work?"

"LVP Partners. Associate level. Very low pay. Not enough to live on and take care of Çidde."

"Is there more?"

"My husband supported us mostly. Of course, I have my work at LVP Partners."

"You mean Joe supported you?"

"That's exactly what I mean. Joe—my husband."

I cringed as the building began burning down around me. While Joe and I were technically medical partners, we kept our medical practices separate. We were two LLCs practicing in partnership in name only. We had done it to get a huge break on our medical malpractice insurance, and it stayed that way throughout our time in the same office. Why was this particularly relevant just then? Because, as separate entities, we also kept our own books, our own accounting systems in place.

The bottom line was I knew no more about Joe's finances than he knew about mine. True, we each contributed ten-thousand a month to our joint bank account for household needs, but beyond that, we never actually knew each other's bottom line. Could Joe have been supporting a second family without my knowledge? Hell, he could've been supporting a half-dozen families, and I would never have suspected. It just wasn't my business to know. Nor did he know—or need to know—how much money I sent out to orphans in Latin America, diasporic polar bears, or blue whales threatened with extinction by Japanese sailors. Go *Sea Shepherd!* I had my things. Evidently, Joe did, too.

Nevertheless, I was stunned by what I heard despite our economic sovereignty. Joe didn't have orphans, polar bears, and whales; no, Joe had a second wife and a third child. A wife who was sharpening her knives as she surveyed my office out the corner of her eye, taking in my Louis XIV pieces, Chinese rugs, and Qing vase that had been used as a milk bottle in someone's kitchen. My buyer brought it to me for $2.3 million. Where did I get that kind of money for a Qing vase? Joe's insurance money. That's right, I spent every last dime of the insurance money—and then some—on the Qing vase. A ridiculous purchase, but it completed my financial bucket list.

Elise's eyes rolled back in her head as she recognized my treasures for what they were: *Ka-ching!* The worst had happened. Joe had not only taken up with another woman and married her under the laws of a foreign nation, but the woman was also a connoisseur of expensive and rare art. It was all she could do to tear her gaze from my Qing vase and re-establish a more or less vacuous manner of eye contact with me.

"Well," I sniffed, "Joe didn't support me. I worked our entire time together, contributing my fair share. I felt I owed him that."

"Exactly! Which was our plan, too, until Çidde's problems developed. My degree is in finance, Mrs. Ipswich. My Ph.D. is from the London School of Economics. It's all I can do to scare up enough time to write scholarly papers at work. It must be wonderful to be the mother of such healthy children as yours."

"Fate has certainly blessed our marriage," I tossed off, referencing Joe's love of fate, which I had begun to detest—both him and his fate mojo. It had been so charming in our youth but now seemed a gas bubble from Joe's ass. Damn him to hell! What else had he left me with but a Ph.D. in economics who possessed a practiced eye for Qing Dynasty pieces and a troubling tale of motherhood guaranteed to give even the most hardened Chicago jury pause?

Suddenly I realized she loved our husband much more than I. It was time to end our visit.

"Elise, I don't know why you've come here today, perhaps to introduce yourself to me and clear some air you believed needed clearing. Whatever your purpose, I have patients to see and obligations to fulfill, so I'm afraid we'll need to break this off now. I wish you all the best and my prayers for your Çidde, but I really must return to my calendar."

A hasty smile returned and then faded. "Of course. My lawyers will be in touch, Mrs. Ipswich. Please keep my husband's things intact, including his tangibles and intangible assets like stocks, bonds, and funds. I'll be seeking a full accounting as well as one-half of all life insurance proceeds."

"Life insurance?" I said it with the sound of one swallowing walnut shells.

"Certainly. We surviving spouses will recognize codicils to Joe's will and beneficiary amendments to his insurance policies, won't we? Just to keep peace at home?"

"You have a codicil to his will?"

"Of course. Joe remembered everything, just like the dutiful husband he was."

"You have beneficiary amendments?"

"Of course. New York Life, Hamilton Life, Fidelity, J.M. Watt, Inc. I have it all in my safe in Paris. Oh, and I want that Qing vase."

My breath snapped in my throat. I stood and spread my arms as if taking a bullet for the president. "Impossible! That is my personal asset, not Joe's!"

She smiled and brushed her hand at me, waving me off. "Well, we'll be in touch. Give my best to my children-in-law."

"What?"

"Or something like that. Joe talked so much about his American children that I feel a special kinship to them. They might as well be part my own. In fact—"

"Really, I have to get back to my work. Can you find your way out?"

"I'm on my way," she said in the dearest tone. "And I do hope we can make all the transfers and sell-offs happen without worry. I know your home will literally fly off the market. So, there's a start."

"My home?" I managed to say, more walnuts going down. "I'm not selling my home!"

"Oh, when you see the quitclaim deed where Joe gave me his one-half, I'm sure you'll reconsider. You certainly wouldn't want me and Çidde moving into the top level, now, am I right?"

"Goodbye, Miss—Miss—"

"That's all right. It'll come to you eventually, from one Mrs. Ipswich to another. Good day."

Then she was gone. I hurried into my bathroom and stuck two fingers down my throat. The bile was quick to dislodge. This was when I noticed: those same two fingers were shaking uncontrollably, as were my hand, arm, and upper body.

Joe's ashes inhabited my Qing vase. But he wouldn't remain there for long. I couldn't wait to dump him into the toilet and introduce him to the City of Chicago sewer system.

And as to my Qing vase. No one could have that but me. I'd die before I gave it up. There's only one other in the world. The man who sold me this one owned the other. But he wouldn't part with the last one.

He felt like I did.

Chapter Six

MICHAEL

Two days later, I was outside the Cook County Courthouse, slogging along with the crowd, trying to keep up with the crush headed for the courthouse that morning. I was to appear as the guardian ad litem for a little boy whose divorcing parents couldn't share. Just as I was entering the building, I heard my voice called from behind. "Hey, Michael Gresham!"

I turned to look. There was the waving hand, the hand of Marcel Rainsford, my investigator. I stopped and waited for him to catch up even though my case was scheduled to begin in four minutes. It was 8:56 AM, summertime in Illinois, I was half soaked in sweat, and I was feeling miserable. The day was only just getting started, and here was Marcel flagging me down, which meant something important was afoot.

"Meet you in the lobby!" I called to him and turned to resume making my way toward the entrance and the air-conditioning awaiting inside.

My back was hurting because I was old, and that's what

backs did when you were old. They hurt. But I tried not to show it. I tried to keep an upright posture, bright and strong, because a trial lawyer must be attractive to juries and appear young, bright-eyed, and hungry if they are to be liked and pass muster.

It was a hurrying bunch all around me, springing ahead on young legs and ready to engage with anyone who stood in the way of them getting the justice they were entitled to that morning. I knew the feeling; I had been there and had been that voracious at one time myself. But not anymore. I was no longer hungry, and that's when trial lawyers should bow out gracefully.

Anyway, I was lugging my briefcase full of law books that I had packed in and out of these courthouses for thirty years. The case was banging against my bum knee and making me wish I was back home in bed, enjoying a second cup of coffee and the sports page.

Then I was inside the courthouse and making my way through security with their conveyor belt and their magic wand. Off came my belt, my shoes, and my watch while coins went into the plastic tray to be X-rayed. When they were satisfied, at last, that my name wasn't Hamid or Hussein, they allowed me passage into the courthouse.

I went to the far wall, leaned up against it, and flattened myself. I checked my watch and searched the crowd for Marcel. He should be coming through at any moment.

He snuck up from the side. "Your friend, Jennifer Ipswich, she's holding on the phone."

"Why so?" I asked. "Isn't one calamity a day enough?" I was referring to the child custody case at which I was to serve as guardian ad litem. The parents wished to own the child, to make sure the other never got to see their offspring again, and they had both been courting me for weeks with invitations to lunch "to see if there's any common ground" or to investigate "whether it's worth pursuing" this or that angle. Whatever. It meant they would wine me and dine me and hope that I would return home, sated, my opinion of them notched up a peg or two, their chances of making off with Robbie upsized.

"Here, I've got her on the line." He handed me his cell phone.

"Jennifer? Michael Gresham speaking. How can I help?"

"Michael, thank God, I reached you. Here's what happened."

"All right. I've got three minutes."

"More than enough."

"Please go on."

"The police called me. The detectives want to take my official statement. I'm afraid to talk to them, and I refused to make an appointment until I talk to you first. I know you will want to be there. I told them I didn't even know if you'd let me make an appointment. Would it be best if I talk to them and try to explain that I knew nothing about Joe's wife in Paris and that I had no motive to murder him? Or should I refuse to speak and just assume the worst?"

"I never allow my clients to speak to the police. I'm so glad you called me. If they call you again, give them my phone number and tell them I am your attorney. They have absolutely no right to contact you again at that point."

"Oh, thank God. That makes me feel so much better. It's not like I have anything to hide. I didn't know about Joe's extra wife until he was dying. It's not like I poisoned him beforehand because I had known beforehand. Nothing like that. So they're really barking up the wrong tree. I'm as innocent as the new-fallen snow. I hope we can get that across to them somehow and you can make them go away and leave me alone. Will that be possible, Michael?"

"I'll do everything I can to make it go away. I can't promise anything, but sometimes the detectives can be reasoned with, especially where there isn't a strong case. I don't believe they have a strong case against you unless they find some kind of poison in your medicine cabinet, which I assume they are not going to find. Am I correct?"

"You are absolutely correct. I would never be stupid enough to keep some kind of poison around my house."

"Is there anything else you're not telling me?"

"Not telling you? Not telling you like what? Like I killed Joe? Do you think that I did?"

"Jennifer, I don't have opinions one way or the other, and it doesn't matter what I think. My job is to defend you, regardless of what happened. And that's exactly what I'm going to do."

"Well, you're going to be defending an innocent person. I can assure you I had nothing to do with Joe's death. Now that I know he was married to another woman, I'm not sure I wouldn't have poisoned him if I had it to do over again. But that's not the case. I didn't find out about her until the moment when he was dying. I hope you can believe me about that."

"It doesn't matter whether I believe you or not. What matters is whether the police believe you. Beyond that, it also might matter whether or not a jury believes you. But I just need you to trust that I'm in your court, either way."

"I trust you, Michael. I know you're going to get me out of this. I'll let you go now, and I'll tell the police 'no way' if they call again."

"All right. Have them contact me if they feel a further need to talk."

"All right, Michael, bye for now."

It was now 9:01. I was late to be the guardian ad litem for the little boy whose parents wanted to cut him in half. I was beginning to see how Joseph Ipswich might've felt, a wife in Chicago and a wife in Paris.

I wondered, had anyone cut him in half?

Chapter Seven

JENNIFER

Well, the same day I flushed Joe's ashes, the police came and arrested me. One detective said my refusal to give a statement made me look bad. But I had Michael waiting in the wings because I had expected them to come for me. They had their reasons.

Michael said we would take them to court, but that didn't help me today where my world was inhabited with zombie women in the jail's common room, watching TV, rubbing against each other, and ganging up by color swatches—skin color, I mean.

I hate it here. I also hated Joe for dying and leaving me in this mess. There was no one else to blame for his death, so they chose me, and here I was. What they had on me was motive, Michael told me. Motive to kill Joe because of Elise.

My first week of jail. Michael Gresham filed motions for me to be released on bail, and the motions should have been allowed but weren't. The judge didn't allow me to get out on bail because he felt I had money planted overseas that I was going to run to so that I wouldn't have to stand trial. Which was ridiculous, given that I have two children, Abel and Sarah, nine and eleven, who I love more than anything in the world and who I wouldn't uproot from their lives just to run off to Switzerland and hide.

Abel had special needs; he was learning challenged. As a pediatrician, I knew how important it was for him to have continuity in his learning environment and his life. He attended the Chicago Northside School, and he loved it there. Especially, he loved sports and playing his trumpet in the band. To me, these connections he had meant everything. I tried to make Judge Stormont understand how Abel's needs and school anchored me to Chicago. But nothing I said seemed to make any difference. Judge Stormont was going to keep me in jail regardless.

I also told him about Sarah, my eleven-year-old, who was having a terrible time adjusting to her father's death and clinging to my parents and me in Schaumburg. While she went through all of this, I wouldn't uproot her either.

Any pediatrician in my shoes would immediately know that removing either of these children from their customary environment would be irremediably damaging. It just wasn't going to happen.

But Judge Stormont was adamant. No matter how hard I tried to make him understand my ties to Chicago, it seemed like he only wanted to listen to the State's Attorney. It was the first time in my life I'd been ignored in a professional setting. On appeal—if there was one—I hoped they understood that, as a doctor, I wasn't accustomed to being disbelieved by people, including some judge sitting in some courtroom like a blackbird on a wire.

My sister Janet moved the kids in with her while I was away. It was only for another couple of weeks, Michael said.

The Cook County Jail was located in South Lawndale in Chicago, and it was operated by the Sheriff of Cook County, according to the one-sheet we were all given when we were processed in. It happened to be the third largest jail system in the United States and was located at 2700 S. California Ave, Chicago. And yada yada yada. No matter, it sucked.

I was single-celled because my so-called crime involved violence, which was extremely upsetting given that I had never committed a single violent act in my entire life. Even when I was little and going through that phase that all children go through where they are mean to animals and stuffed toys, my touch of the terrible threes was moderated even then by my ability to see myself from an outside point of view and control my actions. Having not been a violent child then, when most children go through such a year of aggression, I hadn't committed a violent act against any person, animal, place, or thing in my less-than forty years.

I was struggling. My cell was hardly big enough to turn around in. It was only six feet wide, two steps for me wall-to-wall since I was five-foot-seven and my steps were probably larger than the normal woman's steps. It was also four steps deep, which I guessed made it about six-by-twelve altogether. There was a single bunk with a one-inch mattress, no pillow, and a wool blanket for protection against the all-night noise, the screaming and crying out, which was silenced only by pulling the blanket up over my head and holding it there until I slept. There was also a commode without a toilet ring. There was only enough toilet paper at any given time for one good bowel movement. Also, there was a sink with one faucet, cold, and no soap. It was like they thought we might try to commit suicide with soap.

They allowed me to keep my courtroom dress in my cell, including my gold cross and the gold ring Michael Gresham provided. I didn't believe in anything the gold cross represented since I was a scientist and way down the road on medieval beliefs. As for the gold ring, Joe would have never had me wearing a plain gold band. My real engagement ring, two carats, and my wedding band, both platinum, were held with my other personal belongings that I wore to the jail on the day I was arrested. I didn't know if I'd ever see those things again, but Michael wanted me to wear a plain gold band anyway, his preference.

What did I do with my time each day? I was allowed to have a legal pad and one ballpoint pen. Truth be told, as a physician, I would find it much easier to commit suicide with the ballpoint pen than soap from my sink, but again, I wasn't in charge of such things. At any rate, I spent my days writing, like I was right now. Michael wanted me to keep these notes so that he had a recorded history of my thoughts and feelings to rely on should he need to tell the appellate court personal things about me in the event of an appeal. Also, he wanted me to write down those areas of testimony in court that I considered to be wrong, lies, or presented in error.

"I'm horrified the jury won't understand just how much I loved Joe," I told Dr. Roach.

Sylvie Roach, M.D., was the jail psychiatrist. I would see her every day during my trial. She was easy to talk to, fifty-ish, with silver hair and turquoise eyes and a manner of listening that immediately put you at ease since there was no judgment in her whatsoever. She was wiry but short, maybe five-foot-one, and wore her hair in a bun most of the time.

She carried a black satchel like most doctors, but hers was filled with medical charts and legal pads like the one the jail gave me. In my cell, she sat on my bunk at one end, me at the other. Then she pulled out her pad, dated the next clean page, wrote my name (I can read it upside-down), and started writing.

That second day of trial, I complained that I felt like we were losing the jury. They were buying into what the State's witnesses were saying about me. It took everything I had not to stand up and shout to them that I didn't kill Joe, no matter how those witnesses were trying to make it appear.

Dr. Roach made a note in her dainty hand on the yellow patient sheet that would find refuge in my permanent file. She asked me, "What can you do or say to help them understand the depth of your love for your husband?"

"That's easy," I said. "I loved him more than life."

"Did you get to say that in court today?"

"Not a word of it."

It had been a long, terrible day, listening to chemists and crime lab people. "They talked about chemicals in court. Poison I might have given Joe. It was horrible."

"Are you going to testify?" Dr. Roach asked me.

"No."

"So the jury won't find out you majored in chemistry in college because you wanted to be a doctor?"

"Michael Gresham says they're going to find that out anyway. They have all my school records. They're going to call the records custodian of UCSD."

"And present your college transcripts so the jury finds out?"

"Finds out what?"

"Finds out you know more about drugs than the great Louis Pasteur?"

I ran my tongue across my lips and felt that damned sore bump under the skin. If I wasn't mistaken, it felt like a herpes sore was about to make its semiannual appearance. *Great, and right in the middle of my damned trial. The only people who catch herpes are the people with loose morals. Isn't that what everyone thinks?*

Does that make me a killer?

Chapter Eight

MICHAEL

At the trial, I was to defend Jennifer on charges she murdered Joe with poison. The toxicologist had found trace chemicals in Joe and believed those trace chemicals were left from poison. I felt it was a feeble case and thought the prosecution was, in part, inspired by Jennifer and Joseph Ipswich's considerable contributions to the political party on the other side of the fence as the State's Attorney. At least, Jennifer led me to believe that's what was happening.

How did I view the case? Even from the beginning, I was uncomfortable. I hadn't done my due diligence—and I hurry to add that wasn't all my fault. So why didn't I fully perform with the due diligence?

For one, as a medical doctor, Jennifer assured me there was nothing to be gained by raising any defenses based on her mental condition. She convinced me there were no cognitive deficits despite her last go-around with some psychiatric counseling.

But deep down, I wasn't altogether convinced.

As the trial date neared, I began to ask myself, had I failed her? Would a more skilled practitioner have gone into court and claimed mental impairment? Should I have at least insisted on testing? I usually would without questions, but she was a physician, so I had listened to her.

Here's reason number two why I didn't have her examined by a psychiatrist. She convinced me that if mental issues became public, it would ruin her medical practice and leave her no way of supporting herself and her children.

"Don't bother me with that," she said dismissively with a wave of her hand when I mentioned it the first time. "Absolutely not, I need my job."

So, as I rode the courthouse elevator up to the fifth floor on the second day, I was apprehensive. I was kicking myself, and that's no way to defend a case.

The elevator doors split open, and I was swept into the crowd headed for courtroom 506.

As I proceeded inside and took my seat at counsel table, I looked around, waiting for the jailers to bring Jennifer into the courtroom. She would be wearing the little black dress I brought from her walk-in closet. Around her neck would be seen the gold necklace with the relatively large cross that I purchased for her. Also the wedding band, big as a spoon handle, around her finger—which I also purchased for her. Back in jail, she got to wear none of those things. But when she came to court, the jailers were required to dress her as I dictated.

Then she arrived in a waist chain and handcuffs, doing the jailhouse two-step because of the manacled feet—wearing heels yet. No smile—which was a change for the lady who ordinarily caused the sun to rise with her smile.

The matron walked her up to counsel table. She

unlocked her manacles and unclasped the chain. Ankles freed, Jennifer passively sat down beside me, and I caught the odor of stale sweat. Showers were weekly in the Chicago jail system, and the scent signaled to me she hadn't been allowed to bathe for a while now. I would need to take that up with her jailers after court. I scribbled on the yellow notepad on the table before me. *Shower??*

She read it and sat back. "Not in eight days. Sorry."

The prosecutor opened the case by pointing his finger at Jennifer and claiming she had poisoned her husband. He had it all figured out: Jennifer was a doctor with access to all kinds of medicines, including poisonous ones. She was also a chemistry major in college, so she knew all about chemicals, including poisons.

And he knocked it out of the park.

I gave my opening statement and stumbled around, unable to find the ball because there was none. They had no case against Jennifer except inference, and inference is hard to deny because it's mental, not evidentiary. And so I struggled. I knew it. I could see how the jury looked at me with distaste, maybe even disgust.

Then it was time for witnesses.

First up, the State of Illinois—the "People"—put Runyon Abernathy, Ph.D., on the witness stand to prove some poisons disappear in the human body. Why was that important? Because Jennifer was accused of poisoning Joe. That's right, the government witness gave testimony trying to convince the jury that Jennifer murdered Joe, her husband of fifteen years, with potassium chloride. It was a chemical deadly to humans that's assimilated by the body and ends up dissipating into the normal chemistry of the body, making it all but impossible to identify as a death-dealing substance. He said all of these things elaborately, like he had written the periodic table himself.

I stood up from counsel table and approached the lectern to begin my cross-examination.

"Doctor Abernathy, you told the jury that autopsies had reached a point in the modern world where poisons are generally detectable, correct?"

He stretched and worked his jaw before answering, "Correct."

"And you've carefully schooled the jury how the best poisons are ones that break down into elements that occur naturally—poisons such as succinylcholine and potassium chloride. You told them that succinylcholine causes asphyxiation and paralysis, an excruciating death. You even acted out what the dying victim looks like by sticking out your tongue and pretending to gag. Do you remember doing that?"

"Uh, yes. Correct."

"Now, potassium chloride causes severe heart arrhythmias. You told them that and then clutched your chest and kicked your legs out. Remember that?"

"Uh, yes. Correct."

"Most notably, you testified how these chemicals break down into elements natural in the body and would easily be overlooked at autopsy: succinic acid and choline for succinylcholine, potassium and chloride, of course, for potassium chloride, which is common in heart attack victims due to muscle damage. However, both need to be injected, you said, and leave an injection site. You said injection sites are, as you put it, 'pesky.' Remember that?"

"Correct. The examiner easily visualizes injection sites."

"Were there injection sites on Joe?"

"They couldn't find any."

"So your answer is No?"

"Like I said, they couldn't find any."

"Which is a negative, correct?"

"I guess—correct, it's a negative."

"So, we have that settled. No injection sites means no succinylcholine and no potassium chloride, correct?"

"Correct."

"And you talked about aconite. Recall that?"

"Yes. But there was no gas chromatography. He was cremated, so no chance to study for this poison."

"So there was no aconite used to poison Joe?"

"I don't know that."

"Sir, you don't know there was, correct?"

"Correct."

"Which means there wasn't as far as this case is concerned, correct?"

"I guess."

"Correct?"

"Correct."

"I have to say, Doctor Abernathy, you were good, damned good. A little theatrical, but our jury here in Chicago is mostly housewives and men on Social Security. You probably thought a little drama was what they were here for, correct?"

"I don't recall having that exact thought, no."

"Well, a little playacting helps make your points come alive, as it were, correct?"

"I don't mind demonstrating— "

"Yes or no, doctor. This is cross-examination, and I asked you a yes or no. Let me repeat it. A little playacting brings your points to life, correct?"

"Correct."

"When you were finished, had you told the jury everything about untraceable poisons?"

"I believe so."

"So, there's no evidence in existence that Jennifer Ipswich poisoned her husband, as far as you know?"

"I don't—I don't—as far as I know, yes. But there might have been."

"Well, sir, we don't convict people on what might have been, do we?"

"No."

"Gentlemen," said the judge. "It's noon, and we're going to break here. We stand in recess until one-thirty."

The court went on break, which I, as the defense attorney, didn't find helpful because it meant all this testimony could evaporate before I pounded it home. At one-thirty when we re-convened, I was anxious when I stood to continue to cross-examine.

"Doctor Abernathy," I said, slowly drawing out his name as if the name itself were suspect, "you came here today sworn to testify to the truth of things, isn't that correct?"

"Why, yes, I mean—"

"I asked, yes or no. No need to explain. You'll get that chance when your lawyer gets to undo any damage I might do. Fair enough?"

"Yes."

"Let's take a moment and tell the jury some truth about my client, Dr. Jennifer Ipswich. In truth, there was an autopsy, correct?"

"Correct, but—"

"Ah, ah, ah, yes or no, remember?"

"Yes."

"There was an autopsy, and it showed no abnormalities, correct?"

"Correct."

"All right, then. So, you coming in here and rattling off a bunch of chemicals that can poison someone and not leave a trace... That has nothing to do with an autopsy that finds no trace of any of the things you've mentioned, isn't that true? Isn't it true your chemistry set is irrelevant?"

"No, not if—"

"Ah, ah, yes or no?"

"No."

"You want the jury to believe the crime lab probably missed something?"

"Yes."

"So, at your request, Joe's body was exhumed?"

"No."

"Tell the jury why not."

"He was cremated."

"And the ashes?"

"Lake Michigan. That's my understanding. No gas chromatograph—no telling what that might have told us."

I stood there and gave him my dirtiest look. Then, "You do want to send my client to prison, don't you?"

"No."

"Even if she didn't do anything wrong, you want her in prison, correct?"

"No."

"Would that be because you didn't make it into medical school, and you're jealous of her because she did?"

"No."

"Sure of that? Ph.D. Versus M.D." I stood there, moving my hands like balancing a scale.

"No."

I turned and looked at Jennifer, asking with my look: Is there anything else you want me to ask him? She waved me over, and I returned to counsel table and cocked my head down to her so she could whisper. "Ask him why he hates me," she whispered.

"No," I whispered back. "He could kill you with that one."

She sat back. "Then I don't have any other questions. I just know he hates me."

I returned to the lectern. "Doctor Abernathy, isn't it true you strongly dislike my client?"

"No, I've never met your client and have no feelings one way or the other."

"But you've tried to convince this jury to find her guilty, isn't that true?"

I had him there. Why else would he have come if not to influence the jury?

"Have I—have I—? No, I mean yes."

"You've indeed tried to influence this jury to find my client guilty because that is your job and not because you really believe it yourself, isn't that correct?"

"No."

Now, the road to hell is paved with trial lawyers who asked "why?" at this point. "Why are you trying to have the jury find her guilty?" is the next obvious question. It was also the question that could send my client to prison.

So I didn't ask it because, you better believe, he would tell me if I did. I would have opened the door to it, and any trial lawyer in her first year in law school knew better than to open the dreaded door, the door that allows a witness to go off on you and eat your lunch.

So, I didn't ask it.

Which meant my job there was finished. Now, I had really accomplished nothing as far as totally disproving his earlier testimony about deadly poisons that didn't leave a trace. Inroads, maybe, but there was still a question. But the jury—ah, yes, I had confused the jury with words and innuendoes. As far as the jury knew, I had done something. Which meant reducing the obvious to the absurd. By not doing anything, I *had* done something. *Reductio ad absurdum.*

Mission accomplished.

Of course, I still didn't know whether Jennifer murdered Joe, and neither did our jury.

More was needed. The State called the Medical Examiner, the crime lab people and the crime scene techs. They even called a human factors expert. I still don't know why, on that one. Junk science.

Then we finished for the day.

When I returned to counsel table, Jennifer was studying her fingernails. "Nice," she whispered through clenched teeth. "A whole lot of nuttin."

"Which is something. Never forget. In a court of law, nothing is something."

"Jesus," she said. "I've fallen down a rabbit hole, and I can't get up. I'm dialing nine-one-one."

"Get a shower tonight. You smell like a trout."

"You get one, too. You smell like a mechanic's butt crack."

We smiled. We had grown to know each other well over these past weeks, and we had even formed a bond.

Enough, my look told her. "No, I'm serious. I don't want the jury smelling you. That could wind you up downstate for life. Soap and water tonight, please."

"I'll see if my hosts will allow that."

"I'll call and pave the way. All parts, remember."

"Honestly? There are so many I've forgotten."

"I'll make some calls and make sure you get a chance. Bye for now."

"Thanks, Michael. You were great today."

"We're doing all right."

"Guilty or not guilty?"

"As it stands right now? I don't want to jinx things, but I'm thinking not guilty. But make your notes for appeal tonight anyway."

"Will I testify?"

"I'm still deciding that."

Chapter Nine

MICHAEL

Ordinarily when I go to trial in a criminal case, I know why we're there and I have a pretty good idea how much trouble my client is in. But there was a glitch in this one. Because, so far, the state hadn't really proven a nexus between Jennifer and the death of her husband.

I think all of us in the courtroom assumed that the next witness to testify, Detective Richard Rodriguez, was going to provide that nexus. He was being called out of order. The state ordinarily would have made him its first witness, but he had been unavailable since he was appearing in another court on Monday when we began taking testimony. Today, he was freed up to come testify in our case. I believed he would offer testimony to make a case against Jennifer.

After all, Rodriquez had done the full workup, had interviewed Jennifer, knew all of the evidence, had testified before the grand jury, had seen the indictment come down, and he was the real reason we were all collected there that day on this criminal case.

And so, when the state called him to testify from the

witness stand and he came forward, there was a certain ripple of anticipation that passed over the jury and the spectators. I knew that I was on high alert since I expected some pretty damning testimony to come from him. I wanted to be ready to cross-examine and strip the meat from his bones with my questions.

Listening intently and making quick notes about questions to be asked was how that's done. A good lawyer in a criminal case knew the recorded statements forwards and backwards, knew the police reports forwards and backwards, and knew where the witness has made prior recorded statements that could be used to contradict anything he might say from the witness stand that disagreed with what he'd said before. I was that competent lawyer that day, and I was ready for whatever.

But the smoking gun never came.

First, Rodriguez testified that he had been one of the first law enforcement officers to begin asking questions after Joe's death and autopsy. The medical examiner had called him and said there was an air of suspicion about the death.

As his first duty, he had gone to the medical examiner and had talked to him at length and had then requested the chromatography study be done.

That study was an extra expense on the County and was never undertaken lightly. He testified he had then followed up that first visit to the ME with a visit to Jennifer herself. He had gone with his partner, Teresa Patel, a week after Joe's death. They had called Jennifer's office and made arrangements to meet her after work at police headquarters.

Jennifer had arrived there alone, he testified, and it was clear she had no reason to expect that she herself was the subject of any investigation.

"You mean to say, she appeared at the police station without an attorney?"

"Without an attorney," Rodriguez testified. "That isn't unusual, and nothing was said about it."

The assistant state's attorney then asked, "Please tell us what she said to you that night and what you asked her about the death of Joseph Ipswich."

Detective Rodriquez stroked the side of his face thoughtfully then made eye contact with the jury like all good witnesses do when they are about to lower the boom on a defendant.

"Jennifer told me she had a lawyer and he had said not to talk to us. But she said she wanted to clear up just one or two things so this whole thing might just go away. First, she wanted us to know that she and Joseph had been on good terms, that they were both fully committed to the marriage. As far as she knew, he was loyal, trustworthy, and had never roamed. I asked her if at any time there had been another woman, and she replied in the negative."

"What have you since found out?"

"I have since learned that, in fact, there is another woman. She lives in Paris, France, and her name is Elise Ipswich. What's more, it appears from my investigation, that Joseph and Elise were married in France."

"Are you telling the jury that Joseph was a bigamist and was married to more than one woman at the same time?"

"I'm telling the jury exactly that. Jennifer and Joseph were married on July 4, 2005 and were still married at the time of his death this year. Joseph and Elise were married in Paris France in 2015, and were still married at the time of his death this year."

"When did Jennifer learn about his second wife?"

"Before he died. She said she had guessed it for some

time just by the way he behaved at home. We had our motive."

The jury rustled awake—motive? A ripple passed across the spectators. The scratching of ink pens on notepads could be heard coming from the jury box. They were madly writing down what the detective had just told them.

"Object, motive is irrelevant." My objection. Mostly useless because the cat was already out of the bag.

"Sustained. The jury will ignore the comment about motive."

I cursed under my breath; the state had just given the jury Jennifer's motive for poisoning her husband. It was a simple leap to consider that, number one, her major in college was chemistry, number two, she was a physician with access to drugs, number three, she was a married woman who had just found out that the father of her two children was claiming to be married to a second woman at the same time he was married to her, and number four, he had died under mysterious circumstances with trace chemicals found in his body that could indicate the presence of a deadly drug in his system at the time he died.

Bingo! The state had just made its case. My hopes that I would be able to get the court to grant a directed verdict at the conclusion of the state's case—in other words, dismiss it without further proceedings—were dashed. The case would be going to the jury, and numbers one through four would be going into the jury deliberation room with them.

At that moment, it occurred to me that I was going to have to put Jennifer on the witness stand and have her deny she knew about the second wife.

But—and this is huge—to any trial lawyer, in a criminal case, it was very risky to put one's client on the witness stand. Criminal defendants, according to the defense bar, were never to take the witness stand because they were so easily misled on cross-examination into convicting themselves of the crime with which they were charged. Or maybe they were unlikeable and that was enough to get you convicted in a close case.

In our case, I had no problem imagining Jennifer taking the stand and denying that Joe's marriage to Elise had anything to do with his death because she had only found out there was another woman when he told her he was dying.

However, cross-examination would go into the fact that she could have known much earlier that Joseph was married to Elise. "How might that have come up?" she will be asked. Well, as the cross examiner's questions would suggest, she might have found out by going through his financial records. Or she might have had him followed to Paris and watched because she was suspicious. Or he might have confessed it to her at an earlier time. Or the French wife might have contacted Jennifer herself, for any number of reasons, giving up the fact that she was married to Joseph. Or maybe a wife just knew. Never forget the power of intuition. Female jurors knew all about that.

But even in the case of these terrible possibilities of what might come up during cross-examination, I still felt compelled to put Jennifer on the witness stand and have her deny any prior knowledge of Joe's marriage to another woman until the moment of his death when he confessed to her in the hospital. After all, juries are not stupid, and they are not to be disappointed, and they would expect Jennifer to testify and give them the opportunity to hear her, see her in action, and size her up. What if I disappointed them? Did I dare? I didn't think so. It looked to me like the detective, with his testimony, had successfully put Jennifer on the witness stand by making her come up and deny.

The detective went on, and the gist of it was this. Some women, upon hearing the news of a second wife, would immediately call a lawyer and seek advice. Jennifer had not done that. Jennifer, instead, had done nothing until the police contacted her and asked her to come down to the station and talk to them. That was one strike against her. And it was a big one. He was wrong, of course, for she had contacted me. I would clear that up on cross-examination and show him a copy of the check with which Jennifer retained me.

The odd thing was, though, even up until that moment in court that morning, Jennifer had made no arrangements with any *family* law lawyer regarding the situation she found herself in as a result of Joe's philandering. It was as if she were ignoring the whole situation. That might've been understandable when one was in shock, or it might've meant she had another plan in mind for the second wife. Or it might have been she was simply counting on me. Again, I'd clear it up on cross-examination.

But innuendoes. It was a trial by innuendo, the worst kind. The jury smells smoke and the prosecution yells "Fire!" and Jennifer goes on trial.

Chapter Ten

JENNIFER

Freedom finally came down to money. And the Founding Fathers said there would be no debtors' prison in America. Hooey.

I cashed in a CD and paid my $100,000 bail over the lunch hour, and now I was free.

It was a hassle getting out of jail even after I paid, and it took those lunatics six hours to process me out while I was in court. Do they have any idea how much money I lost in six hours away from my medical practice?

My partners had been covering for me there, but they kept the money I would've made. What's even worse was that some of my patients will wind up liking the substitute doctor better, and I would probably lose 10 or 15% of my patient load.

It's very competitive out there, and attracting new patients is very difficult. I just hated to think what this kick in the butt over Joe's death was actually costing me altogether.

Chapter Eleven

MICHAEL

Back to the trial after lunch. It was my turn to cross examine the detective. I stood and hurried to the lectern, indicating that I could hardly wait to sink my claws into the guy.

"Detective Rodriguez, isn't it true that you have no factual connection linking Jennifer to the death of Joseph?"

"No, that is not true."

"Isn't it true that the only link you do think you have is the tenuous one made by the medical examiner who whispered to you that Joseph died under mysterious circumstances?"

"No, that isn't true either."

Again, we're back to that point in cross-examination when the foolish attorney would ask the witness what link he knew of between the defendant and the cause of death. No one in that courtroom who knew me had any doubt that I was not about to ask that question. So, I moved on.

"Isn't it true you went to Paris, France to interview Elise Ipswich?"

"I did go to Paris to interview her. And I did, in fact, interview her."

As he was testifying about going to Paris and meeting the second wife, I could sense the jury watching Jennifer for her reaction, and I knew she was behaving viscerally. I wanted to turn and see what was going on with her—whether it was body language, facial expression, or a sudden intake of air when she heard about the other wife—but I didn't turn around and look. I didn't want to blow it up into any more than what the jury had just witnessed.

"All right, you did go to Paris and interview her. How old is this Elise?"

"She told me she's early thirties."

"Did you believe her?"

"She looks much younger."

"While you were in Paris, did you conduct any independent investigation of your own?"

"I did. I went to the place that amounts to what we call the County Clerk, being the place where marriage licenses are recorded. I requested a copy of the marriage license between Joseph Ipswich and Elise Ipswich, and I was given a copy. I brought that copy back with me to Chicago, and I believe a copy of it was turned over to you, Mr. Gresham, during the discovery portion of the case."

He was right. I had received a copy of the marriage license, and it appeared in all respects to be valid. What the witness didn't know was that my office had researched the legal effect of a marriage license and marriage ceremony in France where the bride is unaware her groom is already married to someone else.

For Jennifer's purposes, the result of that research was not pretty. It was not pretty because, under French law, if one party innocently relied on the other party who was representing that he was free to marry, and if that one party had no indication that the other party was in fact married, then the innocent party could, in good faith, marry and receive the full benefits of a married spouse. Meaning, she could require her spouse to support her, to support the offspring of the marriage, and to stand by his marriage vows in all respects. Most importantly, she could inherit from him.

Which meant that, under French law, Elise was entitled to everything that Joe owned when he died. What hadn't been said yet, and what remained to be gone into, was that under American law, the innocent spouse had the exact same rights.

That being the case, both spouses were entitled under the law of their lands to inherit Joe's assets. The setup was terrible. The setup was an inevitable lawsuit and the inevitable costs of emotional and financial involvement. Even worse, there were children of both marriages, one of whom, Elise's daughter Çidde, had ongoing medical problems that were expensive.

"Detective Rodriguez, it only makes sense to me that if you were to take the viewpoint that my client would be so upset to find out that her husband was a bigamist that she would poison him, then what if you put the shoe on the other foot and also considered that Elise, the French wife, finding out that her husband was married to an American woman, would be equally upset and equally capable of poisoning the man? Have you, in fact, weighed that in your own mind? I'm asking for a yes or no answer."

"Yes, I have considered that the French wife might be equally angry and upset."

"And yet, you've selected the American wife as the one who actually did the deed, rather than selecting the French wife as the guilty party. Without telling me why, I would like you to answer whether or not there was some reason you chose the American wife over the French wife as the guilty party?"

"There was, yes."

"Thank you."

He then nailed me.

"I chose the American wife, that is to say I focused on Jennifer Ipswich, mainly because she had access to the type of drugs it would take to poison Joseph Ipswich in such a manner that the poison would be untraceable. The French wife had no such access and no opportunity since she is employed as an economist. It was my opinion that she knew very little about the chemistry of poison after speaking to her only for a few minutes."

Rat had snuck it in on me. An end-run.

"So you made a choice based solely on your opinion."

"On the one hand, I had the American wife who had majored in chemistry and who, as a physician, had access to any chemical she wanted on the planet, versus the French wife who had access to the latest financial filing on any given corporation with the SEC, but who knew zip about chemicals. It was an easy mental process for me from there. My guess was it would be equally easy for the jury to make that connection. Not opinion, sir, but fact."

"Having said everything you just said," I began, slowly coming back around, "it sounds to me, and it sounds to the jury, like you still have only the most tenuous connection between Jennifer Ipswich and the death of Joseph Ipswich based entirely on the fact that she is a physician and therefore must've been the one doing the poisoning. So, I ask you, sir, isn't it equally likely that the Hippocratic oath she took, which commands that she do no harm, would have an equal place in your logic, and that because of that Hippocratic oath to do no harm, she in fact has done no harm?"

"Hippocratic oath or not, even doctors sometimes do bad things. That's my two cents."

I had them there. I had made the point that one assumption was just as valid and just as likely as the other assumption. I knew that I was not going to do any better than that, and I knew that one of the goals of cross-examination was to end on a high point. I was definitely not at a low point, so I told the judge I had no further questions. I returned to counsel table and took my seat beside Jennifer.

Then I stood right back up, theatrical as hell, but we must use what we're given.

"Oh, yes, Detective, before I forget. You've told the jury you told the medical examiner you wanted a gas chromatography study done on Joe's body. How did that go?"

I knew the answer, of course. But I saved this for last.

"It didn't go well. The ME forgot to run the test."

"And then?"

He spread his hands, looking helpless. "And then Joe was cremated. Up in smoke. So, no gas chromatography or exhuming the body."

"So the jury can assume there was no poison in the body because you can't offer one shred of evidence there was, isn't that correct?"

"Objection!" cried the State's Attorney.

I didn't bother to answer, and the objection was sustained. I had made my point, and it was a good one: the State dropped the ball by not running the study. And then Jennifer had cremated the body.

Almost as if she knew, too.

The judge had other "pressing" matters in his court that afternoon and so he excused us until the next morning.

Chapter Twelve

EMAIL FROM ELISE IPSWICH

To the addressees below
Michael Gresham
Frank Wilder
Jennifer Ipswich, M.D.

My name is Elise Ipswich and I live in Paris, France at 1114 rue Dumont. I live with my daughter, Çidde, and our Portuguese Water Dog, Max. I'm the widow of Joseph Ipswich, to whom I was married in 2015, and of this marriage our Çidde is the only offspring. I have been married once before, I have no other children, and my age is 34. I was educated at the Université Paris II Panthéon-Assas in economics, and I finished my graduate degree in economics at the London School of Economics.
I'm an associate account manager at LVP Partners, a European private equity firm based in Paris, France. It is one of the oldest firms in the sector with its origins dating back to Lavas Affaires Industrielles, the historical principal investment activity of Paribas, which started operations in 1872.
LVP manages €13.5 billion of dedicated buyout funds. Since 1994,

LVP has completed 65 LBO transactions in 11 European countries, representing over €48 billion in transaction value. LVP has 62 agents from 10 countries in Paris, London, Madrid, Milan, Munich, Stockholm, Tel Aviv, and New York City.

I met Joseph as a patient when I went to see him about a disease I thought I had contracted from my first husband. Joseph was very kind and very interested in my case. He told me it was an infectious disease that could become an epidemic because it was so easily transmissible, and that that was why my own doctor had referred me to him.

He treated me with various medications, and in six months' time, I was cured. Possibly three months into our relationship as doctor-patient, he asked me one afternoon if I would like to have dinner with him sometime.

Joseph was a very attractive man, and I was very lonely so I accepted. That first night, we talked about our backgrounds and our education and we both confirmed to each other that we were single and looking for a long-term commitment in a relationship. It wasn't said that way specifically, but the clues were there, and we both knew why we were together that evening.

Approximately six months later, after taking some visiting friends to the Louvre that afternoon, Joseph and I snuck away for dinner alone and he surprised me with an engagement ring. It was a very beautiful ring, and I was very much in love with Joseph, so I accepted his proposal of marriage.

My parents announced the engagement in the Paris newspaper, and my best girlfriend from college fêted me with an engagement party.

Approximately one week before he died, Joseph sent me an email and told me he was very ill. He was home with Jennifer. He had always told me that Jennifer was his sister who took care of him and his business affairs while he was in America. He also told me that Jennifer ran his medical practice in Chicago and that if anything ever happened to him, I should contact her.

After I received his email, I called his medical practice in Chicago and

*was told that he had passed away. Then a nurse in his medical practice
in Paris—who knew about such things—told me the truth: my
husband was married in the USA.*

*I cried for three days and couldn't get out of bed. You must understand
that I love this man deeply, that he was the first real love of my life,
and that for the most part, I had lived a very cloistered life before I met
him. Occasionally, I would go out for a glass of wine with a friend
from work, but for the most part, I spent my evenings and weekends
with my daughter and with my computer working on my accounts.
Our life together was quiet and studious as we were both involved in
our professions and preferred spending quiet time together at home in our
townhouse on rue Dumont as opposed to spending lots of money eating
out and buying special clothing and things of that nature. We have both
been very circumspect in our spending, in fact, and we have together
purchased and half-paid for the townhouse in which I now live with
Çidde.*

*I'm writing to say that I certainly do not wish to disturb anyone's life
and to tell Jennifer how very sorry I am that Joseph died. In the most
difficult way, I can share that pain with her since I'm going through the
exact same loss. Joseph was a wonderful man, and I'm sure we will
both miss him very much.*

*My main concern is our daughter Çidde. She is HIV positive as a
result of a blood transfusion she had when she was six. This happened
when a tonsillectomy resulted in an emergency surgery. As a result, she
lost two pints of blood and had to be transfused. That's when she got
the bad blood.*

*She also has other congenital problems, and because of these things, I
must pay approximately €1000 per week for her medical needs.
Joseph always promised me that he would take care of those payments
for me, and he always did. Now, however, I find myself in a situation
where, with the other overhead in my life and the low pay which
associates receive at LVP Partners, I'm unable to keep up with the costs
of our daughter's medical needs.*

For this reason, I'm writing to find out whether Joseph had assets or insurance that maybe someone would be willing to share with me in order to help defray these costs. I'm not looking to win a case, and I'm certainly not looking to take away Joseph's assets from Jennifer. My main wish is to see if I can bargain away enough assets to help pay the approximately €4000 per month our daughter requires for her treatment and maintenance.

Please take my situation into your hearts and sit with it while plans are being made about what to do with Joseph's second wife. I know that you will be fair with me and we will all come away from the situation as friends, or at least as acquaintances who respect one another. I wish I knew more about what happened to Joseph, but I know it's a very difficult time for Jennifer, and I do not wish to pry.

With God in my heart I pray, peace be with you.
Elise Ipswich.

Chapter Thirteen

MICHAEL

I checked my email after court. That's when I received the email from Elise Ipswich. It was puzzling, to say the least. I remembered my first meeting with Jennifer, in which she described Elise as somebody cool and appraising, someone who told her she wanted one half of Joseph's assets and that Jennifer should even be prepared to sell her house. The email I received from Elise sounded like none of that. In fact, she sounded like a very reasonable person.

I was at the office the next morning at six. Coffee and beef jerky. I keep a couple of bags inside my Everything drawer in my desk for emergencies. The trial was going all right. We would win because the State just didn't quite have the smoking gun it needed. The beef jerky was like cardboard and tasteless. I knew I'd reek of garlic all morning. Floss, toothpaste, and mouthwash. Followed up by Juicy Fruit. Then I was off to court again.

Before trial resumed, I had a few moments with Jennifer at counsel table while we waited for the judge. I opened my laptop to the Elise email and turned the screen to where it confronted Jennifer. "Have you seen this?"

"I have. It looks like she's after money."

"I have to admit," I said, "she sounds pretty reasonable. It looks to me like we'll be able to make a settlement with her of some kind and she will go away happy and able to care for the child Joe had with her."

"I don't think so," said Jennifer coolly.

"How's that?"

"Read it again, Michael. She's after $4000 per month from me. I don't have that to give to her."

"Thinking back, I believe you told me at our first meeting that Joseph wanted $1 million of the $2 million life policy to go to Elise. I'm sure if that were done, she would go away happily, and the two of you could consider your lives disconnected in a peaceful way for both of you. As a practicing physician with a busy schedule and probably umpteen patients per day, I'm sure you're looking for a quick out like that. I would suggest you let me contact her back and make such an offer to her."

"What, you're suggesting I actually give her one million?"

"Yes, that seems to be what was in Joe's mind at the last minute. What would be wrong about it?"

"That money is *mine*. I paid one-half of the premium on that for ten years. Why should I give away any part of it now to some hussy who bedded my husband, knowing he was a doctor and probably making good money? I don't want any part of that. No, you do not have my authority to make that offer."

At that moment, Judge Stormont entered the courtroom, and we got back down to business.

Chapter Fourteen

JENNIFER

Elise had told me she wanted my vase. I would die first.

It was a Pinner Qing Dynasty vase. It was on record as one of the most expensive antiques ever sold—the Chinese vase sold for $1.5 million, after-tax, at a private auction in London. There were only two known in existence. They boast the Imperial seal, indicating that they were likely explicitly designed for Emperor Qianlong in the late 18th century.

Now I'm going to tell you the true story about how this vase wound up on the auction block in London and made its way to my office in the medical building.

When I was a small child, I spent my summers and holidays at my grandma's house downstate. She lived on a farm with her husband and four boys.

Like all farmers, my grandpa and his four boys were always ravenous. Grandpa kept six dairy cows on the farm just for his family. Milk was plentiful and free. All you had to do was squeeze the teats, skim the cream, take it in the house, and put it in the refrigerator, which is where the Qing vase comes in.

The first time I remember seeing the vase was in my grandma's refrigerator. It was filled with cows' milk. It was filled and refilled every day with milk fresh out of the cows in the barn. The men preferred drinking the milk straight out of the vase. The top was fluted, the neck perhaps four inches long, and then it spread into a vase approximately 14 inches high. It held exactly one gallon of milk. Embossed on the vase's front was the Emperor's seal, a gold circle filled with the blue sea and two goldfish swimming in the sea. The entire bottom two-thirds of the vase looked like a basket weave. Above that, the vase was yellow and covered with blue branches and red and white flowers.

All in all, it wasn't a particularly attractive antique, but for me, it was emotionally powerful.

Grandpa went first, and grandma went ten years later. The vase was sold at a farm sale, I later learned, while I was in college in Chicago. It brought exactly one dollar.

It then found its way into the hands of a woman in Albuquerque, New Mexico. She gave it to a traveling antique buyer who paid ten dollars for it. He then took it on the TV show called *Antiques Roadshow* and learned that it was priceless.

From there, the trail got vague, but I did know the vase made its way to London and was sold there to a man from Monte Carlo.

Now he had two of them, the only two in existence. He decided to sell one, and it was my grandma's vase that showed up online on the Sotheby's website. I attended the auction by proxy, determined to repurchase it. Joe had died, and I had collected two-million dollars on his life insurance. Plus, I had some liquidity of my own.

My proxy attended the auction in New York City, but at the last minute, the item was withdrawn from the auction and its owner returned with it to Monte Carlo. However, we had learned his name, which was Monsieur Jamison Ellington.

I decided to hunt him down and buy it for myself. This was a week after Joe's death. Of course I was dying inside over the loss of my Joseph. But the vase was there and Joe wasn't. That made all the difference. To me, at least.

I flew to Monte Carlo and put out my feelers from the hotel where I was staying. I was in luck because word came back to me through the art dealer representing me that Monsieur Ellington would sell. The price: $2.3 million. I was given directions to follow exactly or I would lose the purchase.

They sent a car for me, a long black Cadillac Escalade, and put me in the backseat. Then I was blindfolded and told that if I touched the blindfold, I would be returned to the hotel and the sale would be canceled. I agreed to keep my hands to myself.

The drive took all of an hour, and distances being so limited in that country of Monaco, I didn't know whether we ended up in Monaco or France.

At last, we came to a stop, and I was assisted in stepping down from the Escalade. Since I was wearing heels, my feet did a tattoo along the walk, which seemed to be stones laid at odd angles, causing me to stumble two times.

I then heard the creak of a door and was told to step up. There was an arm on either side of me, escorting me at this point, and a voice told me I was being taken into a room where I would be able to remove the mask and view the vase.

I proceeded several steps, took a left, walked ten paces

or so, and was then told to sit down. I followed instructions, the blindfold was removed, and I found myself sitting in a darkened room with a lamp in front of me on a small desk.

After several minutes, a man wearing a black suit, a white shirt, and a black tie appeared before me from out of the shadows. He was wearing white gloves, and he placed the vase before me on the desk.

I was handed gloves and told to turn the vase for inspection once and then remove my hands. I followed instructions and confirmed that the vase was my grandma's vase. A small chip, a careless bump in grandma's refrigerator perhaps, left one goldfish at the bottom of the sea without a dorsal fin. While the item was flawed, it had never affected the value of the piece. I was ecstatic to again be in the same room with Grandma's vase. After several minutes, the black suit man stepped out of the shadows and removed the vase.

A voice boomed forth from speakers set in the corners of the room. It said, "You have seen the article. Do you wish to purchase?"

"More than anything," I said. "Now, more than ever."

"How is the vase important in your life?"

"My grandma had it in her house. It's the only connection I have to myself at that age. Just seeing it takes me back, and it's all I can do not to break out crying. I have the money. I'm willing to pay if you're still willing to sell."

"You got my instructions about the wire transfer?"

"I did. I have to text my bank, and the money will be transferred to your bank. Should I do that now?"

"Yes, do it now while we are preparing the vase for shipment. My courier will bring it to your address in Chicago as we have agreed. You will assume responsibility for the item at your front door. Delivery will occur one week from today. Are these the terms you have agreed to?"

"They are exactly as I agreed."

"Excellent. You will now be returned to your hotel. Thank you for your courtesies."

"Thank you, sir."

I was then driven back to my hotel—the same blindfold along the way—and I was let out at the main door. I intended to treat myself to a drink at the Bar Hemingway in celebration. After all, it was the Ritz Hotel.

Now you know how I came to possess the vase, and you understand just how priceless it is to me. For that woman from Paris, that Elise woman, to now think that she was somehow entitled to a part of it puts me into a rage. It will never happen. I promise you that.

Chapter Fifteen

MICHAEL

That night after court, Jennifer's medical office was broken into. It was her first night out of jail. The drugs were untouched, the money was untouched, the equipment was untouched. Only one item was taken.

Jennifer came to see me about the burglary the following day. "Whoever did it," she said in my office, "knew exactly what they wanted. The only thing missing is my Qing vase."

I asked her, "Tell me about the vase."

We were in the lunchroom in my office complex where I was eating a sandwich. I held out a bag of Fritos to her and asked if she wanted one. She shook her head.

"The vase is what I purchased in Monte Carlo. It was and wasn't an impulsive buy. My grandmother had the vase in her kitchen when I was little. I had extremely good memories attached to it from my childhood. Then after she died, the vase went here and there and finally wound up in the hands of a man in Monaco who paid over $1 million for it. Well, this is the questionable part. When Joe died, I took his life insurance money and went to Monaco and bought the vase back."

"All right," I said. "Tell me how much you paid for it, and I'll try not to holler out."

"I paid $2.3 million for it. I know I'm in the middle of litigation over my assets and had absolutely no business doing that, but it was a once-in-a-lifetime chance. He had listed it through a private house, and it wasn't going to be on the market again in my lifetime. So, I jumped at the chance, and now I own a Qing Dynasty vase valued at $2.3 million."

You never knew with people. I tried not to judge.

"Did you have it specifically listed on your property insurance policy?"

"I did because my property insurance guy told me it was necessary. I have pictures of it, and I have copies of the bank documents used in the wire transfer that I made to purchase it. So, it's all documented, but I really want you to submit the claim to the insurance company for me."

"Why would that be?" A red flag went up. When people are indicted for insurance fraud, it's because they have made a phony claim. If someone else makes the claim for them, it makes it that much more difficult for the prosecutors to prove the insurance fraud. If she got indicted, she would claim that it was all my idea and try to put the blame on me. There wasn't any way I was getting into this.

"I want you to do it because you have a lot more weight than I do. They're going to listen to you, and they're gonna laugh at me. Would you please help me with this?"

I still wasn't going to take the dive for her. "It would be very unusual for me to ever list an insurance claim for someone. Even a client as important to me as you. I will assist you in making your claim. But I'm uncomfortable doing it for you. No, I won't do it myself. When you're ready to fill out the forms, let me know and I will look them over for you. But as far as submitting a claim myself, sorry, no can do."

She looked crestfallen. She gave me a look like I was letting her down, and I suppose I was to her way of thinking. But I was firm in my decision, and she could see that.

I asked her, "Why don't you tell me about the break-in itself. What happened at your office?"

"Someone jimmied the lock on the front door and then somehow short-circuited the alarm system. The detective I'm working with said the person was very knowledgeable and had probably done this type of break-in dozens of times without getting caught.

"He said that most likely they had scouted my office, noted the alarm system I use, then gone to the manufacturer's website, found the owner's manual and schematic, and figured out how to short-circuit the alarm.

"He also said it might be an inside job, and the company that installed my alarm system might have an employee who pulled off this kind of crime.

"What gets me, though, is how they knew to go for the most priceless object in my office. Ninety-nine out of a hundred people wouldn't know that Qing vase was worth as much as it is. The detective said someone had been in my office who knew what the vase was worth and wanted it."

I sat back and let this soak in. I already knew the answer to the question I was going to ask. "Do you have anyone in mind who might know the value of that vase?"

She sucked down a lungful of air and looked at me with a depth of sincerity in her eyes I hadn't seen before. "Elise."

I nodded. "Agree. Didn't you tell me the first time she

visited your office she said she wanted that vase? I'm pretty sure you did."

"You're right. She did say she wanted that vase. But how in the world would she know how to short-circuit my system? It takes a pro for that."

I could only shake my head. "She obviously used a pro. She knew or found someone who had the chops and he needed the money she was willing to pay for the job. My guess is she paid someone between fifty and a hundred-thousand. Why would she even care? The item has a value of over two million, so the cost of acquiring it wasn't a big consideration for her. My only question is, where did she get that kind of money to buy someone to do the job for her? I thought we were dealing with someone who was broke and couldn't afford her little girl's medicine on a weekly basis?"

Jennifer grew flustered. Her mouth opened and closed without words, then, "I could kill that woman. I really could. That vase is priceless to me. No one in my office knew how much I paid for it. It wasn't even that pretty. But the dynasty it represented was rare, and most artifacts were gone to the four winds. That's what made it so valuable. So, what should I do? Break into her house and steal it back?"

"I only hope you're joking around. While she didn't get caught, I'm sure you would. Plus, it's really difficult to break into someone's home without leaving traces of evidence that can come back and put you in prison. Moreover, unlike you, she has it hidden somewhere. Probably somewhere away from home."

"Like where?"

"Like a family member's home. Or friend's home. Or maybe even one of those large safe-deposit boxes. They're expensive, but they work."

She helped herself to a handful of Fritos then opened

the refrigerator door. She chose a Diet Coke and popped the top. She took a long drink and began munching Fritos while she stared blankly at the floor. "Oh," she shuddered. "If I could only get my hands on that woman, what I'd do to her."

"Please don't tell me that. You're making me a witness. And you don't want me to be a witness against you, I can guarantee that. I'm not listening anymore."

"Michael," she said between mouthfuls, "please don't take me so literally. I would never hurt someone. I'm a doctor, remember? Remember the Hippocratic oath?"

"Are you under a physician's care by any chance?" I suddenly had to ask.

"Why, no! What a thing to ask! I've told you we're not going there!"

"Yes, but your anger just erupts at times. It's frightening to people on the outside. But I also remember that vase is priceless to you. Anyway, I need to get back to work. Please be sure and bring the claim form and let me have a look at it before you send it in."

She nodded and took another handful of Fritos. "Will do. Thanks, Michael."

I shrugged and walked out of the room, leaving her with Fritos and a Diet Coke.

For now, that would just have to do.

Chapter Sixteen

JENNIFER

It's tough to sit here at my trial and say nothing. Every sentence someone says from that witness stand contains some untruth. At times, it's all I can do not to stand up and scream and tell them to stop, they're getting it all wrong, and they're sitting in judgment of the wrong person as they're making me out to be. If they had any idea what it took me in my life to get to the position where I am today as a physician and pediatrician, they would totally understand how impossible it would be for me to take the life of another human being, much less someone I adored like Joe.

Joe and I did everything together. When he was home during his two weeks with me, we went to all of the museums and art shows, we spent Saturday afternoons together reading in front of a fire, and we spent our nights together propped up against each other in bed, watching John Wayne movies and eating popcorn.

The children lived for the weeks when Joe would be home. When it was just me, we had our routines, and we seldom varied from those routines. But with Joe, anything could happen. He was mischievous and spontaneous, and you might think you were on your way to the dentist's office when suddenly he would take a right turn, and you'd find yourself at 31 Flavors getting ice cream instead of Novocain. That's just how Joe was. Nothing was so serious it couldn't be dealt with, and if it couldn't be dealt with, it could be changed.

To even suggest that someone in my position, and someone who loved her husband as desperately as I loved Joe, could somehow harm them was the height of conceit. It took a very small person sitting in a very dark office with all the lights out to imagine a scene where I would harm my husband, Joe. Any mind that could conceive that was not a mind that I could relate to and was certainly not someone who knew Joe and me.

But in the month before his death, the earth shifted beneath our feet: something between us had changed.

The last time he was home, I could tell something was troubling him. He arrived on a Saturday afternoon, sent the children off to their rooms, and sat me down in the kitchen.

"Jennifer," he said to me as if in a trance, "there's something I just have to tell you. It's something that's going to break your heart. It has already broken mine, and the burden has become so great that I can no longer carry it alone. I must share with you."

"Joe," I said, "come over here and sit down and let me fix you a drink before you take off on this. I know you're heavily burdened, and I know you need to relieve yourself of whatever is bothering you, but I want to see you take a drink first and try to relax. You're bordering on meltdown.

Your face is red, your voice is elevated, and your hands keep opening and closing randomly. I've never seen you so exercised."

I got up from the table and went to the cabinet, found a highball glass, and poured two fingers of Joe's favorite bourbon. I dropped in three ice cubes out of the ice-trays—ice I had personally prepared—and set it down in front of him. "Please drink," I said. "You're going to feel a lot better."

Joe did as he was told. He nursed the drink, sitting back and shutting his eyes. I could see the lines on his face relax as the bourbon did its work on the central nervous system. His fingers released, and he relaxed his grip on the arms of the captain's chairs at our table. He slumped back in the chair and began nodding ever so slowly.

"All right," I said in my most soothing voice, "let's talk about what you have on your mind now."

Joe continued nodding. "I don't know, Jennifer. With all this mileage I'm putting on and jetting here and there, it seems like problems snowball. Lately, I've probably been making mountains out of molehills. That bourbon you just gave me is the best medication I've had in six months. How about a refill?"

"Coming right up," I said and went through the highball ritual a second time. This time, he nursed it I guess for the rest of the night. I was certain that that would be the end of what he had come to say. There are certain things a wife does not want to hear about, especially from a husband who's away a lot on the road. What about those road problems? They come unstuck and disappear after only a few swallows. So, we came to that place together where he knew that I simply did not want to hear what he had to say.

Was that so wrong? Was it wrong for a wife to want to keep her life like it was? Was it wrong for a wife to erect a wall and tell the world, "Thou shalt not cross here"? I didn't think so. I had my life as I liked it, except I didn't care for Joe being gone two weeks out of every month. His absence just made my job that much harder with the kids, the bill paying, the friends who wanted to see you, and all the rest of it. It would've been much easier with him at home full-time. But that wasn't the road he had chosen for his professional practice, so I had let go of that part.

So I sat in my trial, and I listened to the witnesses try to poison the jury's mind. I wondered how anyone could ever make them understand what Joe and I really meant. As the days went by inside that courtroom, it became increasingly clear to me that this jury was going to decide about me and about my life without knowing anything real about me.

And if they put this girl under oath, if they tapped into my empty core, they would know even less.

And that scared me to death.

Chapter Seventeen

JOE'S TAPE RECORDING

Jennifer found the key to Joe's bank box, and off she went. The next day, she appeared in my office with a tape recording. We listened together:

Son of a bitch, girl, I really screwed the pooch this time. Here goes nothing.

I'm Joe Ipswich. I was born in Arizona and raised by my single mother until her death from an automobile-pedestrian accident while she was running behind my jogging stroller one morning on Camelback Road and 24th Street. From the asphalt, they took me to St. Joseph's Hospital and, three days later, the social workers' calls had turned up no family to take me on, so I was placed with Christian Social Services. Eventually, I was adopted by a woman who taught remedial mathematics to middle-school children. Every night after school, she returned home without fail to dote over me during her private hours. My take-over mother was loving, supportive, and my best friend for many years. But the death of my birth mother had carved a hole deep inside my heart that no make-up mother's love could ever fill. Maybe it was a weakness about me or maybe it's always that way. I don't know, and I never beat myself up about it. But I did start looking, about my eleventh year, for the love of a woman to fill that hole.

My search continued up to my marriage to Jennifer and after. Why did it continue after Jennifer and I married? Was it because she wasn't enough? That's like asking why the sky is blue. It's blue just because. I kept looking just because. It was Elise's turn next, and it was Elise I married in France. Her love came as close as any to filling that hole and freeing me from that old, gnawing pain. Lovely Elise, I couldn't do enough for her.

I wasn't rich in that I never had a huge corpus of money to buy a building or a staffed yacht or a Johnny Depp dollop of island. But I earned fifty-thou a month into my forties, so there was always more than enough to go around.

Naturally, the nascent millionaire seeks to fix himself the more he gets, and so I took that French wife for myself.

Elise knew about Jennifer and my American family—the French are savvy like that and can take in sunlight when it's available, accepting that sometimes there will only be shade. Americans, not so much. Jennifer, you knew nothing, suspected nothing, and would never find out until after I had passed on. Poor Jennifer, but that's how it is with Americans. Americans demand a perfect place-setting and woe to the idiot who brings along an extra fork—you understand what I'm saying. Shade, sunshine, forks—metaphors for worldly.

On 9 October 2014, the French authorities reported an autochthonous Zika virus case in France. The client reported symptom onset on 29 July 2014. No travel history to Zika endemic countries was reported for the patient or partner. Since this notification, French authorities reported an additional two probable autochthonous Zika cases, identified through active case-finding in the same area and same timeframe (symptom onsets of the three cases from 6 to 15 August 2014). All three patients had recovered.

Epidemiological and entomological field investigations by French authorities were still ongoing to determine the possible route(s) of trans-

mission for these cases to prevent further spread and detect possible associated cases.

It was probable that the three cases resulted from the vector-borne transmission of Zika in this neighborhood in late July/early August. This was probably the first episode of local vector-borne transmission detected in metropolitan France and in Europe.

Elise Ipswich (née Umana) was the first patient.

I met Elise Umana during that investigation into the Zika case. She was early twenties, highly educated, and needed treatment. The afternoon she came in to see me, she was voluble. Not angry, just full of questions. She wanted to know how she might have contracted the disease. Turned out that a pianist from French Guiana was the likely contact, likely transmitted by sexual intercourse. That didn't sit well, but she held her tongue.

Elise was tall, willowy, with dark, flashing eyes and European teeth—never perfect like the American smile but perfect in their naturalness. She was married to Howard Umana. She told me she was an inveterate world traveler, a member of the French women's Olympic water polo team, and a once-a-week teacher of French to people whose native language wasn't French. The kind of woman that men find immediately attractive and valuable, the type of woman who is so seductive in her exemplary life that she attracts not only good men, but the worst of men as well. Zika is why she came to see me in my medical practice. When I met Elise, I knew my search was over. She filled my heart and then some. She divorced Umana.

Çidde quickly joined us, and she was just a bonus because she was a genius at knowing how much I loved her and responding in kind. Doctors keep track like that. Quid pro quo—the kid's love for her old man was just what I needed when I felt my sails buckle in the headwind.

Here's how the kids stacked up. My two American kids received the daddy gene. Our son is a water skier. He's had his chance at a National Scholastics mathematics award at the ripe young age of nine and has immediately blown it off in favor of the lake. His choice, and he was entitled to make it, right? My daughter is eleven and has already skipped fifth grade because there was nothing there she hadn't already taught herself online. They are gifted in mathematics, but custom water skis and computers running Mathematica stole away their hearts. Who was I to complain? I'd served in the Army, to the horror of my mother, even dropping out of med school to go to war. Carriers always swim upstream against their better talents, and neither their mother nor I could prevent that. So, we didn't even try.

Now I'm sick. I've been to my internist, and he can't find the reason for my illness. He's recommended two specialists, a cardiologist and an infectious disease specialist, and they can't seem to give me anything definitive. I only know I'm unhealthy, and I'm fading. I believe I'm dying and am powerless to stop it.

I will die before I try and explain Elise to you, Jennifer. If I tell you about her now, I will die alone, and I cannot stand that—the hole in the heart and all that. But I will say her name on the way out the door, a warning of sorts.

"Elise," I will whisper.

Elise, indeed. She is a gentle soul, a butterfly. She will not harass you or fight with you. She'll let her needs be known from my estate and gratefully accept what can be worked out. Please don't try to beat her down or let some greedy American lawyer sue her just to run up his bill. She doesn't deserve all that. She's as innocent as you, my precious Jennifer.

Chapter Eighteen

MICHAEL

I received a very distressing phone call one morning before trial. The call was placed from Paris from Elise Ipswich.

My secretary buzzed me and told me it was long distance and that the woman on the other end was crying. She didn't quite get her name but thought it was Lisa. I picked up the phone and said hello.

"Mr. Gresham," said a crying voice, a woman's voice that sounded distant, "you don't know me, and I'm sorry I'm calling you like this, but my name is Elise Ipswich and I need desperately to talk to someone who knows Jennifer Ipswich. I got your name from Dr. Ipswich's medical practice when I called her office. They told me you might be able to help me with my problem."

I said, "Why don't you take a deep breath and see if you can pull yourself together just a bit. You're coming across a little garbled, what with your crying and all. I'm very sensitive to what you're going through right now, Mrs. Ipswich, and I'm certainly going to listen to you and do whatever I can to help your situation. Let's just both count to five and try this again."

We counted to five.

"All right," I said, "I understand you were married to Joseph Ipswich in Paris. Is that correct?"

"Yes," she said. "Joseph and I were married for five years until his death. We had a very warm and loving marriage, and he met all of my needs and the needs of our daughter, Çidde. Our daughter is a special needs child because she is HIV positive and has a congenital blood problem on top of that."

"Yes, I read your email."

"Well, thank you. Her diseases are held at bay only by the medications I give her daily. Those medications cost one thousand euros per week. Joseph was paying for those while he was alive. I work as an associate agent at LVP Partners here in Paris and I take home four thousand euros per month. Like I said, I'm just an associate, and competition for these jobs is very heavy, I'm lucky to have my job, and I will certainly not be making any more money until I become a full agent."

"You realize my client is Jennifer Ipswich, yes? You probably shouldn't be baring your soul to me."

"Please, I have nowhere else to turn except to my husband's assets and to try to make sense of what he owned and see if I can come to some sort of agreement with your Jennifer."

"I understand. Please tell me what you would like to do."

"Previously, I sent the email and asked for one half of Joseph's life insurance. He told me he had the policy and that I was a beneficiary on the policy. I called the life insurance company, but they wouldn't give me any information at all. They did tell me, though, that I was not a beneficiary on any policies with their company. That broke my heart. I had always trusted Joseph to take care of our daughter, and I'm still in shock that he never got around to putting me on that policy, or at least putting Çidde on that policy."

"I can really sympathize with your situation, Mrs. Ipswich," I said. "To be quite honest with you, I approached the topic with Jennifer. She thought about it just for a fraction of a second and then immediately discarded the idea of parting with any portion of the life insurance proceeds."

"Oh, that's almost hateful, isn't it?"

"Her position is that she has paid for half of those policy payments ever since the policy was issued, and she doesn't feel like her investment should be rewarded to someone else. I hope you can understand. I know this doesn't help your situation, but all I can do is report my client's position."

"Do you think I'm going to need a lawyer in America?"

"Honestly? I don't know how else you're going to have your needs met except by getting a lawyer at this point."

"I've been in touch—"

"I cannot advise you, but if you were my family member, I would definitely say you needed a lawyer. Please do let me know if you contact an attorney by having her or him give me a call. My hope is that this matter can be resolved with a few telephone calls and maybe a conference between the four of us. Any more than that, I'm not allowed to say at this time. I hope you understand."

"All right then. To be honest, I've already spoken with someone, and his name is Frank Wilder. I will have Mr. Wilder call you today, and maybe we can get an agreement right away so I can continue paying for my daughter's medications and pay my mortgage on our *maison de ville*. Thank you so very much for speaking with me and we will talk again soon, I'm sure. Goodbye for now."

"Goodbye for now and thank you for calling."

Chapter Nineteen

MICHAEL

I hung up from that telephone call and immediately called Jennifer. They said she was busy with a patient. She called me back five minutes later.

"Michael?" she said. "Am I late or something? I thought we weren't starting until nine today. I had just enough time to see some patients before court. Is that why you're calling?"

"No, we do start at nine o'clock, and I'll be leaving for court in about half an hour and will see you there. But in the meantime, I just had a very distressing telephone call from Elise Ipswich in Paris."

"Why is she calling *my* lawyer? To make more trouble for me?"

"To make a long story short, she has now hired an attorney, and his name is Frank Wilder, who I know to be a very competent domestic relations attorney here in Chicago. In fact, Frank is known to be a family law attorney who will stop at nothing to win a case for his client. I cannot think of an attorney I would less rather have come into this case than Frank Wilder."

"You will crush him, Michael. I have great faith in you."

"Well, while it might be my goal to arrive at a quick settlement of any disputes between you and Elise, my opinion is that such an opportunity will not present itself until Frank has run up one hell of a bill with his client."

"Did you warn her about him?"

"No, because she is going to demand that you pay him because you refused to settle this case the first time Elise came to you. He is devious, and he will stop at nothing to win. He will be able to make a pretty good argument that you should pay his legal fees because you have, as we both know, refused to bargain with Elise. Right now, I'm awaiting his call, and I'm assuming you will want me to represent you in that case just like I'm representing you in the criminal case. Would that be correct?"

"Of course, I want you, Michael. Why would you even ask? As far as Frank Wilder, one of my physician friends had him in her divorce maybe a year ago, and she wound up owning the entire house. So, I'm a little bit familiar with how capable he is. But on the other hand, I feel like the equities are with me because I neither created the situation nor am I responsible for it."

"Sometimes judges can overlook the equities and make a mess of things. Settlement is always best."

"This woman entrapped my husband, I'm sure, and I believe that any family law judge is going to be sympathetic to my position. I cannot imagine being ordered to turn over one-half of anything Joe and I owned together. In fact, I would be shocked if that actually happened."

"You need to hear me, Jennifer. It does happen, it can happen, and in this case, there's a good chance it will happen. There's a good chance she'll be awarded fifty percent."

She ignored me. "Let me be clear. I'm going to ask you to be even tougher than this Frank Wilder and tell him that under no circumstances will I negotiate and under no circumstances will I agree to turn over half of anything I worked so hard for."

"You need to re-think your no-negotiation position."

"Michael, please understand that while my father was a surgeon and did very well, he had his children on their own as soon as they graduated from college. There was no money after that."

"Well, college is often the end of parental—"

"No! My situation was a little bit different because I was going to medical school, but after those four years, no more checks from home. If you can imagine, I was a resident physician sharing a two-bedroom apartment with two other resident physicians and my husband. It was a situation where one of us occupied the bed in our bedroom while the other one was doing rounds at the hospital. So that's how I went through my residency, paying my own way every step of the way. I do not appreciate someone coming after me now and trying to walk off with one half of everything I put together since then. No, I will not negotiate, and that's final."

"I'm going to put in your file that I have recommended upfront that you agree to share one-half of the life insurance proceeds with this Elise Ipswich. I think that she is entitled to that, and I think you're making a big mistake in not negotiating with her and trying to find a quick out."

"Paper my file like you're doing CYA? I don't like you doing stuff like that, Michael."

"Like I said before and I'll say it again, if you insist on taking a position of no negotiation, there's a very good chance Frank Wilder is going to wind up having his legal fees paid by you. It's not a financially healthy situation, and I do not agree with the direction you're going with this, Jennifer. However, I'm only the attorney and will do what you say."

"Yes, please do what I said. I'll see you in half an hour at court, and maybe we can get this damned criminal case over within the next few days. Thank you, Michael, for calling, and goodbye."

MEMO TO THE FILE:
I need to specifically recount that I have, number one, advised Jennifer that she should offer one-half of the life insurance proceeds to Elise Ipswich. Number two, that she will likely wind up paying the legal fees of this Frank Wilder if she insists on no negotiations. Number three, it's going to be expensive for her to hire me to represent her in a family law dispute at the same time as defending her on a criminal case. I'm going to make that clear to her this morning and tell her that I will be sending her a fee agreement to be signed and returned to me before I speak with Wilder. Wilder is a good name for Frank because he is wild. I only wish I could've made Jennifer understand that.

When I first met Jennifer at the swimming pool, I was bowled over by her smile and her warmth and her grace around people. I can see why any medical school would have accepted her as one of its students. She's just that kind of person who's going to make any medical school proud that it educated her.

But something else is developing. It seems to me that since we've gotten into the question of finances in her personal life, there is a different persona lurking just below her surface. She is angry and hurt, and she is being very possessive right now. I'm putting these impressions here in her file because I want to be able to report to any Medical Association or Bar Association what I was seeing at the inception of this dispute with Elise Ipswich.

Chapter Twenty

JENNIFER

Whenever I'm blessed to take a newborn into my arms during their first office visit, I always come away with tears in my eyes. They are a miracle, the little ones.

My first day back in the office, early in the day before trial began again, my first patient was one of those little ones, a three-month-old named Sara Mae. Sara Mae was feeling "puny," as we say. She was off her feed and was restless, not sleeping well at night. That was directly from Mom's intake sheet notes.

"Tell me what's changed with Sara Mae," I asked her mother, a pretty twenty-two-ish girl with very short black hair and a nostril ring. She sat her baby on the examination table and, as she held her there, I could see the arrowhead tats running up the inside of the mother's arm. Tats that meant, in the parlance of today's youth, that she had been smitten for life by cupid, a pledge of undying love to her husband—or some such thing.

"She's hot and cranky lately. Am I keeping her too warm? How do I know?"

They were always afraid they were going to break their new thing. Truth was, they couldn't. The human baby was more resilient than that prehistoric creature still among us and doing well, the cockroach. Babies bested them ten to one.

"Cindy, let's talk about her nutritional status. Is she breastfeeding?"

"She is. She does very well with breast milk, too."

"But you wrote on the intake sheet that she's started pushing your breast away?"

"Exactly. It's never happened before."

"Is Sara Mae getting stronger?"

"Yep. Every day she grips my finger harder when she's in her bath."

"How often do you bathe her?" I asked.

"Every day."

"Too much. It'll dry her skin. Every other, try that."

"Okay."

In my fast approach that the mother would never know what was going on, I assessed Sara Mae's nutritional status, level of consciousness, lack of toxicity and distress, absence of cyanosis, cooperation, hydration, and her mental state. The last one was part of the regimen of the pediatrician and all but impossible. I mean, a three-month-old's mental state—really? Actually, I really did do that.

I checked our prelims—accurate height and weight. Next I felt her skin and slyly moved into her lymph nodes. This one scares the mother much more than the baby. Next I moved to Sara Mae's fontanelle and noted the size and shape for the chart. Scalp, hair, and eyes. This was all preliminary, and then I began my gross assessment.

I listed them so you get a good idea what each of these little people get:

Nasal septum, mucosa (color, polyps), sinus tenderness, discharge. Then I moved to that favorite baby place where everything eventually goes, the mouth. Mouth and throat, lips (colors and fissures), buccal mucosa, tongue (color, papillae, position, tremors), teeth and gums (number, condition), palate (intact, arch), tonsils (size, color, exudates), posterior pharyngeal wall (color, lymph hyperplasia, bulging), gag reflex—here's where she'd start crying. Who wouldn't?

Then I moved to her neck, thyroid, trachea position, masses, top to bottom, lungs came next and her thorax before inspection of pattern of breathing. I told little Sara Mae's mom that period abdominal breathing was normal in infants where there was a pause less than fifteen seconds.

Then I moved onto the large muscles: use of accessory muscles, retraction location, degree/flaring.

I looked at the chest wall, noting configuration. Then auscultation, confirming equality of breath sounds. I noted rales, wheezes, and rhonchi. I listened for upper airway noise. Then the heart: auscultation, rhythm, murmurs, and quality of heart sounds. While on that topic, pulses: quality in upper and lower extremities.

Another five or ten minutes, and I'd completed my examination of Sara Mae.

"Perfect," I told the anxious mother. "In every way."

"You're sure?"

"Positive."

"Thank you!"

"Okay," I said after my exam and charting, "any questions?"

"How is she again?" A second time around was predictable. The mother's lip quivered in anticipation. So tender toward her baby.

"How is she? Sara Mae is a healthy, normal, female baby, three months old. She's good to go until six months when we check her again."

"Six months? That long?"

I smiled and rubbed Sara's chubby leg. "Six months is standard. Of course, if anything comes up between now and then, I know you'll call me."

Didn't I know it? I received and answered just about sixty mother calls every day of my life. And that's on a good day without a bug. When the bugs are out, I might get twice that in one day. Plus treating a full patient load.

"All right," said the new mother. "Six months, it is. Uh…"

Here it came. I could predict this. Third time's the charm.

"Are you *sure* she's normal and doing okay?"

"Pushing the breast away means she's getting her strength, and her arms are able to do more. Nothing else. It has nothing to do with feeding time or your milk or you or the stars in the sky. It's normal."

I waited while Sara Mae was dressed and buttoned into her sweater before I abruptly exited the examination room and hurried to the next one. Usually, I was trying to duck out quickly for urgent appointments. They came in-between patients and made the next one in the exam room wait and wonder why I was so late. So, after Sara Mae, I all but ran down the hall and stepped into the next room.

And so my day began, then off to my trial for murder.

You can't make this stuff up.

Chapter Twenty-One

JENNIFER

Here's the thing about doctors, especially psychologists. They always want to know how you wound up in their office. Dr. Verona Gresham asked me that question the first time we met.

"How did I find you?" I said. I didn't want to tell her I came to her because she was Michael Gresham's wife. So I sat there and looked around her office as if I were searching for an answer. I was sitting on the loveseat beside a lamp with a table built into its waist. On the table was a box of tissues. I got the idea.

Dr. Verona Gresham was sitting across from me.

Dr. Gresham was a psychologist trained in Russia who had moved to the United States with her husband, Michael. This had happened several years ago. As I said, Dr. Gresham did not know Michael was defending me in a criminal case. And Michael did not know that I was seeing his wife, Verona, about my feelings. Really, my feelings for *him*. It made me feel close to him to be close to his wife. Dr. Gresham's office was my private place to go with my mind and feelings to construct a relationship between blue sky and sunshine and closeness with his wife.

Sometimes, as a woman, it's hard to admit I feel like that. But I tried very hard not to fool myself. Michael was special. He was brilliant and handsome—although his face was scarred. Someone had said a client tortured him one time and burned his face. But he was way more than looks. He was all man and capable and looked at me a certain way.

"How did I find you? Well—" I thought I would skip the Michael feelings—thoughtful of me, yes? "I found you because I'm a baby doctor, and I know lots of doctors and get lots of recommendations. My husband's death has hit me very hard, and I just need someone to talk to. You should know that they have me on trial right now for my husband's death and have accused me of murdering him."

"Did you murder him?" asked Dr. Gresham. Her face was compassionate and open, yet she was all business.

"Of course not! I loved my husband dearly, the light of my life, my whole reason for being. Joseph and I were as close as any man and woman have ever been. I cannot tell you what it's been like since he died."

"Well, try telling me what it's been like. I'd like to know that."

"Well, I don't sleep, I've lost my appetite, and my children don't even know who I am anymore. We seldom talk to each other; we're like ships passing in the night. Most of the time I get through my days as a baby doctor almost reactively. I know I'm not thinking straight, and I'm just praying that I don't make a mistake and injure someone. And the depression—unthinkable."

"It sounds like it might be best if you took some time away from the office and concentrated on your children and yourself. Do you have other physicians in your practice who could share your patient load with you?"

"I could never do that. My little guys love me too much. And their mothers—they think of me as a god. Which I'm not, of course, but they rely on me totally when it comes to their children."

"Yes, we can begin to feel indispensable. We're not."

"Half of my calls every day are from mothers who want advice on child-rearing. There is no way I could break away from all that. Nor is it what I really want. No, I need someone to talk to and get through this time of adjustment. I'm glad I found you, but I will stay involved in my practice and come here to let off steam if you allow me."

Dr. Gresham smiled. "You're always welcome here. Moreover, if you ever need to talk during the day and have a small break, please try my phone. You can leave a message at any time, and I'll get back to you between patients."

"That's very kind of you. I'll try not to bother you with calls as I know how they can start to eat into your patient time. But one never knows."

"Anytime. You're welcome to share."

It was my opening, the therapist's keyword: *share*. I was so, so prepared to share, so off I went. Also, I had cut my risperidone in half two days running. Sometimes I just needed to elevate, to get my feet up off the goddam ground.

"Do you know what I mean about feelings so deep, so enveloping, for your husband that every day you're a chrysalis reborn into his light and warmth? Do you have that in your life, Doctor Gresham, so that you can understand me?"

She looked at me, unsure. Was I trying to cross a personal line that she wouldn't allow? Or was I sincerely seeking to connect with another human being as therapy?

She hesitated, but the therapist always won over the individual. It was their training, trust me, to never self-disclose, but she took a chance this one time. "Yes, I have that. I'm born to my husband every time he enters a room. Each time he touches my hand as I'm stirring our spaghetti sauce, I can feel a part of me recover from the day and melt just enough to want to rub—"

"Well...?"

"I mean, that's very personal. But I do, I do understand you, Dr. O'Connor. It's a universal feeling, what a wife might feel for her husband."

"And what you feel. I can almost feel what you feel for Mr. Gresham."

If I were a man, I could say I had just undressed her.

She stopped and put aside her pen. She tugged a tissue from the box and cleaned her eyeglasses. Holding them up to the light, I could see her thinking her way ahead of me, trying to get ahead of the patient.

Dr. Gresham bent to her notes and entered her thoughts into my chart. She was sitting with her back to her roll-top desk. On either end were green-shaded lamps, a triptych behind, portraying a river rolling along from a waterfall down to a pool of water beneath a tree.

"Now, Dr. O'Connor, why don't we try to set up a more structured day for you, morning and night?"

Oh, a hard right turn, off through the ether. *Come, angle off through the ether with me*, she said with that sidestep, that right turn, that phrase following a hard comma.

Ah, yes, structure. We had exhausted our *share*. Brief but emotional, dare I say, climax? Was that saying too much? Probably.

She had just called me "Dr. O'Connor." I smiled at her. I had changed my name for the patient records so that

Verona would never put two and two together and know that I was Michael Gresham's client. And vice versa. I was Jennifer O'Connor in Dr. Gresham's office and Jennifer Ipswich in Michael Gresham's office. It was a nice play, and I had to congratulate myself on my thinking.

"What do you mean by more structured? You mean like prayer and meditation, jogging, writing my memoirs? What kind of structure would I be looking at?"

Dr. Gresham smiled at me as a parent might smile at a child. "Yes, it might be all of those things, one of them, or something entirely different. Let's start by you telling me what kind of things you enjoy doing in your time away from your medical practice."

"Well, Joe and I have a lakeside home, and I enjoy going there to fish, believe it or not. I never fished in my life until I met Joe, and we spent hours out on the lake in our boat, catching all kinds of fish. I never wanted to keep them, but sometimes we took one or two and ate them that night. Anyway, with Joe now gone, it makes me feel close to him to go throw my line in the water and talk to him as my imaginary partner while we fish. Is there anything wrong with me talking to an imaginary partner? Am I just going crazy?"

Oh, the people I talked to! I didn't dare introduce her to my entire supporting cast. So I kept it focused on Joe. He was the only cast member she needed to address. At that moment, at least. The rest could be shuffled in and out of our sessions PRN, pro re nata, as the need arose.

"It's only human nature, Dr. O'Connor. It's very natural for people to continue to talk to their loved ones after they passed. I would be surprised if the newly widowed denied doing that. Often, people will ask for a loved one to appear to them and tell them they're okay. Knowing that a loved one who has passed is okay and not in pain anymore is a widespread human experience. So, yes, your talking to Joe is not only okay, it's healthy. I would certainly encourage that. What else might there be besides fishing?"

"Well, both of our young kids now know how to waterski. Joseph and I would take them out and ski them up and down the shoreline just about every weekend in the summertime."

"I love waterskiing. Michael and I go."

"Joe would drive, and I would be the spotter. With him gone, now I don't have a driver. And you can't be both the driver and the spotter. It's against the law. So I don't know what I'm going to do. I suppose I'll have to learn to drive the boat and let one of the children be the spotter. I don't even know if that's legal at their age. My God, I have so much to learn, and my life has changed so dramatically."

The baby doctor began weeping softly at that point—I was referring to myself, the baby doctor. "The baby doctor"—me—reached over to the tissues, clutched several and dabbed at her eyes. She was amazed at herself, surprised at how adaptable she was. The tears were real, even though the feelings were not. Joe had been a bastard for what he had done. She would never forget. *Note to self: it seems you can only admit your hatred for Joe in the third person. Buck up, you can admit this to your real self: he was a bastard for what he did. He broke your heart!*

I knew before he died he was involved. What wife wouldn't know? Then that last time when he tried to unload it on me and ease his guilt. But I didn't allow it, did I? Ice cubes and whiskey. Next thing, he's telling his internist he's not feeling so good. They decided it was exhaustion from working too much.

"Are you feeling better?" Dr. Gresham asked me.

"I can't stop thinking about Joe. I cry a lot."

"Of course, and you will."

I don't know that I'll need her yet. But if I do, I'll nudge Michael, "Michael," I'll say, "what if we called my psychologist to testify about my feelings for my husband? Would that make sense?"

Dr. Gresham looked at the clock on the wall and nodded. I looked as well and understood our time together was up.

Dr. Gresham said to me, "Same time next week?"

"Same time. And thank you for listening to me today. I feel much better just being heard by another adult. All right then, I'm off to my practice and a room full of runny noses. Ciao."

Dr. Gresham smiled. "That's right. Until next week, take care."

Chapter Twenty-Two

MICHAEL

My investigator is Marcel Rainford. He came to me via Interpol in Europe and the U.S. Army in Iraq where we were friends. He was the most capable, competent finder of lost items—people, places, things—I'd ever known.

It seemed like all I had to do was tell Marcel I needed something and, in the blink of an eye, it was sitting in the middle of my desk. I didn't remember asking, but I suppose I must have told him I would give anything to see Jennifer's medical records from the psychiatrist she was seeing when she started medical school.

At that time, Marcel spent about half his working days in his office and about half in the field. The field could be anywhere in the world, and he'd be pulling together facts and information that I needed in my litigation practice.

Here's what happened with Jennifer's case, as I've pasted it together.

The day after Christmas, Marcel was sitting at his computer, and that's when he made his decision. He was going to obtain Jennifer's medical records and he was going to justify it by the fact I was defending her in a criminal case. He was going to say that my defense of her in the criminal case made her medical records relevant and provided a basis for us to go after them. In retrospect, I agreed. She hadn't been forthcoming, and it was simply a matter of doing the due diligence. Good lawyering demanded no less. So, Marcel knew my thinking, and he went after the records.

MEMO TO THE FILE:
Jennifer had previously refused to allow me these records. I am making a decision that she's in no frame of mind to make that decision. I'm going after the records.

So, Marcel created the California version of an authorization to release medical records. Next, he filled out the authorization and addressed it to Dr. Samuel Erickson, 1101 S. Norridge Road, San Diego, CA. He then left the office with the authorization and took a taxi four blocks north to a storefront payday loans joint. He went inside, walked up to the window, and said he needed his document notarized.

"And whose signature might I be notarizing?" asked the man behind the glass.

"The signature is the signature of Jennifer Ipswich. She just happens to be one of my boss's clients."

"Is Jennifer present to confirm that the signature is hers?"

"No, but I can attest that it is her signature."

At that point, by law, the notary should have told Marcel to go jump in the lake, that he would not and could not notarize the signature of someone who was not present. But that isn't what happened.

"If Jennifer Ipswich isn't here, then I'm gonna have to charge you the full five-hundred dollars for the notarization. It costs more if the person signing isn't here at the window with you. That will be five hundred in cash."

Marcel reached into his pocket and pulled out five $100 bills. He slid them under the glass opening and smiled at the man. "Will that do?"

"That's exactly what's needed." The man then reached beneath the counter, pulled out a notary seal, signed the authorization as a notary, and sealed it with a notarial seal. He slid the authorization back beneath the window and said, "Will there be anything else?"

Marcel told him that's all he needed.

Marcel then left the payday loans storefront and took a taxi back to our office. He took the elevator upstairs and went back into his office.

This next part is a little unclear, but here's what I think happened. Marcel created a letter on my law firm letterhead and stamped it with my name, then sent it with the authorization form to Dr. Erickson in San Diego. He then got up and went out for a cup of coffee.

Several days later, Marcel received a manila envelope with the mailing label from Dr. Samuel Erickson in San Diego. It was addressed to me here in Chicago. Marcel opened the envelope and began studying the medical records of Jennifer Ipswich. He saw that they pertained to her treatment with Dr. Erickson.

The records were fifteen years old, and they did not indicate whether there had been follow-up treatment with any other psychiatrist since the time Jennifer left San Diego after medical school. However, when Marcel gave me the records, he was quick to point out that Jennifer had continuous treatment with Dr. Erickson all through her education at UCSD.

He gave me the records, and I quickly scanned down to what I was looking for. Marcel had highlighted it in yellow. It read it out loud:

"The patient describes experiencing several psychotic episodes over the past half year. During these episodes, she feels very paranoid and sees people in the shadows, waiting to jump at her. She sees people in parked automobiles, waiting to jump and grab her. She sees people in the bushes at her front door, waiting for her. All of these threats are coming after her. She also describes having, quote, otherworldly 'feelings,' as if she is outside of her body, watching herself. These psychotic breaks are episodic; they might occur two or three times in a month, or they might occur two or three times in a week. She never knows. Treatment will consist of risperidone and lamotrigine as a mood stabilizer. She will be closely monitored, and I will adjust her medications as we go along."

I looked up. "Bingo," I said. "Now tell me how in God's name you got these records. I know that Jennifer did not agree."

Marcel shook his head. "Boss, there's some things you're better off not knowing. This is one of those things."

"In a way, I'm glad we have these records. If push comes to shove at the criminal trial, I can introduce them into the record and amend her defenses to include a mental defense. I don't think the case is going to come to that because, frankly, I think we're winning the case and don't need it."

"Are you going to confront her about these things?" Marcel asked.

"Not at this point. If she denied the psychoses, then I

would be forced to show her the records, which, I can only assume, we obtained without her knowledge."

"Only doing my job, boss. It's a criminal case, and I was worried. I know you always want to know every last detail about your client, and I felt like I was letting you down by not obtaining this. I think my efforts have paid off grandly."

"Your efforts have paid off for now. Let's put the records into her file. We won't mention this again. But if I need them, I have them. Good work."

"Always glad to be of service, boss."

"Just don't ever do this again."

"I understand."

Chapter Twenty-Three

JENNIFER

Today, Michael asked me how I felt about settling and getting the Elise case over with—had I given it any more thought? How would I feel if this Elise just went away?

I told Michael I didn't feel like talking about it right then. I didn't want to even think about me giving her $1 million. I just didn't trust what I might say. But something told me the lady couldn't be trusted. I didn't ever want anyone to think I was selfish or I didn't think of other people. But this wasn't that kind of situation.

I knew that Joe was the kind of man who always wore his heart on his sleeve and was easy to read. I could imagine him sitting in his examination room at his medical practice, staring into the eyes of this woman from Paris. She could look right into his face and see that he was probably lonely living there in Paris alone two weeks out of every month. I'm sure that was when she decided to make her move.

I could see them going out for their first dinner, or maybe just drinks, and her sitting there looking lovingly into his eyes and nodding and smiling at everything he said.

Women could be like that. I'd never been like that, because I'd always liked to meet men on a common ground and exchange 50-50 with them. I'd never felt like I had to win a man. In fact, if anything, I'd always let the man come to me. Women who did less than that did not have my respect.

You know what else gets me? I had two children at home, just kids really, and their needs were just as important as the needs of this woman in Paris. It was terrible she had a sick daughter, especially one with HIV. But I didn't cause that, and I couldn't fix it. If she really thought she needed life insurance from Joe, then why didn't she go ahead and have him take out a policy there in France? After all, if you read her email carefully, you could see she was involved in some sort of business that had to do with consulting. So why didn't she consult herself? And get some life insurance? I mean, I wasn't even in consulting, and that's what I did.

I was doing everything I could to hold my feelings in check and not lash out at this Elise. She wasn't innocent, but she wasn't a criminal either.

It was just a terrible situation, and I didn't want to dwell much on it.

It couldn't have come at a worse time, right in the middle of my trial for murdering the man I loved. All I needed was to have a lawsuit piled on me while I was fighting for my life and freedom.

The very nerve of that woman in France to come in and ask for money at a time like this—it just made me crazy to even think of someone doing that to me. No, I had to circle the wagons and protect myself now. That was the best thing for me to do, and I wasn't going to worry about some other woman's problems. I didn't ask her into my marriage and I wasn't going to make her life all okay now that she was in my marriage. She could go jump in the lake as far as I was concerned.

Michael just nodded at me. Sometimes he could get the dumbest damned look on his face, like he was busy with a movie and not really seeing me. Or hearing me. It chapped my ass, but that was my secret.

Wake up, all you people!
I am talking!

Chapter Twenty-Four

MICHAEL

I received a call from Jennifer to tell me the reading of the will would be held late Friday at the office of Cynthia Drake. I didn't know Attorney Drake, but Jennifer asked me to be present, and I agreed.

Friday night, I drove to Evanston, where I was going anyway, then stopped at the office of Attorney Cynthia Drake for the reading of the will. I was shown into the large conference room of Ms. Drake. Already present were Cynthia Drake, to whom I introduced myself, Jennifer, and Frank Wilder, who of course was representing Elise Ipswich in her absence. Without fooling around, Ms. Drake got right to the business at hand. She began reading the will, and I listened with great interest when she got down to the specific distribution of Joe's property.

"To my wife, Jennifer Ipswich, I leave our house in Evanston Illinois one-hundred percent, and to my wife Elise Ipswich, I leave our condo in Paris France one-hundred percent. My United States assets are to be divided between Jennifer Ipswich and Elise Ipswich equally. They are to receive life estates in those assets with the remainder to my children in equal shares."

When Ms. Drake was finished, Frank Wilder couldn't restrain himself from jumping in with his comments.

"Now what we need to do is determine which assets are Joseph Ipswich's and distribute those 50-50 between Jennifer and Elise. Jennifer, are you claiming more than fifty-percent ownership in any of Joseph's American assets?"

I spoke up, "Hold on, Jennifer. This question is really meant for me. Mr. Wilder, this is probably neither the time nor place to be having this conversation as the reading of the will is normally a solemn affair and is not a settlement conference. But since you brought it up, yes, Jennifer Ipswich is claiming more than fifty percent ownership in almost all of the parties' assets. She contributed more than fifty percent as Joseph was investing much of his money in his French family and his French holdings."

"Pure bullshit."

I ignored him. "Jennifer Ipswich will also be making a claim against one half of those French assets. While Joseph Ipswich can, by his will, leave one half of his ownership in the Paris condo, my client is not convinced that Elise Ipswich has actually contributed one half to the ownership of that condo."

"Likewise to the American assets," Wilder said with an angry smile. "So, we'll need her deposition. For starters."

I went ahead, unfazed. "Jennifer will be claiming more than one half of the Paris condo, as to Joe's ownership. And just to let you know, she also has contributed approximately eighty-five percent of the purchase price of the Evanston home. This leaves approximately fifteen percent of the home equity for distribution. Which means, of course, that your client may—but not for sure—own up to seven and a half percent of the home equity. I say that without admitting it, but rather say it only for purposes of information to you, since you've asked."

Wilder was laughing. "You break me up, Gresham," he said and slapped the table.

Jennifer then spoke up. "I'm prepared to spend whatever money I have in fighting off the claim of your client, Mr. Wilder. Also, I don't believe she was acting in good faith when she married my husband for his second time. Surely, she knew that he had a family in America since he kept returning here for two weeks out of each month. I'm certain she would've asked with whom he was spending his time in America and, knowing Joseph, he would've told her the truth. He was a truth teller. And I'm sure he did not try to cover up from Elise that he was married previously in America."

I couldn't resist. "And the fact that she knew before she married him that he was already married gives her unclean hands. Which means that she is not entitled, as an equitable matter, to one half of his assets on either side of the Atlantic. In fact, I'm not convinced she's entitled to any percentage of his assets. Given that she knew going in that he was married makes her complicit in the fraud against my client and my client's children. I'm sorry these matters had to be discussed, Ms. Drake, in your office during the reading of the will. But, evidently, it could not wait, at least in Mr. Wilder's world."

"Right back at you," Wilder sneered at me. "And she didn't know he was married before she married him. You can have your opinion but you can't have your facts, Gresham."

"Oh. You must be right. Isn't that what your wife says?" I couldn't resist, childish as it was.

Girl, Under Oath

We then began gathering our things to leave Cynthia Drake's office.

Outside in the hallway, Wilder buttonholed me off to the side away from Jennifer where he could speak to me outside her hearing. He wasted no time in unloading on me.

"Gresham, I'm putting you on notice that everything you said in there is pure bullshit, and I'm going to be fighting it. My client will offer to settle with your client for fifty percent of all American assets, no exceptions. She is also willing to settle with your client for fifty percent of all French assets. Again, no exceptions. If your client refuses to accept this offer, I will have no option but to drag her into court kicking and screaming and extract one half of all assets through litigation. Trust me, Gresham, you do not want to litigate with me and my scorched earth policy of litigation. Your client could very likely end up with nothing, having spent every dime on legal fees, yours and mine."

I wasn't rattled, of course. I had heard little ducks fart underwater before. Wilder was a blowhard and a big mouth as far as I was concerned.

I said, "I think it would be smart if we got both clients together, with us present, and let them talk through their differences while you and I try to listen and keep our yaps shut."

"Could you do that?" he sneered. "So far, from what I've seen of you, Gresham, I think not."

"I think they will come much closer to an agreement than you and I ever could with our biases and prejudices and your ego."

He knew exactly what I meant when I mentioned his ego. His face lit up, turning red and contorted because I had dared to insult him. But I felt he was the type of attorney who was used to being insulted and probably had a very thick skin. I was just letting him know that I was prepared to go to the mat with him.

"I think you might be right, that it might be good for our clients to talk. While I don't think there has been ego involved on my part, I don't believe I can say the same thing about you, Gresham. You sound pretty mouthy to me. You sound like someone speaking out of school to impress your client. I guess we'll just have to see if you've the wherewithal to back that up."

I shrugged and began walking away. Wherewithal?

That was my middle name.

Chapter Twenty-Five

MICHAEL

It seemed like I was the cooler head, so I called Frank Wilder to set up a settlement conference between the lawyers and their clients. I then called Jennifer to tell her what was going on.

"Jennifer, I just called Frank Wilder. I found out that Elise Ipswich is coming to town to testify in the Temporary Restraining Order hearing."

"What's that?"

"He's asking the court to restrain you from transferring marital assets. Purely an exercise in ginning up legal fees. Anyway, while Elise is here, Frank and I have agreed to set up a four-way conference to discuss the case's settlement. Are you open to that?"

"I don't think a settlement conference will hurt anything," Jennifer said. "In fact, why don't we all go out to dinner somewhere and discuss it over dinner? It seems to me that would be the civilized thing to do."

"No, this won't be a social occasion. There will probably be raised voices and some anger. Fine dining this isn't."

"I was so hoping we could talk about this like adults. Too bad."

"Jennifer, let me say it once again. Frank Wilder does not want this case to settle. He wants to bill, and bill and bill and have his legal fees paid by you. He wants to become your *part*ner in the assets you own. Do you understand what I'm saying? That's how this guy works. That's why I was encouraging you yesterday to get it over with, to bite the bullet, to give this lady one half of the insurance money."

"Well, one half is not going to happen. So let's have the meeting at a neutral place. How about a Denny's?"

"Denny's sounds about right. I'll set it up." I hung up the phone without further conversation.

Chapter Twenty-Six

JENNIFER

"I was reviewing your record before you came in today, Dr. O'Connor," Verona Gresham said to me. "I think we're a little thin on your history around the time of medical school. Long story short, were you under any psychiatric treatment during that period?"

"Not psychiatric, exactly," I replied. "More like continuing treatment for bouts of depression. Plus, sometimes I can get a little hyper and can't sleep for a day or two. Dr. Erickson gave me some pills for that."

"Would you sign a medical authorization for me so that I can get Dr. Erickson's records?"

"Of course, I would. There's absolutely nothing in there I wouldn't want you to know."

"You know we were talking last week about the case. You must have strong feelings over being charged with your husband's death. Is that something you carry around with you every day?"

"Of course, I do. I think about it every moment of every day. For one thing, it's terrifying to think they could put me in prison for something I didn't do. Plus, I feel ashamed being charged with a crime about the man I adored. I know other people know, and I can feel their eyes on me even when I'm just walking to the grocery store behind the cart. Plus, the social life Joe and I enjoyed together is all but dried up. Our friends don't call me anymore. My mother is constantly phoning and asking me if I need anything."

"Mothers do worry."

"I'm getting very paranoid at how people look at me. Even people I don't know. And I can tell you for a certainty, my medical practice has lost patients by the score. Many parents don't want their children treated by some doctor who's going through a trial for murdering her husband. Quite frankly, I don't blame them a bit. If nothing else, this case is going to put me out of business. When it's over, I'm thinking of moving to a new state and starting over. My name has been ruined here, and even a 'not guilty' verdict will not get it back. I'm sure you can understand."

Dr. Gresham nodded. "Yes, that must be very difficult. How are you handling it as far as your feelings? Can you share your feelings with me?"

"I thought I just did. I'm feeling angry, and I feel shame, and I feel like I want to scream. Plus, I want to run and take my kids with me and hide in a new place. Plus, there's the thing with Elise going on. The woman won't leave me alone and keeps texting and saying terrible things about me. She will send one text to me, my lawyer, her lawyer, and the judge on my case, and will say horrible things about me and how I hated our husband and wanted him dead after I found out he had another wife besides me. And nothing could be further from the truth. How I actually felt when I found out, believe it or not, was a certain amount of pity for him. I couldn't imagine how a man could be so needy that he would have to take a second wife."

"What is the timing on all of this? I mean, it can't go on forever."

"Well, tomorrow I'm meeting with my lawyer, her lawyer, and her. We're going to try to settle her case against me and divvy up the assets."

"How do you feel about that?"

"I'm mad as hell. How would you feel if everything you had worked for was up for grabs by your husband's second wife?"

"So, you're feeling a great deal of anger about tomorrow's meeting?"

"Yes. I don't know what I'm going to say. I might just take a gun in there and shoot everyone."

"Please don't say that. People like me are supposed to take those things seriously and report our patients to the authorities. Please tell me you were only expressing yourself, that you would never consider really doing that."

"Of course not. I just want to say that I'm that angry. How I will react, I'm not sure yet. But I might want to bitch-slap that woman."

"What else can you tell me about the meeting? Maybe we can develop some healthy ways to react to what's going to be done tomorrow. How do you feel about your house? Is the other wife after that?"

"She better not be. I've made one-half of those payments all the way through. She's entitled to none of it."

"Did she and Joseph have a child?"

"They did. They have a young girl together. When I found out, I cried for three days. It broke my heart that my husband did that to me. I felt so threatened by the young girl, and yet she was a child, no different than the children I treat every day in my practice. I found myself beating myself up for those feelings. There have been times I have wanted the two of them to just disappear from the face of the earth. I can't even stand thinking about them or thinking about her with him, I mean. I feel so betrayed."

"What are you going to do with all these feelings you're having?"

"Just what I'm doing right now, talking about them. Are you asking me if I'm going to pick up a gun and go after anyone? Not likely. I talk a mean game, but I never follow through with that kind of stuff. I'm way too healthy for that. You've nothing to fear from me, doctor."

"Jennifer, have you ever experienced loss of time, memory lapses, that sort of thing?"

"I suppose everyone has. It happened today. Yes, I have. Is that so abnormal, given what's happened to me?"

"And how long might those periods of lost time last?"

"How long would those times be when I wasn't reacting properly? I don't know, maybe an hour, maybe two. It's very hard for me to say because it's not like all one or all the other. It's like I go in and out."

"At the meeting tomorrow, can you remember that this other woman probably has the same feelings you are? I mean, what if it turns out that your husband didn't tell her he was already married? Wouldn't that make her one of the innocent ones? Wouldn't that make her situation just as sad as yours? Do you know whether she knew when she married him?"

"I have no idea and don't give a damn. At this point, I'm in survival mode. I've been broken by Joe and now I'm looking to put myself back together again. I'm holding on to what I have left. Picking up the pieces and looking for new ones."

At just that moment, we heard a loud commotion just beyond the closed office door. It was coming from the waiting room area. A man's voice had risen and was demanding to see the doctor without waiting another minute. We could hear the receptionist trying to calm him down. But his voice kept growing and sounding angrier with each sentence. Finally, Dr. Gresham looked at me and shook her head. "It appears I'm going to have to go out to my waiting room for just a moment. Can you excuse me?"

"Of course. I'll sit right here and wait."

Dr. Gresham exited her office, closing the door behind her. I waited until she was gone, then jumped up and went to her desk and began looking over her things. There were the usual desk objects—the blotter, the paperweight, the paper tablet holder, the laptop, but what really caught my eye was a silver and turquoise wristwatch. I picked it up, turned it over, and read the inscription on the back of the watch: *Verona, Michael. Let's pass our time together*.

I slipped the watch into my purse and hurried back to my chair. Retaking my seat, I folded my hands in my lap and waited. I could hear Dr. Gresham's voice coming through the door and then heard the tinkling bell of the outer door as the man, I can only assume, had been calmed down and agreed to leave. Dr. Gresham returned moments later. In all, she had been out of the office less than five minutes.

She sat down at her desk and shook her head. "So sorry. Now and then, it happens. I'm sure you don't get that in your practice. Or maybe you do, dealing with babies and small children. I expect you hear lots of crying and see lots of tears shed in your office every day."

"Indeed. My office is a vale of tears," I said with a laugh.

"All right," said Verona. "Where were we?"

"You were just about to tell me how to get through tomorrow's meeting without throttling someone. Please elaborate."

Dr. Gresham smiled and launched into a set of relationship tools she thought I could take with me and try.

I heard none of it. My thoughts were on the wristwatch in my purse. All I wanted to do was get someplace private and slip it on my wrist. Michael would notice me wearing it in court. It would bring us closer together. The first piece added into myself. My *self*, right?

And it wasn't just a mind game. I was way down the road on that. I had real feelings for Michael—Mike?—and needed to let him know that, just like Verona had accepted the watch, I had accepted it, too. It meant just as much to me as it meant to her. Would he be able to understand this? I had to give him credit.

I thought he would definitely understand.

Chapter Twenty-Seven

MICHAEL

Saturday at noon, the four of us met at Denny's restaurant on Warner Road in Old Town. We took a corner booth and ordered coffee. I smiled at the waitress, who looked disappointed, but brightened up when I told her I would leave a hefty tip if she would leave us alone except to refill our coffee. She smiled and said she would.

Elise had just flown in from France and was looking jet-lagged. But there was also an air about her that she was anxious to get going. So, I didn't disappoint her.

"All right then," I said. "I'm delighted the four of us could get together, and it's my sincere hope that we can arrive at a settlement here today. I want nothing more than to conclude this dispute between Elise and Jennifer."

Frank Wilder shook his head. He held up one hand at me like he was directing traffic. "Not so fast, Michael. Not so fast with the hope that we can settle here today. We are here only to investigate and find out about the property the parties claim in common. I know that Elise has a certain amount of property in Paris that belonged to her and

Joseph and that Doctor Ipswich has a certain amount of property here in Chicago that belonged one-half to Joseph."

I smiled and couldn't let it pass. "Wilder, you might know that, but I don't know that. Nor does my client."

He went ahead. "All we want to do here today is discover what that property is and see if we can arrive at a temporary arrangement. Right now, I'm handing you a list of the property Elise knows about in Paris. I know you have a list prepared for me of the property Jennifer knows about here in Chicago. Please pass that to me now."

We exchanged property lists, and then Wilder continued his comments.

"We know that Joseph Ipswich was a very peripatetic man, and we wouldn't be surprised to learn that he had property stashed all around the world. In particular, Elise remembers him talking about bank accounts that he might have opened in the Caribbean. We would be very interested in hearing about those, as well."

"No such thing," Jennifer interjected. "That's a load of you know what."

Wilder ignored her. "If you are not forthcoming about them, Mr. Gresham, then you will leave me no choice except to begin taking depositions around the Caribbean."

"On your own dime," I said.

"Maybe not. I will be looking for any hidden assets of Dr. Ipswich. As you might imagine, those depositions will be costly when you add in the cost of my air travel, my hotels, the cost of the deposition, and my hourly rate. I can promise you that, in the end, Jennifer Ipswich will ultimately be responsible for those costs for failing to tell us about these hidden assets upfront. So, what do you say, Mr. Gresham?

Are we going to have a full and open discussion about Dr. Ipswich's assets? Or are we going to play hide the ball?"

I shook my head. I started to have that feeling in my chest like this guy was after much more than legal fees. He wanted it all. I understood the game. He was going to create chaos and uproar and disagreement because he knew that all those difficulties would result in additional legal fees for him for having to go to court and straighten out the turmoil he had caused. I was going to try to avoid that, if possible.

I said, "It really disappoints me to hear you take such an aggressive attitude right out of the gate, Mr. Wilder. At this time, I can only tell you that Jennifer Ipswich is unaware of any assets owned by Joe Ipswich beyond the borders of the state of Illinois. Should you decide to back up your threat of depositions around the Caribbean by going there and taking depositions, it will be my client who has her costs paid for by your client. I can also guarantee you that these hidden assets are figments of your imagination and not based on true facts upon which the court would award legal fees to you. I have handed to you a four-page document signed and notarized by my client. It includes every asset of the marriage known to Jennifer Ipswich. Maybe we can take a couple of minutes now and go over each other's lists with our clients."

Chapter Twenty-Eight

MICHAEL

It was at that moment, at that Denny's, that it happened.

In looking back, I remember that I was at first stunned by what Jennifer had to say. But then it came back to me in a rush—her medical records. The doctor had said she had a tendency toward psychoses. That she saw things in bushes. That she saw people in the shadows who were waiting to jump out at her and grab her.

In retrospect, all I could think about was her outburst. For, out of nowhere, she said, "You're much more handsome than the Chicago Bar Association directory makes you out to be, Mr. Wilder. If I were you, I would change my picture for one more attractive. If you do that, I can assure you your law practice will double from the female population alone."

For just the briefest of moments, no one said anything. Then Wilder laughed, tossing his head back before leaning forward. As usual, he was not at a loss for words.

"That's very nice of you to say, Dr. Ipswich, but look," he said, holding up his left hand. "As you can see, I'm wearing a wedding band, so I must decline any stirrings you might have toward me. In other words, doll face, I'm taken. I'm a married man. Please get back to reading and get ready to explain what assets are being hidden on this half-assed list your attorney has come up with. Your efforts at clouding this discussion with your comments about me have failed."

I remember I leaned over to Jennifer and whispered in her ear, "What in the world, Jennifer? Are you losing it here?"

Jennifer reached out and covered my right hand with her left hand. "Darling man," she whispered back, "I'm only trying to get inside his head. If it's a game he wants to play, then I'm ready to play it with him."

"You're going to have to leave that to me," I said. "If you refuse, I'm going to conclude this meeting, and you're going to be shortchanged in finding out what assets your husband owned overseas. You know what else? Those comments are nothing like you. And they border on the ridiculous."

Jennifer then said in a firm voice, one I know was heard several booths away because I saw the startled looks, "Say what you will, Michael. I find Frank Wilder very attractive. I might even have a drink with him sometime."

Again, I was totally stunned. That time I just didn't even have any words.

"Maybe we can shelve that for now," said Wilder. "I think we all understand what you're trying to do, Doctor Ipswich. So you can consider it done. You've gotten inside my head and played your little game. But now, let's try to get down to the business at hand. And thank you."

I just couldn't believe it. I took a long drink of my coffee and sat there with my eyes closed for several moments. Then I put my mug back down on the table.

I said, "So, it appears that Elise, with Joe Ipswich, had thirty-five-thousand euros in liquid assets at the bank known as Banque De France. That thirty-five-thousand is a marital asset. So, it's subject to equal division between Elise and Jennifer. I'm going to put it on a piece of ledger paper in a column that I will title 'marital assets.' I understand there was also an American Express account with a credit balance of fifty-five-hundred dollars. I'm going to put that in the same column as well."

"Not so fast, Mr. Gresham," said Wilder. "The truth of the matter is, the thirty-five thousand euros bank deposit represents the work of Elise Ipswich in Paris. It is her sole and separate property and not subject to division."

"I disagree. The asset should be split fifty-fifty. We have to agree to disagree. Because the assets you're talking about in Paris, even if they were separate property, in the beginning, they have now been co-mingled. That makes them the property of the marriage, and Jennifer Ipswich is going to make a full claim against that property of the marriage in the full amount of one half of thirty-five thousand euros."

Wilder smiled. "We strongly disagree. Disagreements like this are what cause lawsuits. Moving right along, Elise Ipswich claims one-half of the bank deposits at Bank of America in the sum of one-hundred-twenty thousand. She claims one-half of the assets in the sum of sixty-five-thousand dollars at the Fifth Third Bank. And she claims one-half of the assets at the Bank of Chicago in the sum of eleven-thousand-seven-hundred dollars. Also, I can see that the medical practice account at the Bank of Chicago is for one-hundred fifty-five-thousand dollars. Elise Ipswich claims one-half of that by the equities."

"Are you finished?" Jennifer asked. "Does she want one-half of my underwear, too?"

Wilder continued, "All in all, my client is laying claim to one-half of each of these accounts. Any attempt on your client's part to avoid immediately making available to my client one-half of the sums will be raised at next week's hearing for temporary orders." He handed me a pleading. He had filed with the court a request for an accounting of all American assets and a request for a temporary distribution of those assets. She wanted half and wanted it right now.

"All right, Gresham? You've read my pleading? There is absolutely no reason for your client to walk out of here today without turning over to my client a check in the amount of one-half of the total balance in those accounts. So put that on your ledger sheet—that's joint property."

And then Jennifer spoke up again. It happened so quickly there was no chance to stop her. "Pure nonsense," she said. "Except for the medical account funds, all of that money belongs to me and me alone because I earned it in my medical practice. I earned it while Dr. Ipswich was away in Paris enjoying his sleepover with your client, Mr. Wilder."

I remember I nudged her quite hard and then leaned over and whispered that she would have to shut up and let me do the talking. Yes, I was really upset. I was pissed with her. I also told her she was going to have to keep her opinions to herself or give them to me after the meeting when it was just she and me.

"Then why am I even here?" she said in a loud voice. "If you won't let me talk about how cute this man is, and you won't let me talk about the assets that belong to me, then why am I here? Anyone?"

"You're here because you're trying to hide assets, and we know it," said Wilder. "And while you're so outspoken, maybe you can divulge the other assets that you are trying so damned hard to cover up. I'm waiting…dear."

Wilder took a big drink of his coffee, and he scowled. He waved at the waitress. "This crap is cold!"

He then continued. "The second area I would like to take up is real estate. It appears that Joseph Ipswich owns a house in Evanston, Illinois. Jennifer has put on this paper the house is worth two-point-one million. It just so happens that I've had that house appraised, and I've learned the value is more in the neighborhood of six-and-a-half million. So, we are about four-point-four million apart."

I stepped in. "Amazing your man could appraise a house without entering it. Did she enter while my client was away at work and didn't know? Burglary, Wilder?"

"Again, we will be taking this up with the court next week when the court hears our motion for temporary orders. It is Elise's position, however, that she will accept three million for her share of the house. Failing that, we will establish at the hearing next week that the house should be immediately listed on the market at eight million."

"Utterly ridiculous," muttered Jennifer.

"Dr. Ipswich," said Wilder, "you might think it's ridiculous. But if I were you, I would begin packing my suitcases. Long story short, you should stop by U-Haul on the way home and pick up a whole bunch of packing boxes. You're going to need them. Your house will be sold in the next thirty days because I understand it's a hot market up there. No sooner are houses listed than scrappy buyers grab them. Don't like it? Tell it to the judge next week."

Jennifer turned to me and said in her loudest voice, "Michael, is this lunatic serious? Does he really think I'm going to allow him to sell my house? Please tell him that's never going to happen. Even if I have to appeal this case to the United States Supreme Court, it's just not going to happen."

I tried to ignore her. Instead, I said to Wilder, "While we're on the subject of real estate, I don't see any real estate assets listed by Elise Ipswich in Paris. Or anyplace else in the world, for that matter. Would you care to explain that to us?"

Wilder shrugged. "That's an easy one. Elise and Joseph owned no real estate together. It's all in Elise's name, and she makes the payments, which she can hardly afford since Joseph is no longer helping support his French daughter."

I said, "She's told us she earns next to nothing at LVP Partners. How in the world has she afforded a condo in the heart of downtown Paris?"

"You've just nailed it, Gresham, part of the problem that Elise is facing at this moment. She needs support for herself and her sick daughter. As to the Evanston home, Judge Adamson will immediately see the inequity of the situation and award my client three-point-two million, constituting one-half. It seems to me your client has some serious banking to do to make my client an offer. If she doesn't offer complete payment, we will be in court next week, and I will make my case there."

I smiled. "You can try. Can you pull all this off? Impossible, Wilder."

"I can promise you Judge Adamson will have no difficulty selling your client's house and splitting the proceeds. Judges do that every day since they see it's the only fair way to divide up marital homes."

I could only sit there and shake my head. Inside, I knew he was probably right. But this was a contest, and I couldn't totally ignore Jennifer's wishes. So I said, "As far as Judge Adamson, it's going to be very clear to him that you are doing nothing more than trying to run up legal fees with your grab-and-run tactic. This scam might work well for you in other courts, but it's not going to work in this one. My suggestion for you is that you accept the sum of one million for any interest your client might have in my client's real estate and be damned glad she's getting that. Because, otherwise, she's going to go to court next week and be sadly disappointed when Judge Adamson finds that the real estate in Evanston is my client's sole property."

"Pure BS."

"Not so." I sighed. "Moving right along. I see where your client has listed two Mercedes automobiles paid for. She has listed those with a total value of fifty thousand euros. Without going to the *Kelly Blue Book*, I know that those vehicles are worth a minimum of a hundred-fifty thousand. So, I'm going to put that value in the marital property column and make a claim on my client's behalf for seventy-five thousand euros."

"Mr. Gresham," said Wilder, "you just said something significant a few moments ago. You made an offer of one million. I'll tell you what I'm going to do. I'm going to tell my client to accept that offer of one million in partial payment of what she's owed. I'm going to suggest we then have our appraisers get together, yours and mine, and arrive at valuations for the home."

"Appraisers make sense."

"If we can do this, we can avoid going to court next week. Also, my client will accept one-hundred thousand in full payment of her interest in those accounts. I have discussed this, and she has authorized me to settle in these amounts. So, it's a steal. Your client pays one-point-one million and gets out from under what she owes on the life insurance of two million and on the bank accounts. Then we will split the difference on the house valuations, and your client can then refinance and pay my client one-half of that valuation. Or we can agree to sell the house on the best terms possible to the best buyer possible."

I looked at Jennifer. She was noncommittal. I was exasperated. She should've grabbed that offer and run.

Wilder plunged ahead. "This will forgo a court-ordered sale and will put more money in the pockets of both our clients. I can't think of any way to be fairer than this. And I think you'll have to admit, it's a fair offer. The only requirement is that your client brings a passbook with one-point-one million to my office by five o'clock today."

I looked at Jennifer again. She nodded. "Okay on the one-point-one million. No, on the house," she said.

"Have the money at my office Monday by five p.m.," said Wilder. "No bait-and-switch, or I'm calling the judge and the sheriff."

"Will do." Jennifer smiled benignly. "Will do."

Chapter Twenty-Nine

MICHAEL

We broke from court on the criminal trial Monday at 12:30. We went over by half an hour because the assistant medical examiner was available to us for testimony only in the morning, and my cross-examination of her didn't conclude until 12:30 on the button. Right after that, when court was recessed, Jennifer disappeared without telling me where she was going or asking whether I needed to confer with her over the lunch hour. I saw her an hour later when she came into court with a smile on her face. She sat down beside me and said, "Well? Are you going to ask me where I've been?"

"All right, where've you been?"

"I've been to the Bank of America. I opened a savings account in my name and the name of Elise Ipswich, and I put one-half of the life insurance proceeds into that account. Here is the passbook, which I want to give to you and ask you to give to Elise in hopes that we can settle this matter once and for all. I thought about the things you cautioned me about after we hung up this morning. One

134

thing I don't want to do is get into a land war with Frank Wilder after all the things I've heard about him."

I smiled and slapped the table. "Smart lady!"

"Right now, there's one-point-one million in that account, which should be enough to settle all differences between that French hussy and me." She held up a hand. "I don't really mean that. I know she's a good person, and I know she probably got taken in by Joseph. He had his weak moments, and I have to admit there were times with him when I just had to look the other way and shake my head. 'Boys will be boys,' is what I told myself. Anyhoo, the money is there, and now you have the passbook, so please do whatever legal mumbo-jumbo you have to go through and get me out of this little mess. Thank you very much."

"This is great, Jennifer," I said. I exhaled a great sigh of relief because nobody in their right mind wanted to go up against Frank Wilder while he raped and pillaged someone's assets. Plus, it made sense to me what she was doing. I made a note to myself to call Frank after court that day and try to escape any litigation he might have in mind. We then continued with the criminal trial.

Later that afternoon, I managed to get Frank Wilder on the phone, and we had our back-and-forth about the case.

"Frank, this is Michael Gresham. To make a long story short and cut right to the heart of the matter, I have in my file a passbook at Bank of America, an account which presently has one million in it, earmarked for your client. I hope that your client will accept this amount in full settlement of any claims she might have against Joe Ipswich's property. Please let me know if it's going to settle matters between them."

"Haha, Michael Gresham. I'd heard that you're one of those guys who does like to cut right to the heart of the matter, but only when that heart favors your client. No, Joseph Wilder's assets are worth much more than one million, so consider your offer declined. But we are still waiting for the money, as we discussed Saturday, in full settlement of the insurance policy and bank accounts. Your client should jump at that, or else she's as crazy as the loon she likes to portray."

Portray? I asked myself. At this point, I wasn't so sure it was all an act. Anyway, I plowed ahead. "Wait, Frank, aren't you even going to take the offer to your client? Doesn't the law require you to do that?"

"Oh, we've already talked, and she's told me that anything less than fifty percent of Dr. Ipswich's other assets should be rejected."

"Wait a minute, the assets owned jointly by Joseph and Jennifer include just about everything in her life. What are you going to try to do, put her on the street?"

"Yes, Michael, that's exactly what I'm going to do if that's what it takes to make her sweetly reasonable and willing to settle this case for fifty percent to my client. As you and I both know, nothing makes a client more sweetly reasonable than restricting their access to their bank accounts, cash accounts, and cash flow. I'm going to ask the judge for a conservator. I'm going to have my runner bring these documents to your office tomorrow morning, and I hope you will stipulate there's no need for formal service of process and that you will file a response without wasting any time. Is that fair enough?"

"It's fair enough that you can send those documents over to me, and I will prepare and file responsive pleadings. What isn't fair is for you to think you're going to go into court and tie up one-half of all of my client's assets, just to make her come around and surrender to your client. That just isn't going to happen, and you can be aware from the get-go that I will be seeking legal fees from your client for having to respond to such a ridiculous assertion as the one you're about to make. Your client has no claim against the marriage assets that are in the name of Jennifer Ipswich in her own right. Yet it sounds to me like she will be going not only against joint marital assets but against assets she holds separately."

"That is exactly right. It's going to be my client's position that even assets held in Jennifer's name, she earned those assets while in a marriage with Dr. Ipswich, and thus they are assets of the marriage to which my client is entitled to fifty percent. See you in court, old man. Please get ready to get your ass kicked."

"I'm going to be ready, all right, but I would suggest you prepare to get your ass kicked in return. Goodbye now, Mr. Wilder, you have a good rest of the day."

"Have her here by five with the one-point-one million."

We hung up at that point, and I instructed my paralegal to prepare responsive pleadings when the Wilder pleadings arrived. I already knew that the guy would be asking for the moon, and I already knew that I was going to be fighting everything he was seeking. Already, this case was going south, and my client stood to lose a huge amount of money in legal fees because Wilder was going to stir this thing up.

While I was sitting there contemplating appearing in court against Frank Wilder, he called me again—another charge of a ten-minute legal fee.

"Mr. Gresham, I forgot to say one thing. My client does accept an additional two-thousand euros per week as temporary child support for their daughter, Çidde, who currently needs her medications refreshed. When my runner arrives with the documentation, please have the account book ready to turn over to him. Are we in agreement with that?"

"Yes, we will turn over the passbook. While I'm not sure the estate of Joseph Ipswich owes child support to your client, the agreed money will be turned over. Just let the record show that the money turned over is not for child support. At this point, there is no proof whatsoever that Joe Ipswich was the father of that child, and we're not going to go into this thing admitting parenthood from the get-go. That's something you're going to have to prove to me. Now, you want to play hardball, how about that hardball?"

"My my, you must've been reading some of my articles, Mr. Gresham. Proving that Joseph Ipswich is the father of Çidde Ipswich is a very simple matter. But the issue will increase the legal fees your client is going to owe to me, so I can only say you're making a mistake by taking that position. For now, thank you and goodbye. I'm billing your client three-hundred and seventy-five dollars for this call."

"Thank you, too. Goodbye."

Chapter Thirty

JENNIFER

Bank of America, Schaumburg branch, was on Golf Road just off the freeway. I took the Golf Road off-ramp, went up two blocks, and pulled through the drive-through banking. When it was my turn at the teller window, I put the Jennifer Ipswich–Elise Ipswich savings account passbook into the tray. The woman inside the bank booth asked what I would like done.

"I would like you to move the money out of that account and back into my personal account. I'm going to send you a deposit slip for my personal account."

The teller called right back. "Ma'am, this one-point-one million was just moved into this account this morning earlier. Is there some problem that you're moving it right out?"

"Not at all. Just do as I say, please." I then placed a deposit slip into the transfer box, but the agent made me enter the bank. When she was finished, she put the savings account book and the receipt for a $1.1 million deposit into my personal account back into my hands. I went back out and drove away.

I turned my car around at the intersection and headed back toward the freeway, where I went underneath and then made a left curve to head home.

It was just too much to ask of me, to give away a piece of myself.

The money was back where it belonged.

Chapter Thirty-One

MICHAEL

After criminal court Monday, around 5:30 p.m., Wilder called me. It seemed like the impossible had happened. Jennifer had failed to show up with the savings account book.

I called Jennifer. "My God, Jennifer, what have you done? You actually took the money out of the savings account and put it back into your own account? What in the hell are you thinking?"

"Well, I'm not going to support her love child. When I heard that it was going to be used for child support, I decided hell no. I wasn't going to play that game. Funny thing is, I might have done it before if she had come to me in a civilized manner and asked me for it. But, so far, all she's done is demand, demand, demand. I'm not gonna let her get away with that. She already stole half of my husband; she's not going to steal half of my money. So yes, I put the million back in my account, and they can sue me."

"They've already sued you! Get ready for that dam to burst! This is not a smart thing to do."

The line went dead. She had hung up on me.

It wasn't fifteen minutes later that I got a call from Frank Wilder. I could tell at the beginning that this wasn't going to go well. He was furious. "Will you please effing tell me what your client is thinking, taking the one-point-one million away like it was a baited trap?"

"Frank, I'm still trying to get a grip on that myself. I just want you to know that it was against my advice. And it certainly wasn't done after consulting with me. After we hang up, I mean to talk to her. I'm going to strongly encourage her to put that money back and go ahead with the original plan."

"Ha ha, Gresham. That offer's off the table. I'm preparing an amended affidavit for Judge Adamson right now. I'm gonna tell him what kind of games your client is playing with my client's life. Knowing Judge Adamson, he's gonna be pissed and won't let your client get away with it."

"Give me until tomorrow at noon. I need to talk to her in person."

"Too bad. There could even be a fine involved. Maybe even jail time. At the very least, the court will sequester one half of Doctor Ipswich's assets and grant my motion. I want you to know that I'm also going to be amending all my pleadings and asking for a conservator over the medical practice, too, at this point. I want someone appointed to take full control of all of Jennifer and Joseph's assets. That way an accounting can be done. Then I can set the matter for hearing and ask for a fifty-fifty division. Your client isn't going to play any further games, Gresham, not on my watch. Tell her to pull her head out of her ass before I pull it out for her."

The phone went dead. I looked down at the phone, and the button was red. Terminated.

I then called Jennifer.

When she picked up, I didn't wait to charge in. "Congratulations, Jennifer, you just started World War Three. Frank Wilder is totally pissed, and he's going after blood. If I were you, I wouldn't hesitate to give me authority to give Elise one half of Joe's assets. If you don't, the court is going to do it for you, and you're gonna wind up paying one-hundred to two-hundred-thousand dollars to Frank Wilder's in legal fees because you wouldn't cooperate. I can't urge you strongly enough to authorize me to make that offer. What do you say?"

"Michael, I think the court will take notice that this woman entrapped my husband. The court will know she's nothing more than a common leech. It will send her away with nothing. In fact, I'm wondering why we aren't going for one-half of her assets? Isn't it possible we could file a pleading and ask for half of what she has?"

"Yes, we could do that. If you really mean it, you need to send me an email telling me to do it. You need to confirm to me in writing that it was your idea. Because believe me, it is going to cost you more money than you ever imagined if you do something as foolish as ask for half of her assets."

"Should I send it to your regular office email?"

"Yes. That will give me evidence when the shit hits the fan that all of this was your idea."

"Ta, Michael."

For the second time that day, someone had hung up on me.

One of the hang-ups had been justified. The second one was going to be enormously expensive, and I would've given anything not to have to be there when it happened.

Chapter Thirty-Two

MICHAEL

On Tuesday, the jury came back with a verdict in Jennifer's criminal case.

Speaking with the jurors after they had given their verdict, I kept hearing the same thing.

Said one, "We thought something funny was going on, but we also thought the State hadn't proven its case beyond a reasonable doubt. So, we had to find your client not guilty."

Said another, "They simply didn't prove their case. There was no connection between Jennifer Ipswich and the death of her husband. It was a very sad situation, and I think most of us felt very sorry for her. But most of us also felt a little suspicious. But they couldn't prove anything beyond a reasonable doubt, so we found her not guilty."

After the verdict, Jennifer and I hugged, she thanked me, and then she left to go back to her office. Marcel and I returned to my office. We gathered around my desk to wrap things up. I said to him, "I didn't tell you this, but Saturday when we had our settlement conference, I saw in action what Dr. Erickson said about Jennifer and her medical chart. It was like a light switch had been thrown, and she was suddenly a woman on the make. There she was, flirting with Frank Wilder. She might even have given me the eye a couple of times."

"Oh, I could stand that." He chuckled.

I ignored Marcel. "Honest to God, I've never seen anything like it in thirty years. I feel sorry for the woman. But at this point, I'm wondering whether I should just jump out of the property settlement case. Maybe I should just tell her to get another attorney. Those medical records have really jaundiced my view of her. I no longer trust her, and I don't like her all that much—which is a sad commentary on me because I need to remember the things she is doing are not her, but are her medical condition acting out. God, that's hard for me to remember sometimes."

"I have great sympathy for the situation," said Marcel. "I know a lot of stuff can be controlled with medication. But there's still crap that slips through the cracks. Plus, sad but true, sometimes patients don't take their medications. But even then, I'm not faulting them for that. Many times, it's the illness itself that whispers to the patient to skip the meds. Nobody is responsible for that. That's more a matter between the patient and her angels and hope nothing bad happens during those times. It's just too damned bad in her case."

"What do you think of me staying on her case?" I asked Marcel. "Leave or stay?"

Marcel said, "It doesn't matter what I say. Knowing you, you're going to stay on the case and try to help her regardless. I've never seen you return a dog to the dog pound. I don't think you're about to start now."

"Pound puppies. God love 'em."

Marcel clapped his hands together and sat up straight in his chair. "All right, how do we get ready for Wednesday and the hearing to end all hearings? Wilder is going to be loaded for bear, and I want us to be loaded for bear-plus-one. What do we need to do, oh boss of all bosses?"

"First, I have two appraisers out at the home doing a structure appraisal and a lot appraisal. They both agreed to be present at the hearing tomorrow. And they've both been paid by me. Both are young women in their thirties, and Judge Adamson will be impressed with their credentials. They are both master level MBAs, and they know their stuff forward and back. Now what about the bank accounts? What do we know about those so far?"

Marcel held up a finger. "I've collected the bank balances as of the date of Dr. Ipswich's death. It seems the balances at that date totaled around three-hundred and twenty-thousand dollars. I've had a forensic CPA do the workup, and of that amount, two-hundred eighty-five thousand was contributed directly from the medical practice of Jennifer Ipswich. This means that Elise has a very small claim of thirty-five-thousand dollars against the parties' joint efforts. So the judge will give seventeen-thousand five-hundred to her and give the other half to Jennifer."

"So far, so good. What else?"

"Your witness is a CPA with an MBA who is prepared to testify that he was trained at Yale University and has his MBA from Wharton Business School. He's also working on his PhD at the University of Chicago and has testified in similar hearings no less than fifty-five times. He wears thick glasses, Brooks Brothers, and a class ring on his right hand with stones that sparkle in the dark. Judge Adamson is going to be impressed with his credentials, impressed with him, and I think we will walk away with her two-hundred eighty-five thousand plus another seventeen-five."

"I can hardly wait to see that ring. What else do we have?"

"Well, you know there's one other interesting aspect of the case. Jennifer is late thirties and Elise is early thirties. They both have a life expectancy of around 85 years. I've hired an economist, George Smathers PhD, who is going to come into court and testify that Elise, once she becomes a full-fledged agent of LVP Partners, is going to make more over her work life than Jennifer. So, the equities are such that our opponent is going to make more than eleven million more than Jennifer in a normal work life. I think this is going to impress his honor."

I couldn't help but smile ear to ear. Marcel was incredible. "You've done a great job, buddy. Now I know why you're paid the big dollars. And I know why Thaddeus Murphy is trying to steal you away from me by offering up his daughter as a living sacrifice out in San Diego."

"I know you're joking, but I don't find that at all funny. Turquoise Murphy and I love each other very much, and we expect to be together quite soon. I don't expect our marriage to have any impact on my ability to work for you when you need me and work for Thaddeus when he needs me. As you might recall, we now have jet airplanes that fly between Chicago and San Diego in four hours. I can work half day for you and half a day for him and still be home in time for a late supper."

"Whoops, sorry for the bad joke. When you and Turquoise tie the knot, I expect to be there with Verona, and I hope to get together with Thaddeus and Christine for dinner at least once. We'll put our heads together and figure out how to best use you. I only hope you're open to our planning, as you are about to become a very wealthy man."

"Uh, Michael, you might've forgotten, but you and Thaddeus have already made me a very wealthy man. It doesn't get much better."

Chapter Thirty-Three

JENNIFER

"And how did it go with the settlement conference?" Verona Gresham asked me late Tuesday. We were together in her office again, her back against her roll-top desk, me seated on the love seat beside the box of tissues. So far, I hadn't needed one. Today would change that, I decided.

"Well, the Paris faction is nothing but gold diggers. I was afraid it might come down to this. She's asking for one-half of everything I own without regard to the fact that I paid for about eighty-five percent of everything Joe and I owned together. My lawyer has hired people to do appraisals and forensic accounting in order to prove these things. I love my lawyer and am very pleased with his brain and good work. His intentions are also honorable, and he is a very darling man. Take it from a widow, I'm impressed with his good looks and his charm. Sure, he has his scars, but who doesn't?"

I said this last part with a great smile, nodding, and I'm all but certain that Dr. Gresham made a note that her patient—me—seemed to be letting go of her fixation with her dead husband and was maybe opening up to the prospect of other relationships. She was pleased with my growth. She had no idea it was her own husband who was now receiving my admiring looks.

"It sounds healthy. Maybe you moved on from Joseph and are thinking about other men. Is that what you perceive yourself doing?"

"No man could ever replace Joe. He was my everything. No, I'm just talking about men's looks generally. It's not too different a feeling than when I'm in the store selecting a cantaloupe. I check how its looks, how it sounds inside, and I smell it."

Dr. Gresham had to laugh. "Not a bad way to choose someone to have dinner with. Maybe more women should do what you do. Looks-sounds-smell. Write that down."

"Dr. Gresham, one thing is troubling me. My attorney, at times—not all the time, mind you—seems to be undressing me with his eyes. Most of the time this makes me uncomfortable. I'm just wondering if there's anything to be gained by saying something to him to let him know that I'm not interested. The truth be told, I'm a widow still in mourning, and I can't even imagine becoming interested in a man right now. It's kind of depressing that he doesn't realize that and instead keeps devouring me every time he looks at me. What should I do?"

"Are you giving out signals? You know, women can give out signals without realizing it. Maybe it's the way you're dressing, maybe it's the way you smile at what he says, maybe it's what your eyes say to him. If you're having any kind of romantic feelings toward him, then you are probably unconsciously giving off clues. If I were you, I would check my motives and, more importantly, check my feelings. Sometimes, it's easy for the newly widowed to get caught up in the comfort and expertise offered by men in his position. Times like that, women can be taken advantage of. It doesn't sound to me like your lawyer's that kind of person, but please be aware that worse things have happened. So, check your motives and check your feelings about this person. Then I think you will have a much clearer picture of what's going on, at least from your side."

I sat back and shut my eyes. I was thoughtful for several moments. Then I opened my eyes and said, "I am having feelings for him. I think I would like to have coffee or dinner with him. The only problem is he's a married man. If I were to proceed and pursue him, I wouldn't be any better than that French whore who ran my Joe to the ground and screwed him and got pregnant and is now trying to take his assets away from his real wife. That makes me insanely angry at her and her lawyer. I will fight them until the bitter end. Speaking of which, our hearing is tomorrow, and I don't wish to come across as unreasonable. But on the other hand, I don't want to just get up on the witness stand and give away half of everything I own. That would be extremely unfair to me. I wonder if the judge will take into account the fact that this woman moved in on someone else's husband and got pregnant and is now making a run at the real wife's property. I hate her for that. But I know in court I can't come across that way. How am I supposed to cover up my true feelings once I start talking?"

"Would it be so bad if your real feelings came out? Maybe the judge would have sympathy with your position and will understand why you are angry and hurt. As long as you're not letting those feelings interfere with the property settlement itself, I don't think a judge will fault you. Therefore, I would counsel you to be yourself and to reveal your true feelings and let the court know that, despite those feelings, you're still trying to be fair about the property. If you can do that, then I think the judge is going to like you better than anyone else in the courtroom. And I have to agree, the woman who jumped on your husband and made a target of him is quite distasteful. I think any married jurist, at least one who is true to their family and spouse, will empathize with you."

"That's good advice," I said. "I'm going to take it to heart. Tomorrow I will be honest but reasonable. Thank you for that."

"Incidentally, Jennifer, I seem to have misplaced a very important wristwatch sometime last week. It's a treasure, something extremely sentimental given to me by my husband. I'm wondering whether, at our last visit, you happened to see it on the floor or if I had knocked it off something and missed seeing it."

"Of course not. I would've told you right away if I'd seen anything like that. I'm so sorry for your loss. Maybe you can ask the giver to provide you with a replacement. That could be every bit as valuable, couldn't it?"

"With me, it doesn't work that way. I need to find the original, and I'm asking all of my patients whether they saw anything out of the way the last time they were here. Anyway, we're out of time here today. Same time next week?"

"Sounds good."

"All right, I'm putting it on my calendar. And good luck tomorrow."

"It's not about luck, doctor. It's about being honest and reasonable. I have to remember that."

"There you go. Honest and reasonable."

I plucked a tissue from the box and dabbed my eyes and blew my nose.

She could see I was reactive.

Chapter Thirty-Four

MICHAEL

From what we've pieced together, here's the part about Karrol. She's an important player.

In a downtrodden location in Paris, along the north bank of the Seine, stood a row of apartment houses where the rents were very reasonable—€1100 a month for a two-bedroom. Which meant that the place was rundown, usually ran no hot water to the tenants, and was loaded with cockroaches that came out after dark and moved things around in the kitchen.

Inside one of these apartments, in a front room with the window shades drawn, sat two men and one woman, dark-complected, beards on both men, surrounded with automatic weapons and bomb-making materials.

Said the first one, named François, "So, we agree? Our target is to be LVP Partners?"

Said the one named Mikell, "We agree." He turned to his smart phone and began recording the first part of the spiel that would be turned over to TV after the murder: "LVP Partners is active in Israel and has a presence there in the amount of over three billion. They actively help the Israelis spread their insanity beyond their borders and are financing settlements in Palestinian territory. Black December's first target is the same. LVP Partners, we can now claim credit." He paused for further input from his teammates.

The Egyptian woman spoke up. Her name was Karrol. "Well done. I've been looking and have found a Paris target, a woman who works for LVP."

François asked, "Who might that be?"

"Her name is Elise Ipswich. She lives on rue Dumont. She is single with a six-year-old daughter who is looked after by Elise's mother—a sixty-year-old woman who is nearsighted, hard of hearing, and will never know what hit them. We will take out Elise, her mother, and daughter if we strike on a Sunday afternoon. That is my recommendation."

Mikell nodded. "Then so be it. Now, all we have to do is decide which Sunday we are going to strike."

"What about kidnapping her?" asked Francois.

Mikell said, "We might do even better by kidnapping this Elise and making a demand for several million dollars from LVP Partners for her safe return. This would leverage our ability here in Paris to effect our ends. It would put money in our bank account, and we could buy more C4 and plastique and more bullets. Friends, I think we are just beginning here. Let me think more about this, and I will make a decision soon."

"Of course," said François.

"As you wish," said Karrol.

Chapter Thirty-Five

ELISE

Email from Elise Ipswich to the addressees below:
Michael Gresham
Frank Wilder
Jennifer Ipswich, M.D.

Good morning everyone! Tomorrow is the big day when we go into court for our first hearing on Joe's assets. I have to admit, I'm just a little bit frightened at the prospect. So, I have decided to take a few minutes, write everyone, and try one last time to settle without court.
I don't think I can emphasize strongly enough that I would be willing to settle this case for one-half of the insurance proceeds, and then I would go away quietly. That would give me enough to take care of Cidde.
What I mean is, it would give me enough to buy her medicines and maybe even find a nicer place for her to live where there are fewer environmental allergens as she has an impaired immune system and dust and mold all but puts her to bed and keeps her there. Plus, I might buy a house with a yard as she wants a dog more than anything.
Combined with her HIV compromise and the potent drug she is taking,

my little girl is having a tough time. She's uncomfortable for most of the days, and it's not unusual for her to have to come home from school early, maybe two or three times a week. So, you can see, I would really like to get this over with and get home to her and do what I can to make her life better.

While he was here with us, Joseph spent a good deal of time with his daughter. Being a doctor, he checked her regularly, kept up with the literature on her primary diagnoses, and kept things in balance in her life. In other words, she had the best medical care money could buy, except we didn't even have to buy it. It was all Joseph. Now we've gone from 100% to maybe 15% of the same kind of care for Çidde.

She shows it.

I particularly want to speak to Jennifer, who is a children's doctor. I know that you spend your days trying to make sick children well and trying to keep well children well, and I know you must be able to sympathize with Çidde's plight. If I lived here in Chicago, you would be the first person I would bring my daughter to see. I would trust you with her care, and I know that you would have a special place in your heart for her. I'm asking you at this time to have that same special place in your heart for her. While she is not your daughter, she is your husband's daughter, and I hope that counts for something. What I'm trying to say is, she is a piece of Joe left behind, and it's my wish that someday our children can know each other and can remember their father together, all of the separate parts making the whole that much stronger.

Also, I would like to thank Michael Gresham for setting up the meeting we had on Saturday and trying to help us settle this case. Let me ask you a question, Mr. Gresham. Am I wrong in thinking that everyone agrees there's around seven or eight million in assets? And am I wrong in thinking that if I go to court, I will get 3 1/2 million or $4 million worth of those assets? Why isn't it simple, then, for us to settle my claim for only $1 million? Doesn't that seem like the best thing for your client? I don't know if it's you or Doctor Jennifer who doesn't want to *settle, but I'm begging both of you to hear me out and settle with me for half the insurance proceeds and let me go home to take care of my little girl.*

One last thing. My mother is staying with my daughter while I'm here in America. I spoke to her this morning on the phone, and they have taken my daughter back to hospital for asthma. This breaks my heart that I can't be there for her while she's in hospital. One last time, I'm begging you people to settle this case and let me go home.

With great love in my heart, I remain,
Elise Ipswich

Chapter Thirty-Six

MICHAEL

Elise's email fell on deaf ears, near as I could tell because Jennifer didn't suddenly call me up and instruct me to settle.

Crickets.

On Wednesday morning, court began at 9 o'clock sharp. Judge Earnest Adamson was seated on the bench, and he peered through his reading glasses, presumably reading the pleadings filed in the case before things got underway. At last, he said, "Mr. Wilder, it is your petition for a restraining order, accounting and temporary orders of support, so you will go first. Please proceed."

I watched as Frank Wilder climbed to his feet, anxious to get a running start, but instead he made a long, winding, windy, opening statement to the court, outlining the parties' assets, their debts, their earning histories and potential, and telling the court what witnesses he would call. He ended by asking the court to restrain Jennifer from transferring assets.

Witnesses followed. Wilder led off by calling Elise Ipswich. Elise, a pretty woman with olive skin and an ear-length bob, walked briskly up to the witness chair and turned to be sworn in. She raised her right hand, upon which she wore a plain gold ring on her middle finger. She took the oath of witness, smiling slightly, and she then arranged herself in the witness chair and leaned forward in anticipation.

Wilder asked her the usual background questions, including her date of marriage to the decedent, Joseph Ipswich, and the date of her giving birth to Çidde Ipswich, their daughter. Wilder then asked her about her assets. Her testimony aligned with what had been discussed at the Saturday noon meeting. He then got into her need for support, and he spent a good portion of her testimony there.

"How much, Mrs. Ipswich, do you receive each month as payment for your work as an associate agent at LVP Partners?"

"I receive approximately four thousand euros per month."

"Is there any bonus at the end of the year or any other type of compensation in addition to the four thousand per month?"

"No, that is the total pay I receive, about forty-eight thousand euros per year."

"And what, if you know, is the average wage for French citizens as of this year?"

"I believe it's about sixty thousand euros per year. I might be off by about five thousand, give or take, but I think I'm pretty close."

"Suffice it to say, your yearly income is below that of your fellow citizens by a considerable amount?"

"Yes, it would seem so. At any rate, I know that other people my age are buying condos and apartments and have title to many other assets. At the same time, I'm in a small condo that I paid for half with my savings. I still owe half, too. Other people in my office are doing much better than me with their houses and yards."

"Why do you think this is?"

"I know why this is. It's because I must spend one thousand euros per week for the medications my six-year-old daughter needs to stay alive. As you can see, I have no money per month to live on and have just about exhausted the savings that my late husband left me."

"So, this morning, you're here to tell the judge that your circumstances are desperate?"

"They are desperate in the least. I'm here this morning, hat in hand, to beg the judge to help me continue to buy my daughter's medication and keep a roof over our heads. It just seems unfair to me that—"

"Objection!" I shouted out. "The witness is about to make a closing argument rather than give testimony. While the court might sympathize with her position, she is not entitled to give opinions about what's fair and unfair."

"Sustained. The witness will provide testimony of observable facts. She should not offer opinions as to fair and unfair however deserved they may be."

Wilder continued, "How much money are you seeking per month for the court to award you as temporary support while this case is pending in this court?"

"I need at least ten thousand euros per month to supplement my income and allow us to live in the condition we were more or less living when my husband was alive. The other Mrs. Ipswich is living at a much higher standard of living, due in large part due to the earnings and assets of our late husband."

Frank Wilder took a minute to go through his notes, allowing those comments to sink in with the judge. He then looked up, adjusted the reading glasses on his nose, and ran a hand through his hair. "Would it be fair to say that you are only seeking an equal standard of living to that of Jennifer Ipswich, insofar as that standard of living is made possible by the assets of Dr. Joseph Ipswich? Do you understand my question?"

"I understand that you're asking whether I can set aside how much money Jennifer Ipswich earns and set aside how much money I earn and look at only the assets and income from those assets of our late husband. Yes, I can do that, and I can say unequivocally that this is exactly what I'm looking for, a substantial similarity in our standard of living based only on our late husband's assets and earnings. I think that's only fair." She hurried to add this last sentence, fearing another objection by me. I almost made that objection but decided against it because her commentary was really very harmless.

At that point, the court interrupted. "Excuse me counsel, but I'm just now reading the latest of the pleadings, and it's just now becoming clear to me that the litigants, Mrs. Ipswich of Paris and Mrs. Ipswich of Chicago, were both married to the same man at the same time. Is this correct?"

Wilder answered sharply, maybe revealing his annoyance with the judge's dilatory reading of the pleadings, "That is exactly correct, your honor, and it should further be understood that neither woman knew about the other woman's marriage to Dr. Joseph Ipswich. At a minimum, my client did not know about Jennifer Ipswich's marriage to Joseph Ipswich. We are just coming to the point in her testimony where I was going to make clear to the court that she was entirely innocent when she married Dr. Ipswich."

"That being the case," said Judge Adamson, "consider that point made. It won't be necessary for you to go into it any further. Counsel, are there any other questions that you wish to ask of this witness before I allow the respondent to make his case?"

"I think not," said attorney Wilder. "I think we're just about finished here, Your Honor."

The judge looked perplexed, but then his face relaxed as if it had all become clear to him in a rush. He then said, "Counsel—both of you—I've heard all I need to hear from this witness. Please let us proceed and telescope down this hearing by allowing me to move on to the respondent, Jennifer Ipswich."

At that point, Elise Ipswich stepped down from the witness stand and resumed her place at counsel table beside her attorney. The judge then turned his attention to me and addressed me directly.

"Mr. Gresham, I have read your pleadings, and I have read your avowals to the court of what your witnesses would say, your summary of their testimony, and the numbers and amounts they would testify to. The court will accept your pleadings as true as if you had presented this testimony, and I'm ready to make a ruling in this case. Would you have any objection to my proceeding in this fashion? If you do, then I will have no alternative except to make a temporary order for support at this time and continue this matter so that I can get onto my next case, a pressing criminal case."

"Your honor," I said, "I would rather the court take as true those matters alleged in my response rather than continue this matter to another time. My client is ready to hear the court's ruling and will make every effort to comply."

Judge Adamson sat back and contemplated the ceiling for several moments before rocking forward in his chair and fixing his gaze upon a point approximately between the two lawyers' tables. "It is ordered that respondent Jennifer Ipswich make available to Elise Ipswich one-half of the total bank accounts presently held in her name, from whatsoever source and however earned. The court is aware that Dr. Jennifer Ipswich claims that a good portion of those proceeds is her separate property, but the court disagrees. While this is not a community property state, this is an equitable property state, and the court has some leeway in making its ruling. Based upon the petitioner's testimony about her ill child, the cost of that child's medications, and the fact that the petitioner is still working as an associate agent and is living significantly below the average standard of living in Paris, the court makes this order to do equity between the parties. Jennifer Ipswich shall deliver a cashier's check in the amount of one-half of the value of all checking and savings accounts and CD accounts upon which her name appears, no later than five PM this afternoon. That check will be delivered to the office of Frank Wilder, attorney for Elise Ipswich. Gentlemen, is there anything further?"

"Only to ask the date when we may come to court for a full and complete accounting," said Frank Wilder—who, I just happened to think, was always more than willing to come running back to the court if only to run up more legal fees.

As if to make my point, Wilder then added, "And incidentally, Your Honor, we also asked in our petition for temporary attorney's fees of thirty-five-thousand dollars. Will the court care to rule on this as well? The reason I believe it's deserved is that the parties met on Saturday, at which time Jennifer Ipswich stated that she would never even consider turning over one-half of those bank account funds to Elise Ipswich. Thus, she is the reason we are here today without a settlement, and my time and hours have been provided to the court in a separate pleading, which amounts to thirty-five thousand dollars. I would ask the court to award me this amount out of the separate funds of Jennifer Ipswich."

The court looked at me and said, "Mr. Gresham?"

"Your Honor, the demands that counsel was making on Saturday were without basis and were outrageous. He intended to drag this matter into court to be awarded the enormous legal fee he is now claiming while pretending to make it look like it is all occasioned by my client's fault. It is only fair that Mr. Wilder's client pays him herself, at least until we can have a full-blown hearing on this matter and get into testimony on who said what on this past Saturday."

"Yes," said Judge Adamson, "that is my inclination as well, to put off the hearing on legal fees until we can have a full hearing on the entire matter. But in the meantime, to ensure that Elise Ipswich can continue with this litigation, the court will make an order for at least partial payment of Mr. Wilder's fees. Dr. Jennifer Ipswich will pay out of her separate property ten-thousand dollars to Frank Wilder. There being nothing further, this matter stands adjourned."

Chapter Thirty-Seven

MICHAEL

Upon leaving the courthouse and walking across to my office, I could all but feel the steam coming out of Jennifer's ears. However, she was able to keep herself collected until we arrived back inside my office and were sitting around my desk with Marcel present. She then erupted.

"That rotten, conniving woman! I've never been so angry in my life. I've never been so inspired to take matters into my own hands and throttle her myself. The absolute nerve of her to come to the United States and make a claim on my personal property as if she has some right to it for doing the dirty of stealing away my husband and enticing him to marry her. It is shameful, it is degrading, and I hope to hell we can keep it from being published in any legal newspapers or, even worse, the *Chicago Tribune*. I don't even know where to begin."

I nodded solemnly and shifted my gaze over to Marcel.

He spoke up first. "I've been to lots of these hearings, Doctor Ipswich, and it never ceases to amaze me how utterly random the rulings appear to be. The court today could just as easily have awarded you one half of her assets as award her one half of your assets. It seems to me to make no good legal sense. Michael?"

"I was afraid something like this might happen. It's not good law, and it's not taking into account the proffered testimony of my experts. It is very clear, according to my experts, that the amount of thirty-five thousand dollars was the only amount that was in question as to whether or not it was joint property. The rest of the amounts at the banks and CDs, were clearly found to be the sole and separate property belonging to Jennifer. I cannot express to you how sorry I am that the court went this way, and I'm really feeling rocked back on my heels at this point. Not to mention the ten thousand that the court added on as almost a punitive damage. That certainly wasn't deserved."

Jennifer stood and stamped her feet as if she were a child throwing a tantrum. "Isn't there some damned way we can appeal this thing before five o'clock and get another judge to look at it and overrule him?"

"There's absolutely no alternative offered in the law that would accomplish that. Appeals take a long time. They very often amount to Solomon splitting a child in half rather than give real relief to one party or the other. No, I'm afraid you're stuck with the court's ruling, and that all we can do from here on is prepare for the full-blown hearing."

Jennifer then raised her right hand and pointed an accusatory finger at me. She said, as if swearing an oath, "Right? Then that leaves me no option except to do what I can to make things right. I'm not going to be run over by this woman and that greedy bastard she calls her lawyer. I'm just not going to obey the court's orders. You might as well call the judge right now and tell him to send the sheriff after me because there's no way in hell I'm going to raid my bank accounts and give that bitch one-half. That just is not going to happen today. I don't care what anybody says to me."

Now it was Marcel's turn to look back at me. I shook my head. "That is absolutely the wrong attitude to take, I can assure you. If you persist in that, the judge will appoint a special conservator to all assets in your name and will proceed to dole those out fifty percent to the second Mrs. Ipswich. I cannot strongly encourage you enough to proceed to your banks, obtain a cashier's check, and return it to me by four PM so that I can have our runner deliver it to Frank Wilder's office before five PM. I'm terribly sorry to be so blunt, but at this point, it's the only reasonable avenue of action for you to take, Jennifer."

Jennifer folded her arms and glared at me. "You're not hearing me. I said I would never do it. That's all I have to say to you." She then turned on her heel and stamped out of my office without another word. It left me and Marcel staring at each other in astonishment.

"I don't think I've ever had a client talk like this before," I said. "Not in thirty-some years. I have no idea what that woman is going to do, but I don't like it one bit. I can't help but think about the psychotic episodes she experienced during med school, and I'm praying that the stress of today's hearing doesn't send her over the edge so that she has another episode and does something crazy."

I drummed my fingers on my desktop. Then I sighed, leaned back in my executive chair, and rubbed my eyes with my fingertips. I was absolutely worn out by then. I checked my wristwatch and found it was only 10:20 AM. All was not well. I yawned, collected myself, and then came forward in my chair.

"You know, it might not be a bad idea for you to follow her and make sure she doesn't do something entirely off the wall, Marcel. What if you swing by her office, make sure she's there, and follow her home after work and then lurk around until the light goes off in her bedroom?"

Marcel said, "I'm thinking the exact same thing. I'll call you back tonight, boss, after she's in bed."

Chapter Thirty-Eight

MICHAEL

What follows is what we've pieced together.

Just as court ended, Elise, who was planning on flying out within the hour to attend to her daughter in the Paris hospital, happened to pass by my counsel table while Frank Wilder and I were up with the judge. Jennifer Ipswich had moved over by the windows in the courtroom and was using her cell phone. Everyone's back was to Elise as she passed by my and Jennifer's table.

While no one was looking, Elise reached down and grabbed the manila folder off the table as she passed by. She stuffed it inside her bag and kept moving, fully expecting that at any moment, a voice would cry out and demand she return the file.

However, there was no voice with each new step, and it became clear to her that she was going to make it out of the courtroom with the new treasure.

She had no idea what was inside the folder, but she was desperate. Whatever she might find, she hoped against hope that it would help settle the case and give her the money she wanted. Beyond that, there was no ill will, no intent to commit a crime, and no intention to embarrass Jennifer Ipswich in any manner or to take advantage of the situation as it existed.

Instead, she hoped to use whatever was in the file to help the other side see that settlement was in everyone's best interest. If she could make that happen, she knew she could go to Paris and not return to Chicago for the full-blown trial. Nothing would please her more. Nothing would be better for her daughter than to have the money with no further delay to meet her needs.

Elise returned with Frank Wilder to his law office to wait for the 5 p.m. deadline so that she might receive the money the court had told Dr. Ipswich to bring to Frank Wilder's office.

She was anxious but hopeful that Jennifer Ipswich would obey the court's order and deliver the money fully and on time.

Frank Wilder provided a new office inside his law firm complex where Elise could stretch out on a small couch and sleep while she waited. She did just that, and soon it was five o'clock in the afternoon. Wilder had come for her and taken her to his office to anticipate the delivery of the several million dollars from Dr. Ipswich.

At 5:15 p.m., Attorney Wilder excused himself and went out to the reception desk for a word with the receptionist. He came back with a white envelope, business size, and a smile on his face. He sat down at his desk across from Elise and said, "Ready?"

"Ready," said Elise.

Wilder used his letter opener to slice the seam on the

letter. He reached inside and pulled out a cashier's check for $15,000. Along with the check was a note that said, *I believe this is all that I owe. I think that the court was wrong. You will have to take me to court for the full-blown hearing to get another dime out of me. Sincerely, Jennifer Ipswich, MD.*

Tears washed into Elise's eyes as she realized what happened.

"Can she do this? Can she get away with this? What are we going to do?"

"Hell, no, she can't get away with this! I'm going to call the court in the morning and report this fraud and jerk her ass back into court."

"Oh, my God, I'm flying out at seven o'clock to return to Paris and my baby girl tonight. You know she's in the hospital, and I have no option except to go. Please tell me I don't have to be there for court tomorrow."

"No, you're good to go. There'll be no need for you to attend court. I can take care of it without your presence."

"Am I—Am I going to get my money, or is this going to drag on even longer now?"

"I'm afraid it's going to take more time. These things have a habit of going south when something like this happens. I'm going to have to beat this woman down several times before she becomes sweetly reasonable. I can tell you that I can get it done, but I can also tell you that it will take some time. No, you fly back to Paris tonight and take care of your little girl, and I'll take care of court tomorrow. You take the fifteen-thousand.

"I already changed my reservations once today. The airline won't let me do it again without charging me. I have to go tonight."

"So be it. I agree."

Chapter Thirty-Nine

VERONA

"I'm going to kill that woman if it's the last thing I do," swore Jennifer Ipswich at her late afternoon meeting with Dr. Gresham. "Please don't run out and tattle on me. I'm only blowing off steam, but I would like to see that bitch dead. And that lawyer of hers—what a jerk-off. Every time he wipes his ass, he charges me three-hundred dollars for it. How can people like that even sleep at night? I work myself silly each day with a couple of hundred runny noses in my office. I earn my money the old-fashioned way: I work. Guys like that need to be taken down. I've gotten to the point in this litigation where I'm about to pick up a gun and end it myself. Can you really blame me?"

Verona Gresham studied Jennifer and her expressions and tone of voice. She was trying to judge whether she was hearing the usual rants of an upset patient or whether she heard threats that she would be required to report to the authorities before they happened. She decided to test further. "What would happen if Elise were dead? Would all of your problems be solved?"

"I think so. At least those greedy fingers would be out of my bank accounts and not trying to sell my house."

"Yes, but if she's dead, she leaves behind a little girl who would have the same claims against your estate as she does. Would you be willing to kill the little girl, too?"

"I hadn't thought about her. I hadn't thought that she could be just as difficult for me as her mother. In all honesty, she's a child, and my training and oath is to protect children. I don't know what I would do in that circumstance."

"I think what I was looking to hear was that you would have no animosity toward the little girl. I do not hear that, and so your words are frightening me. I'm wondering whether I should call the authorities and warn them about you. What would you do if you were me?"

Jennifer shook her head violently. "Pure nonsense! When the day comes that I can't come into my shrink's office and blow off some steam, then that's the day we might as well all take out a gun and go after our enemies. Dr. Gresham, what I'm saying here is said to make me feel better. It's not actual threats against these people. Nor do I want you to put my comments in my chart. If something bad happens to Elise Ipswich, and if my comments were in my chart and anyone got possession of it, they might come after me. Please be sensible and just put in your notes that your client was distraught and very angry at what the court had done to her. Can we agree on that?"

"I think we can as long as you can confirm with me that you don't have it in your heart or mind to follow through on any of your threats. I think we can keep what you've been saying anonymous and not worry about you killing anyone. I think I'm willing to take that chance with you. You're a medical professional, and I know you understand what my exposure is here. I won't turn you in, and you won't kill anyone. Is that our agreement?"

"That is exactly our agreement. Thank you."

Dr. Gresham didn't respond. She was busy making notes about her patient, who was very honest and upset. That was the extent of what she entered into the patient chart, and after the patient was gone, she did not lift her phone.

For Dr. Gresham, it was over and done.

Just another patient, mad as hell, but manageable.

Chapter Forty

ELISE

Many hours later, Elise's airplane touched down in Paris, and she frantically made her way to the hospital where her daughter was being treated. She was exhausted; the flight had taken almost ten hours with an unexpected layover in London. Still, Elise was determined to see Çidde and planned on spending the day in her daughter's hospital room in the chair beside her bed.

The hospital was *Day Hospital Marie Abadie* on rue Raymond Losserand, a taxi ride of twenty minutes from the Ipswich home. Elise noted on the ride that she had reverted to an old teenage habit of biting the cuticle on her fingers as a way of suppressing her anxiety. She jerked her hand away from her mouth and scolded herself as she looked out the window at the passing cityscape. *You can do better than this*, she told herself. You owe it to your daughter not to regress but to be the adult in the room in all respects.

She arrived at the hospital, paid the taxi driver, and ran for the elevators. Five minutes later, she entered her daughter's room and found her six-year-old sitting up with a children's picture book. Elise's mother, Sarah Milam, was sitting up in the chair beside Çidde's bed, and she turned to Elise when she came into the room and all but burst into tears. But rather than cry in front of the little girl, she kept on a brave face.

"Oh, Elise, we are so glad to see you. Çidde needs to hear one of your stories before she closes her eyes tonight for her sleep. Çidde was wondering where you were. Here, let me get up and change places with you so that you can get right here beside her and hold her little hand."

"Darling," Elise said gently to her daughter, "Mom is here now, and everything is going to be okay."

"Why isn't daddy here? He was my doctor before."

"You know your daddy isn't here. Daddy had to go to heaven and see his own mommy and daddy. One day, you and I will be there with him. But that is a long, long time from now. For now, we're going to stay with you until you get well and make sure you're ready to go home as fast as possible."

A half-hour later, the little girl was sleeping, and Elise's mother had left to return to her home. Elise remembered the manila folder she had taken from Michael Gresham's table in the courtroom. Now, she pulled the folder out and started reading. She hadn't gotten very far before realizing she had taken the medical records that belonged to Jennifer Ipswich from when she was a much younger woman, evidently living in San Diego, California. Elise read on.

Twenty minutes later, she folded the manila folder closed and put it back inside her bag. She was stunned. She had learned that Jennifer Ipswich had suffered psychotic episodes while she was in her first year of medical school and after. She was treated by a doctor in San Diego and took medications to treat her psychosis and bipolar disorder.

Elise had suspected as much from the very start.

It answered a world of questions for her.

Chapter Forty-One

KARROL

After speaking with her terrorist cell and rehearsing her role, Karrol left the safe house with a satchel charge with explosives, fuse, and an igniter.

She took a circuitous route through Paris's back streets, spending almost a full hour making sure she wasn't being followed before arriving at rue Dumont.

She located the front stoop of the flat where Elise lived with her daughter. Just as she was about to duck into the bushes and attach the satchel charge to the bottom of the building, a carload of partygoers pulled up in front, and all four doors opened.

They had been drinking and were loud—two men and two women—laughing and calling out to someone in the flat above Elise's. An upstairs window opened, and a woman leaned out. "You're going to have to stop with the noise," she called down in a sweet voice, "else someone along here is going to call the *gendarme*. Trust me. You don't want that. Our local constabulary takes disturbance of the peace quite seriously, and you might even find yourselves going to jail if you keep this up. Why don't you all come inside, and I'll make coffee?"

The larger of the foursome, a black man wearing a blue suit and an orange Fedora, called back up to the woman. "Sasha, get on down here, girl. We are going to party like there's no tomorrow, and we aren't coming inside your place to get it on."

Karrol waited patiently while this interchange played back and forth. She pressed back against the bushes two doors down, hidden from anyone passing by.

There were a few people out strolling the sidewalks, a few dog walkers, and an ancient man pushing his walker down the middle of the street, hunched forward, muttering to himself as he made his way. *That's all right, old man,* thought Karrol. *We should all be so determined at that age.*

Karrol had just settled in to wait out the others when a second male voice called to the first. "Hey, everyone, Sasha, who is the girl standing in the bushes?"

Karrol stepped back farther, hoping to hide from prying eyes. However, she had been found out, and the two men started toward her to investigate.

She then came charging out of the bushes and ran down the sidewalk in the opposite direction. As she ran, the satchel charge banged against her lower back, and she cursed her bad fortune. She was going to have to wait for another night and could only hope they hadn't been able to make out her face in the low light. She also hoped they wouldn't make a report to the police that she had been there. That would call unwanted attention on her and her future efforts.

In the flat beneath Sasha's, Elise Ipswich turned on her side in bed. She heard the voices outside and heard the laughter. She did not hear the woman running away down the street and had no idea why she had been outside two doors down from her window.

That night, the woman with the satchel did not return. Instead, she returned to her terrorist cell, and it was decided they would try to get closer to Elise with some poison or knife, away from other people.

Karrol decided she would force her way into Elise's flat and stab her.

Chapter Forty-Two

THE RITZ

"Legend has it Hemingway drank fifty-one martinis in a row to celebrate France's victory over Germany in World War Two," Jennifer Ipswich said to Elise Ipswich.

At Jennifer's invitation, they had agreed to meet at Bar Hemingway, the 25-seat bar in the Ritz Hotel in Paris at 15 place Vendôme.

Jennifer had told Michael she was going to settle the case for herself. She also told Michael that Elise had agreed to meet with her only because Jennifer had promised they would "work out" their differences over a martini. She said Elise would leave with a check in her pocket for the $1 million she was seeking, having signed a release and given up her interest in all other Ipswich assets of the American marriage.

Elise looked up from her leather chair at the sidebar and its sweeping leather booth, overseen by the wall-hanging jaws of two sharks, open and ready to inhale whatever sweet mischief came their way.

Elise had never been able to afford the Bar Hemingway

on her own, although Joe had taken her there for a celebratory drink on their first anniversary. She remembered that he'd had to call ahead and pull some strings to reserve a small table for two at 8 o'clock that night. She had worn her Givenchy suit since it had been cool out that night, and the middleweight wool held the night air at bay perfectly. The suit had been given to her by Joe, and she still had it hanging in her closet inside its garment bag. Likewise, Joe had worn his matching Givenchy suit, but no one else had seemed to notice. It was a night of fun and romance. His suit was in his closet, untouched since his death, looking forlorn and useless. So, meeting with Jennifer, she had good feelings about the place, although her feelings about the company were less-than.

Commenting on Jennifer's claim about Hemingway and his 51 martinis, Elise said, "I'm afraid Mr. Hemingway has left me in the dust. After one martini, I get silly, and we don't want me silly. Certainly not on a night like tonight when we're about to resolve our differences finally. I can't thank you enough for calling me and offering me this opportunity, Jennifer. Somehow, deep down, I feel like Joseph is pulling strings to bring us together. I know he wouldn't have wanted us to fight and argue. Like I said some time ago, I hope that our children will become friends, and perhaps even family."

Jennifer nodded and slowly turned the stem of her martini glass between two fingers. "I have to agree. My husband would've wanted to see us succeed at what we're about to do tonight. And like you, I do hope Joe's children can get to know one another and maybe even visit each other during the summertime vacations away from school. I want you to know that I'm here to make a settlement with you out of a feeling of duty to Joe. When he was dying, his instructions to me were to give you one-half of the life insurance policy. I'm embarrassed to say I've struggled with his wish. But it's only because I've been so upset and unsure which way to turn once I found out he had taken a second wife. I didn't grow up that way, where men did things like that, and neither did Joe."

"Of course not. Same with me."

"I'm still in a state of shock, so bear with me as I work my way through my feelings. Also, I've had to work my way through the finances and see how I believed the apportionment of Joe's assets should happen. I want you to know that when I've previously said I contributed most of the amounts to the bank accounts, it was true. For the past fifteen years, Joe has been spending half his time in Chicago and half his time in Paris. I know that he preferred Chicago, sometimes, and he preferred Paris, sometimes. I can only conclude that he felt the same way about his two wives. Sometimes me, sometimes you. It still hurts, however."

"Goodness, I really appreciate your frankness. It's too bad we couldn't have done this sooner without all the lawyers and stuff. I hate going to court, and I hate how I feel when I argue and fight about money. I only want to make you believe that I wouldn't even be here if it weren't for Çidde. Sadly, she was born with that blood deficiency. They told us it was that transfusion that was infected, and that's when she became HIV-positive."

"It happens. Blood is never one-hundred-percent pure."

"Well, whatever, it's all said and done now."

"One thing I wondered... Doesn't France have socialized medicine to pay for your daughter's needs?"

"France is somewhat different. You must have health insurance coverage to live in France. State healthcare in France is not free. Healthcare costs are covered by both the state and through patient contributions. The French national insurance fund, Caisse Primaire d'Assurance Maladie, will then repay you for part of the costs later."

Jennifer nodded. "I think I'm beginning to see. So, it's the upfront cost that is more than you can bear, even though you will be reimbursed on the backend. That makes your situation much clearer to me."

"Now you understand. The reimbursement can take up to eight weeks, and by then, I might have eight thousand paid in for Çidde's injections."

"But why are the injections so expensive? One thousand euros a week?"

Elise took a sip of her martini before she answered. "It's true, you can get cheaper medicine, but as a physician, Joe only wanted the best for Çidde. So she has never received any generic medicine or any treatment that wasn't the best. I won't change that now."

"I see," said Jennifer.

"It has been a nightmare since Joe died. I borrowed from my mother, my brother, even one of my friends from work has loaned me one thousand euros. I must get these people paid back as they need their money. I really hope against hope that we can finally settle tonight, and I can put this all behind me. Jennifer, I'm not only financially exhausted but emotionally exhausted, too. I miss Joe, I cry myself to sleep at night, I don't sleep but maybe two hours, and I wake up exhausted with burning eyes, facing another day at a very high-pressure job. So tonight means everything to me. For the love of God, let's make it work. I'm ready now to sign whatever you need me to sign."

Jennifer reached down on the seat beside her and opened her bag. She pulled out a folded document and handed it to Elise. "Please read and sign. When you hand it back to me signed, I will give you the check. Right now, I'm placing the check on the table between us and ask you to pick it up and look at it and make sure it's filled out properly and in the amount of one-million dollars. The bank should give you the foreign exchange on this value. It's your half of the insurance money."

Elise frowned. "This is the life insurance? What about the vase?"

"The check is for two million. One for the life insurance and one for the vase. It's all there."

Elise didn't believe her and remembered the psychosis stuff from Jennifer's file. But she decided to play along and see if the two-million dollars really came through.

Elise picked up the check, studied it, and replaced it on the table. She then opened the folded document and began reading down through its two pages. Once that was done, she reached inside her purse and pulled out a pen. She signed her name at the bottom of the first page and the bottom of the second page. She also dated the second page and refolded it, and handed it back to Jennifer.

Jennifer opened the document and scanned it, noted the signatures and date, making sure all was well. She then nodded at the check on the table. "Pick it up, please. The money now belongs to you."

Elise reached down, picked up the check, folded it once, and placed it inside her purse. Tears had come into her eyes, and she put out her hand to shake hands with Jennifer. The women shook hands, and Jennifer smiled. "Say, let's have one more drink, and then we'll take you outside and call you a taxi. I don't see how another can hurt."

Elise brightened up. "I usually only have one, but this is special tonight. Just let me go to the bathroom first. She stood, picked up her bag, and headed for the bathrooms.

Jennifer watched Elise walk off. When she was sure she was out of sight, she dug into her purse, removing a small vial. She poured the contents of the vial into Elise's last inch of drink. She then dropped the vial back into her bag and sat up. After a second thought, she went back into her bag and pulled out her makeup mirror and checked her makeup. She refreshed her lipstick and blotted her lips on tissue from her purse. She then sat back, satisfied.

Elise suddenly returned from the bathroom. "Guess what? I threw up in the bathroom. I think I've had enough to drink. If you'll excuse me, I'm going to go outside, catch a cab, and run along home now. Please forgive my sudden departure. I'm feeling dizzy from the drink I've had. I never drink except an occasional wine, and I know better than to have a martini."

Jennifer frowned. "I was expecting we would have one more drink and talk about our children. I want nothing better than to make plans for them for the summer. I think your Çidde might be able to come to the U.S. for a couple of weeks, and then all three of our children could return to Paris for a couple of weeks. That way, they can get the feeling of both homes and make better connections with each other. Please sit down, finish your drink, and let's see if we can firm this up."

Elise sat back down and picked up her drink. She lifted it to her lips and set it back down. "Even the smell, ugh. I can't finish it. But I will order some coffee if we can get the waiter's attention."

The two wives then had coffee, talked more, and then stood to go their separate ways.

Elise promised herself that once she was safely in the taxi, she would hit the bank at 8:01 a.m. and make sure the check was good.

The money on her condo was due in two more days, and she didn't have enough money to pay. So it was urgent she get to the bank, deposit the check, and put off her landlord for a few more days while the out-of-country check cleared. He would be understanding. He was a gentleman who lived two floors up from Elise, and his wife often watched Çidde on those nights when Elise had to work late.

As she rode along in the taxi, she didn't notice the taxi that had pulled in behind hers and was now following. Every time Elise's cab took a different street, the following taxi did likewise.

Then she was home. She headed up the stoop out front and then disappeared inside. The second taxi parked out front and a dark figure climbed out. The figure then hurried from the curbside to the stoop and also went inside the building.

Chapter Forty-Three
MICHAEL

I was waiting in the courtroom for the final hearing to begin. In the end, I had decided to stick with it and finish the case—it was easier, all things considered, for me to gut it out. Jennifer came breezing in. She was wearing a black pantsuit and white shirt with a red tie, and her makeup appeared to be quite thick. Her cheeks and lips were a cerise color, and her deeply-sunken eyes had black false eyelashes that were stark against her white skin. I did a double-take, and I saw Wilder do the same thing. It didn't even look like the same woman.

Wilder told the court that his client waived her presence. The truth was, he'd whispered to me, he couldn't locate her. "Never mind," I told him. "I won't object to her absence."

So, we launched into the hearing. Wilder led off with his first witnesses, who were appraisers who had gone over the house, the medical practice, and the other assets known to exist in Illinois. Those would include automobiles, furniture, and the like.

After they testified, it was my turn. I put my experts on

the stand, and they testified as to the minuscule value of Joe's property in France and depressed the value of all Illinois assets just like I had told them to do. At that point, it looked like Jennifer was sitting on top of a few million in assets, and Elise was sitting on top of about €3500 in assets.

The court found Jennifer's assets to be jointly owned by the parties, so there was $1.5 million ascribed to Joe, and the court awarded one-half of that to Elise and the other one-half to Jennifer. The court also awarded one-half of the insurance proceeds to Elise and one-half to Jennifer, which Jennifer assured the court had already been accomplished. The same division was made with the Qing vase and Jennifer again told the court that was a done deal. The court then had Jennifer sworn as a witness, and Wilder put her on the witness stand.

The judge qualified her as far as who she was, her education, her work history, her earnings, her maternal responsibilities, living situation, and the fact that she was still working full time and making about $250,000 net a year. The court then went to the following litany with Jennifer:

"Do you understand, Doctor Ipswich, my orders here today?"

"I understand perfectly, Your Honor. I tried to settle with Elise, but that wasn't enough for you. You are taking one-half of everything else I worked for and awarding it to this woman from Paris."

"You further understand that I'm appointing a conservator to take over those assets and distribute them in accordance with my order today?"

"I tried to settle with Elise, but that wasn't enough for you. You are taking one-half of everything else I worked for and awarding it to this woman from Paris."

"Do you also understand that you are to refrain from moving, hiding, segregating, transferring, or in any other way interfering with the conservator's control of those assets?"

"I understand that you are taking one-half of everything I worked for all these years and giving it away to this woman from Paris. Yes, I do understand."

"You are making this very difficult for the court, and I have about reached the end of my patience with you. When I ask you questions, I expect answers to those questions, not editorial commentary from you. You understand the difference?"

"I understand that you are taking one-half of my assets and—"

"Enough! I won't have any more of that in my courtroom. Whether you understand or not is no longer my concern. The conservator is now directed to take control of all assets and make the distribution I've ordered here today. The court has seen how difficult this case has been for Mr. Wilder. Hence, he is awarded legal fees of $150,000 to be paid by Jennifer Ipswich. Gentlemen, is there anything further?"

Both Wilder and I answered in the negative. We had nothing further.

When we were finished in court, the judge called us forward, the two attorneys, and told us off the record that my client would go to jail if she, in any way, disobeyed any part of the court's orders. That satisfied Wilder and put the fear of God in me. I wasn't fearful for my well-being; I was fearful for the freedom of Jennifer, who seemed more and more insulated from the reality of what was going on in this courtroom. At any rate, we were excused by the judge, and when we turned around to leave the judge's bench, I realized Jennifer had left the courtroom.

I was shocked that she had walked out without discussing with me what had just occurred. She was between a rock and a hard place, and she needed my counsel. There was action we could take. I could file a motion asking the court to put its order in abeyance while I filed an appeal of the court's order. There were other things, too, but Jennifer was nowhere to be found.

I made my way back across the street to my office, went upstairs, and collapsed at my desk. After several minutes, I picked up the phone and asked the receptionist whether or not anyone had taken calls from Jennifer Ipswich. They said they had not, just as I had anticipated.

I decided right then and there that I was done with the case. If she called me, I was going to respond that I was in the process of preparing and filing a motion to withdraw from her case.

I was finished. I felt a certain sympathy for Elise Ipswich. When an attorney starts feeling sorry for the other side, it's time to bail, to get out of the case.

I did leave a message with my front office people that if a call came in from Jennifer, I was to be interrupted no matter what was going on in my office.

My door was still open, but it was about to slam shut permanently.

Chapter Forty-Four

MICHAEL

Jennifer had interfered with the liquidation of her assets in every way possible. So, the judge called us back into court. I had no doubt he was about to throw her in jail for her obstruction of justice.

By now, Elise had been in France several weeks, and, I understood from Wilder, Elise's daughter was back home from the hospital. He said they had communicated by email only, that his client was extremely busy and couldn't take his calls at her office.

This time, Elise couldn't make it again. She had sent Wilder an email, explaining that Çidde was sick also and Elise couldn't leave Paris. We had scheduled a four-way last-minute settlement conference I had begged Wilder to have. A final chance for Jennifer to sign the paperwork and conclude all problems.

The only problem was Jennifer didn't show up for the settlement conference either, and she didn't call.

So, there we were, the two of us, in Wilder's large

conference room with its dozen leather chairs, drinking coffee as if we had some reason to be there together.

I kept trying Jennifer, her home number, her cell, and her office. Her medical office told me that she had called in sick that day and said she would be staying home in bed. I had sent Marcel to her house when she didn't show up that first hour, and he had pounded on her door and leaned on the doorbell. But still, there was no answer, so we could only assume she was either hiding, or she wasn't there.

At this point in the whole case, I wished to high heavens I had never become involved. It felt like Jennifer had changed. She had been a smiling, sweet blond woman full of self-confidence that day I first met her at the Evanston Racket Club. Now she had changed into an irresponsible, unknown quantity that, quite frankly, I did not understand.

She had become someone or something unlike anyone I had ever known before in her irrationality and irresponsibility. That trick she pulled with the $15,000 after the last court hearing had almost been the last straw for me.

After an hour of waiting with Wilder for my client, I excused myself and returned to my office. Marcel was there and caught me as I came through the front door. "Can you believe this chick?" he exclaimed. "She just doesn't seem to get it, does she?"

"Beats me," I said. "It almost seems like she wants to go to jail again. I'm going to have a motion to withdraw drawn up before I go over to the courthouse this afternoon on the Dunleavy case. I'll file it myself and good riddance."

Chapter Forty-Five

FRANK

Frank Wilder gave up on settlement as well. Frustrated, he decided to go for a long drive in the countryside. He rode the elevator down to the blue level, the door slid open, and he stepped out.

"Hello, Frank," said a voice off to his side.

Startled, Wilder jumped and swung around. There stood Jennifer Ipswich. She was smiling and appeared to pose no threat. Then he saw: she had enough makeup on as to almost be unrecognizable. He was taken aback. *What in the world?*

"I've been waiting for you, Frank," Jennifer said in a lilting voice.

"You've been waiting for me; why?"

"I've been waiting for you to take me out for dinner and drinks. Let's celebrate your victory. I want you to know there are no hard feelings about the money stuff. It's like a seduction to get it away from me, am I right? So, would you like to go out and eat and have some female companionship that's different from what you get at home? Maybe conclude the metaphoric seduction? Tell me, Frank, are we on the same page?"

"You've got to be kidding me! There is no way in hell I'm going anywhere with you, and I can't even believe this is happening. I'm going to ask you now to stand aside and allow me to get into my car and drive away. Or are you going to be a problem?"

"Darling man, I'm never a problem. I'm always the solution." She smiled and leered at him as she moved two steps closer.

Wilder took a step away and began walking rapidly in the direction of his car. His parking slot was down at the other end of the blue level, and he headed in that direction. He realized from the tap tap tap of her high heels that Jennifer Ipswich was following close behind him. Suddenly, he stopped, spun around, and held up an accusing finger. "All right! Hold it right there! If you come one step closer, I'm calling the police, and I'm going to have you arrested for harassment and assault. Now get the hell away from me."

Ignoring him, Jennifer closed the difference between them and reached out and touched the side of Wilder's face. He could smell her perfume—rose water. It was a very disagreeable smell and, in fact, reeked so bad his head snapped back.

He whipped out his cell phone and dialed 911. As he held it to his ear, Jennifer suddenly reached out and swiped her arm across his, making the cell phone drop to the floor. She scooped it up and began running in her high heels away from Wilder, back toward the parking level elevators.

He didn't see it coming, but her car was parked five cars away from his, and she was able to jump inside her vehicle and lock the doors before Wilder could get to her.

She held his cell phone up to the window, taunting him.

She then started her car and backed out with a squeal of tires. Before he could catch up, she was up and out of the parking garage and had made a right with traffic and then another right at the end of the street.

When he jumped into his car and made the top of the exit, he had no idea which way she had gone. So, with a great sigh of dismay, he made a left turn and began driving home.

Jennifer drove a circuitous route back to her home in Evanston. She parked inside her garage, closed the garage door, and went inside, Wilder's cell phone still inside her purse.

She wasted no time running to her bedroom and stripping off her clothes in front of the large mirror on the dressing table wall. She snapped several pictures of herself in the nude with Wilder's cell phone, then put it on the bed while she went to the closet and pulled on sweatpants and a sweatshirt.

She then retrieved the cell phone and went into her office, where she toyed with the phone until she found Wilder's wife's phone number.

She then texted that number and attached the nude photographs of herself. She sent a text that read:

Darling, this afternoon was incredible. I'm sending these pictures to you to remind you how beautiful I looked at the hotel. You said you'd never seen such an incredible body, and had never been so turned on.

She then hit send, and the text went off into the night to the cell phone belonging to Frank Wilder's wife.

Chapter Forty-Six

MICHAEL

That night when I got home, I checked emails. I always check emails when I get home to Evanston from Chicago. I was quite surprised to find an email for me from Elise Ipswich.

Michael Gresham,
I'm writing to you, but I hope this email goes no further and you keep it just between the two of us. I need to be upfront and honest with you. Ever since we met, I can't get your eyes out of my mind. Nor can I get your body out of my mind. You are the exact form of man I have wanted all of my life. Please do not be shocked by this. And please do not think I'm too forward. In France, it's very common for a woman to approach a man. Maybe it's not in the US, but here it is. Let me continue.
We both know I might be a woman on the rebound. But I also know my feelings, and I have been very much in touch with my feelings all of my life. While I still miss my husband desperately and wish he was alive, I have, at times during my marriage, loved other men. Joseph knew that, and I was open about that with him, as we French are. So,

I can tell you that even though I still have my feelings for my husband, I can see you and see that you are someone I would like to be with. Please do not just erase this email and write me off as another crazy woman. I'm not that. I'm well educated, attractive, and am under no duress except for what you know about my financial situation. But now the judge has taken care of that, and there are no longer any disagreements between you and me. You are free to do what you wish to do about me without any problems. You no longer owe any allegiance to Jennifer Ipswich, and so I ask you to please respond to my email and tell me there is at least some interest on your part. For I have seen how you look at me, and I like what I've seen.
Yours, Elise Ipswich.

I read all of this and was shocked. But on the other hand, at this point in Jennifer's case, I had just about decided that nothing would surprise me ever again. Both were in love with the same man, and both were destroyed because that man had died. Now here was one of them reaching out to me in a moment that had to have been a low ebb in her life, but even so, she sounded like she had it together. Elise deserved an answer. So I wrote her the following:

Elise, it is very kind of you to be honest with me, and I feel obligated to respond. First, I'm a very happily married man and very committed to my wife. I would never betray her, no matter what my feelings for another person might be. I say this because I have learned to be distrustful of feelings. Our emotions could lead us around by the nose if we allowed them. But I do not allow them. I have said words and I have taken vows, and I have made commitments. Those are lines that can never be crossed either by an outsider or me. So, I must respectfully decline your invitation to engage with you.
Sincerely, Michael Gresham.

Chapter Forty-Seven

MICHAEL

I sent the email and assumed that would be the end of the matter.

However, later that night, my computer chimed in with another email. I thought it best to look right then and there, so I left Verona in the family room and took my laptop into my office where I could read in private.

I shuddered when I opened my computer because there was another email from Elise. This was troubling, and I was ready for anything as I started reading.

Michael, darling, you can say whatever you wish, but that doesn't change the fact that I cannot get you out of my mind. You are the man for me. I will follow you to the ends of the earth. And I will wait. I'm very good at waiting. If anything ever happens between you and your wife, I will be there. I fear for your wife. I'm the type of person who can lose control and do bad things. I will try not to, and I will try to honor your wife. But if something happens to her, please remember that you were given a chance to avoid that. It would be best if you had not turned me down.

Sincerely, Elise.

To say that I was shocked would be the total understatement of the month. I took the email and forwarded it to Frank Wilder. I asked him to please contact his client immediately and tell her to back off. I also told him that I would not abide threats on my wife's life. That serious trouble could come her way if she didn't withdraw what she had said.

I then heard back from Wilder, and he wanted to know whether the serious trouble I was referring to was a threat I was making against his client.

I told him that he could take it in any way he wished, but I would not allow his client to threaten my wife. I told him that I was willing to go to any length to put an end to that kind of nonsense.

By the time we finished exchanging emails, he knew I was not going to back down. I expected him to contact his client and tell her to leave my wife and me alone.

Then he told me about Jennifer and his cell phone and her text to his wife. He had nearly been kicked out of his house over it. He demanded I return his cell phone. I said I would try, but no promises.

We then left it at that for the night. I expected to hear no more.

Chapter Forty-Eight

FRANK

The wives had met at Bar Hemingway in Paris, and Frank Wilder was finding it difficult to contact Elise.

His paralegal was sitting across from him in his office, a woman named Lana, who had been with him for fifteen years. She looked worried and was nervously fingering her ink pen as she awaited orders from her boss.

"Now tell me again—you tried her numbers, cell and home phone, how many times?

"I have it written down that I've tried her cell phone eleven times just today and her home phone four times. She doesn't answer, and it doesn't go to voicemail on either one. Why it wouldn't go to voicemail is beyond me."

"Tell you what we're going to do. Let's have you contact a private security firm in Paris and have them stake out her home on rue Dumont. Surely, they will be able to contact her at her work, if not at home. I mean, she has her daughter, and somebody has to be coming and going to take care of her while Elise is away at work. And you said you contacted LVP Partners how many times?"

"I've called her office, I can't tell you how many times. I've also talked to her supervisor, a man by the name of Rafael Duchesne. Mr. Duchesne told me just this morning that she hasn't been in now in seven days, and they've been trying to get hold of her. He wanted to know what we wanted to do, and I told him I would run it past you and then get back to him. Is it okay if I tell him about the private investigators?"

"Sure, it's no secret that we're using someone to help us locate her. I'm wondering, too--do we know the names of any other family members that we can turn over to the PIs?"

"I know that her mother was helping out with the little girl. But I never got the mother's name."

"That's your mistake, Lana. Always, always get the names of other family members and their numbers to contact our clients in an emergency. Haven't we discussed this before?"

Lana ignored him, saying, "I think it's time to contact Michael Gresham and see whether he has heard anything about her from his end. Do I have your permission?"

Wilder waved his hand, "Sure, sure, be my guest. I'm sure Gresham hasn't heard anything, but we can at least alert him."

"And the conservator has taken over. The house is set for auction at the end of the month. So we have some good news for Elise."

The meeting broke up, and Lana returned to her cubicle. She dialed the number for Michael Gresham and waited.

"Hello? This is Michael Gresham. My secretary said it's Lana?"

"Yes, Mr. Gresham, it's Lana from Frank Wilder's office.

We haven't been able to contact Elise Ipswich for several days now, and we're wondering whether you've heard anything about her coming and going anyplace?"

"Two inappropriate emails. As far as I know, she's back in Paris and back at work and back with her little girl. I forwarded her strange emails to Frank. Frank called and said he had seen them and for me to wait for him to get back to me. Did Elise tell you about taking a trip out of town or going away on business?"

"No, she didn't. We've checked her home--I can't tell you how many times, and we've checked her office. Right now, we're in the process of hiring someone to go by her house and look for her."

"Well, if we hear anything, I'll call you, Lana. Sorry we can't help more."

The line went dead, and Lana turned her attention to hiring private investigators in Paris.

The hunt was on.

Chapter Forty-Nine

MICHAEL

The first text arrived on my phone Friday night after the end of a long week—but a good one, one without Jennifer.

The text sender was Elise, and the text told me that her husband Joe had raved on at times about the sexuality of his wife, Jennifer.

Elise suggested that I, Michael Gresham, might like to "taste" that.

At first, I was stunned that Elise would send me any such thing. But then I began considering the circumstances. Elise was missing, and Marcel was now on his way back to the States. Marcel told me he had called Elise's mother, who said to him that her daughter had abruptly moved away. A recent relationship with a man had all but destroyed her, so she left Çidde with her for a few weeks while Elise started all over. She said that she didn't want to visit with any family just then but would contact her when she got settled. I asked Marcel how the mother knew these things, and he said she had received an email from Elise.

While I was pondering these things, I received a phone

call from Frank Wilder. I took the call, fully expecting that he had located Elise.

"Hey, Frank, Michael Gresham here," I said. "How can I help?"

"Gresham, there's something odd as hell going on. I just received a text from Elise in which she told me about the sexual abilities of your client, Jennifer Ipswich. I'm stunned. Two things. First, has Jennifer been in touch with Elise that you know of? Second, have you heard anything from Elise?"

"The second question first—yes, I received a text from Elise. She said that I might wish to sample Jennifer's sexual prowess. At first, I was stunned, but now that I've heard from you, something is going on that someone needs to find out about. As to your first question, no, Jennifer has not been in touch with Elise that I know of. I'm sure if they had been in touch, Jennifer would've let me know that. Sorry, I can't help you with that one. I'm just wondering, thinking out loud here, has Elise ever said to you she was having problems with anyone? Has she ever complained of being followed? Or been fearful someone was after her?"

"Never. This is a woman who lives a very quiet life and doesn't get involved in things where there might be a downside like you're talking about. I've dispatched investigators in Paris to check out her flat and employer, but they've come back empty-handed. Nobody knows anything. She's been terminated from her job, and her supervisor told me they've already filled her position. She won't be welcome back there, even if she does surface. Well, Gresham, thanks for the feedback. I trust that if you hear anything, you'll let me know?"

"Of course, I will. I'm just wondering where this leaves us with the wrapping up of your lawsuit."

"I've heard nothing. I'm preparing my final report for

the court and will have something for you by the end of the month after the house sale. Well, please stay in touch, Gresham."

I said I would, and we ended the call.

I returned to work on another case. It wasn't fifteen minutes later that Wilder called me again. This time he was calling to say he had received a tearful phone call from Elise's mother.

The woman had received an email from Elise stating she needed money from the house sale. She had told her mother how to send the money so it would get to her. Her mother had called Wilder, wanting to know whether he thought she should send the funds.

Wilder again asked me whether or not I had talked to Jennifer and whether or not she knew anything about all of this. I told him that I was waiting on a return call from Jennifer. But, as far as I knew, she was back to work in her medical practice and very busy. I told him I would call him back as soon as I heard from her and give him an update.

It was just after noon when Jennifer returned my call.

"Jennifer, I'm calling because Frank Wilder and I have been receiving very strange texts from Elise. I'm wondering whether you've received any such texts?"

"Why, no, Michael, I haven't heard a thing. Last I knew, she was getting ready to go back to work. We had it all worked out and I tried to settle with her but the check had to be stopped because she still wanted half of everything. You told me that yourself when I got back."

It was true. Wilder had filed a motion seeking to set aside the agreement signed by Elise for the two million. It turned out she was now after that and half of everything else as well.

"All right. Well, if you two talk again, I need to know."

"I'll call. Sorry I can't help."

I called Wilder back and told him what Jennifer had told me. We both agreed to keep each other updated if there was any further contact.

So that's how we left it then.

Chapter Fifty

MICHAEL

At home that night, I was balancing the laptop on my knees, reading email, and Verona was watching a movie on HBO. We jumped to our feet, and Verona screamed when the sliding door window leading out to the pool suddenly shattered. A red brick had impacted the glass and crashed into our family room.

The outdoor security lights blinked on.

I was immediately outside with a flashlight kept by the door. I stopped and listened for the sound of someone running, but hearing nothing, I switched on the light and walked through the back gate to check the alleyway.

There was no one, and I didn't hear the sound of anyone making a getaway. By the time I returned inside, Verona was getting off her cell phone, having just dialed 911. "The police are on the way," she said."

I nodded and then noticed the brick had a band of clear tape running around it. I gingerly stepped through the broken glass and picked up the brick and turned it over. A message was held in place by the tape:

You've been very lucky so far because you've ignored me in favor of that tramp you're married to. Have you asked her about Sam Langley, the real estate agent who comes to your house while you're away, Mr. Gresham?
Haha, your secret friend.

I'd never seen anything like that before. The note was a printout, of course, and I was careful not to smudge its surface if fingerprints could be lifted.

I called Marcel, and he headed our way. I wanted to make sure he took the brick for forensic analysis by our team rather than the police. Marcel would get it done much faster and more thoroughly than the Evanston Police Department.

Sure enough, Marcel arrived at our house before the 911 responders. I handed him the brick and explained what had happened. He took the brick out to his truck and locked it inside the glove compartment. He took my flashlight and then headed for the gate and disappeared into the alley.

The police arrived about five minutes later. Two officers dressed in blue. One of them, a black woman, began questioning me and taking my report, while the other woman, a white woman, went outback. I cautioned her that Marcel was out there already and to call out his name.

I could hear her, moments later, calling for him, and then I could see her flashlight beam sweeping around. The officer with me asked about the shattered glass, and I told her about the brick. I told her that I had turned it over to my investigator. I was a lawyer and wanted my forensic team to study it before turning it over to the police. The police officer looked perplexed. Then she said, "You know you're fouling up the chain of custody by turning it over to a third party, don't you?"

"I realize that. But for my purposes, I must get to the bottom of any fingerprints immediately."

"What, you've access to the fingerprint database?"

"I'd rather not say," I told her.

She shrugged but backed off. "All right, have it your way. But be warned, it will never make it into evidence at a criminal trial now that it's been handled by non-police personnel."

"I know that, and I appreciate your concern. But we're fine here."

Chapter Fifty-One

MICHAEL

The next afternoon, Marcel and I met to discuss the findings of our forensic team. The brick was a standard construction-grade brick without any identifying characteristics and was therefore impossible to trace.

3M made the clear plastic tape, and the paper note appeared to have been printed off of a Hewlett-Packard printer. All printers have built-in identifying characteristics by agreement among the manufacturers, so their machines can be easily identified for cases such as ours.

The note contained several fingerprints, all smudged and therefore not usable. Of course, we saved the note so that we might, at some point, be able to match it up to the printer. Likewise, we saved the tape since the ends were serrated as it had been cut from its roll. There was always a chance we could match the serrations between the tape and the dispenser it had come from.

We decided to attempt to entrap the person who had the most to lose by Elise's being alive. That, of course, would be Jennifer. We discussed how we might approach her and finally decided we would play dumb as if we didn't know that Elise had gone missing.

I dialed Jennifer's number at her medical office, identified myself to the receptionist as Jennifer's lawyer, and told her I needed to speak with Jennifer immediately. Sure enough, within three minutes, Jennifer came on the line.

"Michael, is that you? Is there something wrong?"

"It is me, and thank you for taking my call. Why I'm calling is because we've been doing some looking around and have all but decided your husband did not die accidentally."

"What? Please say that again!"

"That's right. We have reason to believe that Joe was poisoned."

"What do you blame this on? Is there some new evidence I don't know about?"

"Marcel inspected Elise's home in Paris. He came away believing that she had something to do with Joe's death. For one thing, as you know, she has been hurting for money. We believe there is a French life insurance policy on Joe that no one knew about until Marcel visited her flat."

"That's fantastic! Please tell me what else."

"Well, it's a short leap in logic, given her dire circumstances, that she would've wanted to cash in that life insurance policy once she found out the truth about Joe."

"What truth?"

"That he was married already."

"Are you telling me she didn't know that when she married Joe? Oh, my God, what a shock to her. Well then, it would only make sense she would poison Joe. So, what are you thinking?"

"I'm thinking I need to get more evidence against her. I want to build a case so airtight that I can put her away for life. If we can do that, then you keep everything. Her claim for any of Joe's property will go away based on the fact that she killed him. She would no longer have the right to inherit or make any other claims based on the marriage."

"In other words, the property would be all mine?" she said in all innocence.

"That's exactly what I'm thinking. If we can make this case against her and she is no longer a problem in your private financial affairs, you win. It's that simple."

"All right, tell me how I can help."

"It would be terrific if you might email her and see if you can get her to say something negative about Joe. That would at least be a start. Can you do that?"

"Yes, I do have her email from that time she emailed all of us. I'll try that and see what I can come up with. And thank you, Michael. This is almost too good to be true."

"Don't thank me yet. First, we have to put together a case against her. That could take quite a bit of work and cooperation from you. I think I'm going to really need your help, Jennifer."

"Michael, you've always known you can count on me. I'll be there for you. I will get an email off to her tonight when I get home. My God, Counselor, thank you again."

I then turned to Marcel after I had hung up the phone. He shrugged and smiled. "I heard every word. You own her, Michael," he said to me.

I could only sit there and grin.

Hook, line, and sinker.

Chapter Fifty-Two

MICHAEL

I was spot on because, sure enough, the next morning, before 8 o'clock, I received a phone call from Jennifer.

"You're absolutely right, Michael," she said to me. Her voice was lilting and determined. I knew right off that she was in. She had bought it.

"Tell me what you found out?" I asked. "I'm assuming by your voice that you've been in touch?"

"We have been in touch, yes. She sent me an email. Can I forward that to you?"

"Please do. Be sure, and don't erase anything from it when you do. We will need that metadata in the header that came with it to prove it was from her computer and IP. I'm very excited about this and happy for you, Jennifer."

"Wait until you read what she said. It almost bowled me over. All right, I'm forwarding now, and then I'm off to work. Please send an email letting me know what else you need, and let's get to the bottom of this ASAP. Again, I'm eternally grateful. Goodbye, Michael."

I set the phone down and sat back to wait for my email

notice to chime. Sure enough, less than a minute later, her email arrived with the email that Elise had sent to her. It read as follows:

Jennifer,
I'm so glad you contacted me. It was so good to hear that someone besides me was upset with Joe and how he was behaving. I think you know already, but if you don't, when Joe proposed to me, I didn't know he was already married. When we got married, he still hadn't told me. I married that bastard, unaware he had another wife in the wings. I would never have married him had I known. I can't tell you how angry it made me when I found out.
I cried for a week straight while he was back in Chicago. I couldn't even go to work. My eyes were red and bloodshot day and night. I had to tell Çidde that Mama had a cold. That's what was making her eyes look bad. That poor little girl didn't know what in the world was wrong with me.
This happened maybe six months before he died. And I have to be honest and blunt with you. When Joe died, I was not disappointed. I know I cried, and I was hurt, but deep down, I felt like justice had been done. I'm a very basic person, and I take things like that very seriously, but I believe that God is looking down on all of us, and there is going to be justice in the end. So, I think that Joe got what was coming to him when he died. I don't want to say good riddance because that wouldn't be loving, but now you know how I feel.

I called Marcel into my office. I turned my laptop around so that he could read the email for himself. When he finished, he whistled softly. "Our Jennifer has been a busy lady. There is no way Elise would've written this garbage. She's French, and without overgeneralizing, something like this would never affect a Frenchwoman to where she would commit murder. She might throw a frying pan, but she's not going to poison him. I think we're on to something, Michael."

"I can only agree. So, where do we go from here? What comes next?"

Marcel looked very thoughtful then began nodding. "Don't you think it would be fantastic if we had Elise admit what she had done? I mean, I doubt if she will ever admit anything directly, but maybe we can start building our case a pebble at a time, getting pieces here and there out of her."

"All right, what if we ask her how Joe might've died?"

"Exactly. Go back at Jennifer and pose it to her that we need Elise to show some knowledge of how Joe died. Anything along those lines will do."

"All right, consider it done."

I then wrote Jennifer and told her we needed, and prayed for, some admission from Elise that she had some knowledge of how Joe died. I told her we would take anything we could get, but the more specific, the better. I didn't lose sight of the fact that I was dealing with a brilliant woman during all of this. I didn't want her to see through me and knew that I must come across as very sincere. And so, I carefully worded my next email to Jennifer, taking care to sound as lawyer-like as possible. I then hit send and sat back to wait.

After dinner, I was sitting beside Verona, my laptop open, half-listening to CNN. They were having a special on Russia, Verona's motherland, and she was intently watching. At any rate, my email notice chimed, and I clicked over to see what had come.

Jennifer had written:

Michael, below is the email I sent to Elise, and right above that is her answer to me. I really think we're onto something here.

Here's what "Elise" wrote:

Hello dear Jennifer and thank you for writing to me again. I'm sure I don't know how Joseph died, but I do know I received a call from one of the crime lab experts in Chicago very early on. She told me that she had been involved in doing a workup on Joseph. She indicated she thought he had been poisoned with a substance called aconite. She said that it is a very deadly poison and one that causes a very painful death. She went into much more than this, and I don't remember much of it. I wish I had written it down, but I did not think to. I hope this helps, and please let me know.
Sincerely, Elise Ipswich.

I started laughing with pure happiness. We had scored again. It was so remarkable to me that the expert witness in Jennifer's case, the toxicologist, had at one point testified the poison that killed Joe might have been aconite but a gas chromatography would be required to prove that definitely. The problem had been, of course, that Joe had been cremated and there was no tissue upon which to do the test. So here we were with Elise—who was actually Jennifer—telling us that Elise knew aconite had been used.

Of course, the second email confirmed a terrible fact. Elise was missing, and Jennifer was doing her talking for her. I had dreaded this moment, but deep down, I had known it would come. Jennifer had done something terrible to Elise, which explained her disappearance. The fact that her mother said she would not stay in contact with her and the fact that she was missing from work confirmed it. Plus, she had not contacted her attorney even once about the money she so desperately needed. It was stacking up to be a terrible situation, and I was sick at heart for Elise. I also knew that I was also building a powerful case for the prosecution against my client with the emails I was receiving. This created all sorts of ethical problems for me as her attorney because I was, in effect, enticing her to compound any crime she might have committed in making Elise disappear.

That was a problem I would have to face, beginning right now.

Chapter Fifty-Three

MICHAEL

Jennifer's texting and behavior had caused me to file a motion to withdraw from the liquidation part of her case. I had it called up for hearing, she didn't show up to object, and the court allowed it. I had no sooner finished discussing the Jennifer strategy with Marcel when I received a text from "Elise" as follows:

Michael, I have it on good information that Jennifer would like to meet you for a drink. Please let me know where and when. She's too embarrassed to ask you herself. Elise.

My pulse skipped a beat when I saw the text. Jennifer had set her sights on me, which was a bad, bad development. In my opinion, and in Marcel's opinion, Jennifer had gone off the deep end. Now, what had happened to Elise that Jennifer was now sending out emails *and* texts, purporting to be from her?

The same night that I received that text, I was sitting in my family room, reading a novel on my laptop, which I read on to keep track of incoming business emails. I had eaten dinner and was getting drowsy when my phone chirped. Another text. Again, from "Elise":

I'm standing outside your window. I can see that you are wearing the yellow shirt that you like so much. Please come out back and let's talk about a meeting. Elise.

Out the sliding door, I ran, heading for the back gate at top speed, which was quite fast, even for a man my age. As I approached the gate, I thought I could hear feet running away in the alley. I unlocked the gate and got it open. Since the brick through the window episode, I had been keeping the gate locked. Having to stop and unlock it meant that I had lost whoever was there because of the delay.

I finally made it out through the gate and into the alley.

Without knowing which way the person had gone, I took a left and ran at top speed.

At this point, I figured I was a good minute behind. Nevertheless, I put my head down and ran as hard as I could.

I made it to the street and looked both ways but saw nothing moving--whomsoever had been there having lost me.

I glumly walked back to my house and back through the gate. Just for a moment, I stood and stared into my family room and realized how easy it was to look at my house at night from the alley. The fence was slump block, six feet high, and was easy to see over by pulling oneself up from the outside. I assumed Jennifer was out there because the text had been from "Elise," and no one else besides Jennifer was playing that game.

I went back inside the house and decided to get Marcel

involved. So I called him and told him what happened and asked him to stake out my back alley for the next several nights. I explained the whole story. He agreed that something needed to be done and said he would monitor the alley for the rest of the week.

When I sat back down after refreshing my coffee, I noticed my hands were shaking. It had upset me to no end to be watched inside my own house. It was virtual trespassing and was as real as someone standing right outside my window.

Now I was in a quandary. Should I go ahead and confront Jennifer? Or should I continue to play the game with her and see how much I could get out of her before the confrontation that would inevitably occur? I decided on the latter.

I decided it would be an opportune time to get back to Jennifer to request more information. I sent her a text:

Jennifer, would it be possible to get Elise to take the next step and admit she had purchased aconite? I need to see her confession, so I'm hoping you can manipulate her into something more substantial. Good luck to you on this one. Michael.

I sent that text out the morning after the alleyway chase. I would've sent it the night before, but I didn't want there to appear to be a connection between the two. How long would I have to wait before I would hear back?

Not long. Less than an hour later, I was in my office and having my first cup of coffee. When my phone chimed, the hair on the back of my neck stood up. I was developing a Pavlovian response to my cell phone.

I opened my phone and read an email from "Elise" to Jennifer and forwarded to me:

Jennifer, I know that it's not that hard to get aconite. Joseph had me purchase some from the chemist when we had a roach problem under our kitchen sink. He told me to line the corners of the underneath cabinet with the stuff, so I did. The roach problem went away. I'm sure other people can easily obtain it as I did without a doctor's prescription or anything like that. You should also know that it is called wolfsbane in some places—best of luck, Elise.

Now, I had "Elise" confessing that she had purchased aconite. I had only to translate that into Jennifer making the purchase, and I would have my case. This was going to require some stealth work by Marcel. I called him into my office. He filled his cup from my Keurig and took a seat across from me.

"What's up, boss?"

"I have Elise confessing she has purchased aconite. But what I need is Jennifer confessing."

"Simple. I break into her house, get into her medicine cabinet, find out which pharmacy she uses, and bribe someone. When do you need it by?"

"Damn it, Marcel, I don't want to know how you do things. Haven't we had that talk before?"

Chapter Fifty-Four

MICHAEL

Burglary is a serious crime in Illinois. There had to be another way than B&E. The other way presented itself.

"I've got a more palatable idea," I told Marcel. "Let me call Jennifer, and we'll make an appointment to meet her at her home. You'll excuse yourself and use the bathroom."

"Her bathroom will be upstairs."

"So, I keep her busy. No one's timing you."

"All right then. Upstairs, it is."

I then called Jennifer and lied to her. I told her that Marcel and I needed to bring her murder case file to her. It was all part of us closing her case. Being a doctor and a non-lawyer, she had no idea what I was saying wasn't true—or so I believed at the time. So, Marcel and I appeared at her front door at seven that night.

"Hello, and thank you for allowing us to come to your home," I said.

"Hi Marcel, hi Michael. Come right on in, you two."

She showed us into her living room—a high ceiling great room with two linen couches, four wingback chairs, and two glass-top coffee tables. The pieces were all modern, and the wall hangings on two walls consisted of Navajo rugs —which I'm sure were authentic—and pastel Southwestern landscapes. Here's a woman, I thought, who would one day retire to the Southwest, maybe Santa Fe, and take up acrylics or oil painting. If she wasn't in prison for murdering Joe, that was.

Once seated, I started right in. "We needed to see you tonight, Jennifer, and really appreciate you taking the time."

"No problem. Think nothing of it. I'm so glad and anxious that we're getting this case over with that I can't tell you. Would you all like something to drink, or are you hungry?"

"No thanks. We ate on the way over, and I'm about coffee'd out."

"Some water? I have ice water?"

"Not for me. But thanks," I said.

"Nothing for me," said Marcel. "But I'm wondering if I could use the restroom. Just a wee bit too much coffee earlier."

"Certainly, you may—that door there and then down the hall, third door on the right. The first and second doors are bedrooms. Those are the kids' rooms. You may ignore those. All right, Michael, what are we going to start with?"

She was sitting on the couch, so I moved from my chair to her side and opened my laptop. "Here is your case file, and here are selected portions of the toxicologist's testimony. I have these marked because they're now a public record and I'm concerned about your reputation. Now, I'm wondering about the expert witness's testimony, the toxicologist who testified about the aconite and the gas chromatography. Do you recall whether you've ever had aconite in your home?"

"Oh, I would never have that horrible stuff around. That's probably one of the most dangerous plants on earth, that wolfsbane. Having it around home—no reason on earth for that. Except maybe—*maybe*—to kill pests beneath the kitchen sink. Don't forget, Michael, I have young children, and they get into everything."

"Would you mind if we check out the prescription list at your pharmacy for you and Joe over the last twelve months? Would that be all right with you?"

Her face grew flushed, and the lines around her mouth tightened. Now I was getting somewhere—she was visibly upset. I had hit a raw nerve.

"It's just so I can see what the public might find out about."

"I don't see what in the world that has to do with anything in my case. Are you seriously suggesting that my prescriptions need to be checked out to see whether there was anything that might harm Joe? Or are his prescriptions to be checked out to see if there was anything he had to do himself in?"

"That's exactly right. What I'm doing is foreclosing a path that I can see the news media going down. At this point, I expect them to stop at nothing because you're a doctor. Now, which pharmacy do you use?"

"The CDN downtown on Birch and Eleventh. Many of my patients use it, too. They carry everything."

At just that moment, I could feel her move closer to me on the couch. It was almost imperceptible and looked innocent. But there we were, our thighs touching, and I'm getting that old familiar feeling from long ago, the sense of the first touch with someone. I wanted to stand and run out but didn't. I was getting too close to finding out what I needed to know. Plus, I couldn't tip our hand to her. She had to think we were acting in good faith and innocently—so I remained in place. As I talked on, pointing out pieces of the toxicologist's testimony that I wanted her to review, I realized she had moved her left arm up onto the back of the couch and that it was slowly working its way down to my neck. Then she grazed my neck with her fingertips. I looked up. I smiled at her, gently reached back, and removed her hand. I held up my left hand and displayed my gold wedding band.

"Sorry," I said as I looked into the soft light in her eyes. "Married."

My mouth was dry, and suddenly that drink sounded like just what I needed. "I'm wondering if I could get water. Possible?"

"Certainly, married man. You can get whatever you need at my house. Be right back. She jumped up and headed—I hoped—for the kitchen. For the kitchen and not into any of the rooms where Marcel might have crept.

While Jennifer was away, I stood and stretched my back, and looked around the room. For a moment, I wanted to bolt down the hallway and retrieve Marcel. Then, just as I was about to do just that, here he came, hands stuffed in his pockets and whistling a non-tune like he did when he was playing Mr. Innocent.

He raised an eyebrow as if to ask what was going on. I shrugged and nodded toward the kitchen, then made a drinking motion with my hand. I then turned and sat back down in the wingback chair where I had started out. Marcel walked around and took the wingback facing me, leaving the couch for Jennifer.

She returned, carrying three bottles of water. Without asking, she handed one to Marcel and then handed one to me.

She looked into my eyes and smiled. I could've sworn she had refreshed her lipstick, maybe even her eyeshadow. In the living room's low light, she was very attractive, but she knew it. She took a seat on the couch, opened her bottle of water, and looked at me again. "Where were we, Michael?"

"We were discussing the toxicologist's testimony. I was pointing out to you the key parts and trying to explain why I needed a list of your medications from your pharmacy to ask the court to amend the record with a list of your medications—just so the news media finds out you're clean. I'm sure you understand."

What a whopper. But she took it right in.

She fixed me with a very firm look. "I think I understand perfectly what you're saying. I'm still not convinced I should let you have my entire list of medications. As a physician, I consider that personal and believe you are crossing a boundary in my private life by even asking. Is there anything else we need to talk about?"

"That's very disappointing. I'm going to send you an email confirming that I asked for that list, and you denied it. I don't consider it a smart thing to do, and I would like to caution you that you're making a mistake. Nevertheless, you've made up your mind, and so there's not much else to say. I think we're ready to leave, so you can get on with your night. At any rate, I'll do the best I can with what I have to work with. You can be sure of that."

Marcel and I followed Jennifer to the front door and went outside after telling her thank you and goodbye. We climbed into my car and breathed a sigh of relief.

"Holy Mother," said Marcel. "She came looking for me and caught me in her bathroom off her bedroom. I didn't even know what to say. Then she said, 'What, you couldn't find the guest bathroom at the end of the hall?' I had no idea what to say. So I told her I thought she said the second door, which I found was the door to her bedroom. At any rate, she gave me a look and turned around. I followed her out of the room, and she went right, and I went left. She didn't say anything to you about it?"

"No, she never brought it up. Anyway, what did you find out?"

"I found out that her medications were many, and she is getting them filled at CDN pharmacy downtown. I memorized what she was taking. First, there was Risperidone."

"An antipsychotic."

"Then there was also one called Lamictal."

"A mood stabilizer."

"There was also one called Seroquel."

"For sleep. She must have insomnia. Who wouldn't after they murdered their husband?"

"We've decided that, have we? I thought the jury found her not guilty," said Marcel.

"I'm just tired. At this point, I'm not sure what I believe. So, what else did you find in her cabinet?"

There was one that was a blue pill."

"What? You opened the bottles and looked inside?"

"I guess I did. Then there was also one called Duloxetine."

"Depression medication. Pretty common. Anything else?"

"Yes, there were several others, but I'm not hitting on them right now."

"You didn't see anything that said aconite or any of the other poisons we've discussed?"

"Nothing like that. There were over-the-counter meds

like Tylenol PM, Benadryl, some cough syrup. Stuff like that."

"Well, the one called Risperidone. That one is the tipoff. That one is an antipsychotic if given in a high enough dosage. You remember how many milligrams?"

"No, I'm lucky I even remember the name Risperidone. Sorry, but it was very fast and I didn't get the amount. She walked in on me just as I had closed the medicine cabinet and was pretending to wash my hands."

"Well, now, if we can just figure out a way to get CDN pharmacy to turn over her purchases over the last twelve months…"

Marcel sat up in his seat. He looked over at me and said, "Let's leave that one to me. This time I won't tell you my methods."

"Fair enough. I'm not asking, and you're not telling."

Chapter Fifty-Five

MICHAEL

The next day, just after one in the afternoon, I was sitting at my desk and looking out my window. It was pouring rain outside, and the raindrops were running down my window in rivulets. I was thinking about Jennifer and her closeness last night. She had turned out to be a 100% different person than when we first met. I didn't know if it was her mental state, or if she was playing me because of her legal problems, or both. I only knew that I was uncomfortable, and I became more certain by the hour that I needed to withdraw from her appellate case.

So when she called me on the phone and asked me to come to meet her down at the lakefront, I agreed. Anything to get an admission about the aconite out of her. I slipped the voice-activated recorder in my shirt pocket. Now I was ready.

Five minutes later, I was headed for the lakefront and the beach. The skies had cleared, and the rain had stopped. Then the sun came out, and it was one of those steamy days you can only get in Chicago.

The taxi dropped me at Navy Pier. I began walking toward the beach until I saw a blond woman sitting down at the water's edge. I stepped onto the sand and kept walking. Fifteen feet away, I realized Jennifer was doubled over in pain and softly crying. Then I saw it—blood spilling out from her thigh.

"My God, Jennifer! What in the world has happened here!"

She looked up at me, her face contorted in pain, tears streaming from her eyes, and moaned, "Elise shot me in the leg. It hurts too much for me to let go. Please dial 911 and get me some help. God, Michael, I'm so glad you came. That woman has gone nuts and is in a rage at me because I appealed the case. She said she wasn't going to leave me alone. If she had to, she would shoot me in the head next time. Honestly, I thought she was going to kill me. Anyway, she threw the gun out in the lake and ran for the sidewalk. I fell on the sand and haven't moved since. I think my purse is over there, behind me, and it has my cell phone inside. I just couldn't reach it. I can't even crawl."

I didn't hear the last of it since I was too busy dialing 911. It didn't take long. Just a couple of minutes and I could hear the sirens coming. Then the paramedics were running across the sand with their gurney. They fashioned a tourniquet and loaded her onto the gurney, and took her back to their ambulance. Then they were gone.

I was totally stunned. Elise in America? I immediately did not believe it. I didn't think Elise had it in her to come to America and shoot Jennifer. But had Jennifer shot herself? I had great difficulty believing that, too. That would take a twisted mind, somebody much further gone than I had thought. So, I collected myself, trudged back across the sand, and hailed a taxi. I rode back to the office and hurried upstairs to get Marcel. I stopped at his office and asked him to come to mine. There, I told him what happened.

"I don't know, boss. It sounds to me like we got a very sick woman on our hands."

"What do you mean? The Risperidone convince you?"

"I mean, I don't believe a damned word of it. There's no way in the world Elise Ipswich traveled here from France to shoot this woman in the leg. Stop and think about it. It's ridiculous. There's nothing to be gained by it. It's the sort of thing only a very deranged mind would come up with and try to get you to believe. You know what I mean?"

"I know exactly what you mean. But you know what worries me? If she would go to this extent and shoot herself in the leg, what else might she do?"

"You thinking what I'm thinking?"

"I sure am. Elise is missing, and we've got a crazy woman on our hands. Someone needs to find out about Elise. I'm very fearful for her. I was before, but now I'm concerned to the point I'm ready to start looking myself. The only thing is, if Jennifer did something with her, she would be all but impossible to find without Jennifer's help."

"We're going to have to keep going at Jennifer like we planned. Take her down one step at a time, and make it fast. I mean, what if she's got her kept alive somewhere? What if she's hurting her? Do we know anything about Çidde, the little girl?"

I got up from my chair and grabbed a bottled water from Marcel's mini-fridge. "Marianne told me she was talking to Janice over at Wilder's office, and the little girl is all right. She's with Elise's mother, who the school called the day Elise didn't come to pick her up."

"Well, that's a relief. So, what's next with Jennifer?"

"First, I need that list of medications from CDN pharmacy. Any luck with that?"

"I just happen to have that list in my office. Don't ask me how."

"Really? How much did it cost us out of pocket?"

"And here I thought you didn't want to know anything about my methods. Don't ask, don't tell."

"Run get your list. Let's have a look."

Marcel left, and I took the opportunity to call Frank Wilder.

Once he got on the phone, I didn't waste any time. "Frank, Michael Gresham here. My client, Jennifer Ipswich, was just taken to the hospital with a gunshot wound to her thigh. It didn't look that serious, but it is serious legally because I think it might prove my client's state of mind. Here's what I'm wondering. Jennifer told me that Elise shot her and threw the gun into Lake Michigan. Here's the sixty-four-thousand dollar question—is Elise actually in Chicago?"

"Michael, of course not. Elise is still missing. If I had my way, I would hang your client up by her thumbs and beat it out of her until she told me what she's done with Elise."

"Actually, I might do some of the beating with you. I'm very worried, Frank, and I'm doing what I can with Jennifer. I've got some more ideas. I'll get back to you in short order."

"Thanks for calling, Michael. In the meantime, I'm off to Paris again since the police think they might have another lead. I'll call you if anything important comes up. You do the same with me."

"You got it. Talk later."

Marcel came back into my office with the printout. We sat down and started going through the pages. It turned out it was mostly the same items over and over again. Most significantly, none of the prescriptions were written by Jennifer Ipswich.

Thirty minutes later, we had finished going through the medications purchased from CDN pharmacy over the preceding year. Nothing had caught our eye.

I leaned back in my chair and stared at the ceiling. "I think we need to have a look at her house without her there. Are you up to that?" There I was, asking Marcel to commit a crime. But, I decided, sometimes it was necessary to commit a small crime to solve a large crime. I had no doubt that Jennifer had done something with Elise at that moment, and I was going to find out what.

"Our minds are operating on the same level," said Marcel. "My only concern is getting inside of her house and having her suddenly return home or having the kids return home from school unexpectedly. Is there some way you can keep her busy?"

I knew only too well how to keep her busy. I knew the gunshot wound was going to turn out to be fairly inconsequential, and she would probably be released home tomorrow. If we were going to do it, we were going to have to do it now.

"Marcel, I would like to see you there within the hour. She's at the hospital. They'll probably keep her overnight, and I'm guessing the kids are still at school. If you hurry, I think there's going to be a window of time for you to get in there and do your thing."

Marcel jumped up. "I'm on my way. Funny thing, this time we both know my methods."

"Yes, this time we both know. So sue me."

Chapter Fifty-Six

MARCEL

The lock on Jennifer Ipswich's door was electronic, and Marcel was inside in six seconds, softly closing the door behind him. He knew the rooms and went straight for Jennifer's bedroom. It was built in an L shape. At the bottom of the L were her bed and the door leading to her bathroom. There was a desk, a file cabinet, and a couch on the vertical of the L. He began rummaging through the desk.

Any evidence that would put him on the trail of what might've happened to Elise and Joe was fair game. He noticed there was a camera, a Canon EOS. He picked it up and examined it. There was still a SanDisk inside and two SanDisks free in the drawer. He pocketed all three disks and resumed his search.

When he had completed his search of the desk, he then went to the filing cabinet and began opening drawers. Patient files back to front, all drawers.

"What in the world?" he muttered. He could not think

why Jennifer would have patient files at home in her bedroom. He continued with his search.

He then went to her nightstand and bent to that. He found a .38 pistol in the nightstand on the right side of the bed and found miscellaneous reading materials on the nightstand on the left. He examined the .38 revolver with his latex gloves. It wasn't loaded, and he didn't see any bullets in any of the drawers. He carefully replaced the weapon and then searched the other two bedrooms, one a girl's room and one a boy's room. Nothing there.

He went into the kitchen and searched through those drawers.

He walked through the other door out of the living room and found her office on the other end of the house. There was a supply cabinet, locked with a padlock, which he picked and pulled open. The cabinet was filled with medications, so he pulled out his recorder and read them aloud. When he had completed his list, he closed the cabinet, relocked it, and continued searching the office. He located typical medical equipage, a couple of stethoscopes, ear, nose, and throat examination lights, and the like. And there was an odd one, a tattoo machine, and needles. Of course, he thought, used for marking IDs on children. He had heard that was a "thing" now with so many children being kidnapped.

Again, he ransacked her desk. He didn't know what he was looking for, but that didn't stop him. All the while he searched, he wondered how he was ever going to get her SanDisks back into her camera and drawer. He said a silent prayer they would reveal something, but he wasn't that hopeful.

Twenty minutes later, he had concluded his search of the house and let himself out the front door, locking it behind him. He stripped off his gloves and headed out the door.

Two of the disks contained vacation pictures, presumably Disney World in Florida. Some of the frames included pictures of Joe wearing a Mickey Mouse hat and eating cotton candy. The third disk was blank and contained no images or files when he reviewed it on his computer.

Marcel decided to take all three disks to a forensic computer scientist he used in Arlington Heights. He drove out there on the freeway after making an appointment. The man lived in a house trailer with a flower bed out front and a relatively unstable set of three stairs leading up to the door. Marcel climbed them and knocked. The man came to the door, wearing a bathrobe and cowboy boots. "Marcel, come right in. Let's have a look at these disks of yours."

The living room area was crammed with electronic equipment, green LEDs, and the whir of fans, and the buzz of fluorescent lights. "Grab that chair," the man told Marcel.

"Emmanuel, I'm particularly interested in the blank disk. It was loose, not inside a wrapper, which tells me there's a pretty good chance it one time contained something."

Emmanuel said, "The process of retrieving digital evidence may seem complex to most people, but I have special software to examine the disk and retrieve any deleted files. Why don't you go get coffee and come back in one hour?"

An hour later, Marcel returned. This time a voice yelled

from the inside, "Come right on in. I've got something here that's gonna knock your socks off."

Marcel let himself in and went to Emmanuel's computer screen. There, on the screen, was the picture of a human foot. He leaned closer.

"Woman's foot," said Emmanuel. "No hair."

"Holy Mother," Marcel whispered. He let out a long, slow whistle. "Looks like it was severed in one swipe with a meat cleaver. Clean margins all the way around. Are there any more pictures?"

"I'm going to page through them. I think there are six in all."

The screen began changing with different shots of the foot. When number six came up, it was a picture taken of the inside of the foot and ankle. There, on the ankle, was a Chinese character. "What in the world does that mean?" Marcel wondered out loud.

"Got you covered, buddy. I shot this picture down to my friend Andy Ling at One-Day Cleaners. The character means 'mother.'"

"Mother? Did you say it means mother?"

"According to Andy, that's what it means. And he's from Taiwan and should know."

"I've got an idea. I gotta get back to the office, Emmanuel. Send me your bill."

"Does five-hundred sound okay?"

"Five-hundred sounds perfect. Just don't say what the work was for."

"Got you."

Marcel left and jumped in his truck. He headed back downtown on the I-90 freeway. He impatiently rode the elevator up, and when the door opened, all but ran for his office. "Michael," he called out as he went past his office, "come on in. You gotta see this."

Chapter Fifty-Seven

MICHAEL

Marcel ran past my office in a huge rush. I turned the page on what I was doing and went to see what he had. He spun his laptop screen around for me to see. There, in red, white, and black, was the image of a human foot. It was a very gnarly image. The foot looked dirty, and most of the toenails were broken.

"All right," said Marcel. "Look at this tattoo on the inside of her foot."

"Wait, why do you say her?"

"Because, like Emmanuel says, there's no hair any place. Guys have hair on their toes and ankles. She does not. Besides, look at the size of it. Now, this right here, this tattoo, a Chinese man told us this is the Chinese character for mother. That's how else I know it's a woman's foot. She's a mother. Do you see where I'm going with this? This came out of Jennifer Ipswich's desk. Somebody did some postmortem surgery."

"Postmortem? How do you know the victim was dead?"

"Michael, so suspicious! You don't suppose—"

"I don't suppose anything. But I know what we need to do next. Elise's mother has to be contacted and asked about Elise."

"I've already got a call into her. I left a message on her machine. I told her to call me collect."

"What time is it in Paris right now?"

"Not for certain, but I think they're nine or ten hours ahead of us. Which makes it maybe eleven or twelve there, I'm not sure."

"Well, when she calls, patch me in. I need to hear this."

"I sure will."

Elise's mother, Sarah Milam, called us at three-thirty. "Hello? Mr. Rainsford?"

"Hello, Mrs. Milam, this is Marcel Rainsford. Thank you for returning my call. You haven't, by any chance, heard from the authorities or anyone else about Elise have you?"

"No. And Çidde is missing her desperately. She cries herself to sleep every night and asks me how come she no longer has a mommy or daddy. It's all I can do not to break down and start crying right in front of that child. I cannot tell you how much I miss my daughter, Mr. Rainsford. But here, let's have you talk. You called me. How can I help?"

"Well, this is going to sound quite bizarre, but I know you probably have pictures of Elise. In particular, what I'm looking for is a picture that shows the inside ankle portion of her right foot. Would you by any chance have anything like that?"

"My, that is a strange request. Let me see. I believe we took pictures at the pool party last summer when my other daughter got engaged. They wore swimming suits that night since it was so hot in the middle of July. I don't know, but maybe Elise was wearing a swimming suit in one of the pictures. I would have to go dig those out."

"Please go ahead and do that. I can wait since this is very important."

Marcel looked at me and shook his head. I knew exactly what he was thinking, and he was praying, like I was, that we would find a picture of the right inside ankle and it would be absent any tattoo. I asked Marianne to bring us some coffee while we were waiting, and she bustled around for five minutes or so before returning with a pot and 2 cups. Suddenly I heard Mrs. Milam's voice erupt on the speakerphone.

"You are not going to believe this, Mr. Rainford, but I do have a picture. It's a picture of Elise's right foot and ankle where she is sitting with her legs crossed, smoking a cigarette, and making a face at the camera. Joseph is sitting right beside her and appears to be laughing at something. Probably one of the stupid jokes he was always telling."

"Let me ask you this, ma'am. Are there any marks or tattoos on the right inside ankle?"

"There is some Chinese writing. It looks like a vertical line with arms and legs and eyeballs, and a hat. It's on my computer. Would you like me to email it to you?"

"Yes. I would like that very much. And thank you for finding that. We're still looking up other leads, trying to find Elise, and we'll get back to you if we know anything. Thank you so very much."

The emailed picture showed these characters:
母亲
They were the symbols on the inner ankle of Elise's foot in the picture.

We studied the Chinese characters from the pool party

picture and compared them to the Chinese symbol on the photograph taken from Jennifer's desk drawer. They were exactly the same. My heart fell. I looked up at Marcel, and I could tell he was feeling as sick as I was feeling. This had suddenly gone beyond the pale. This had suddenly become much more than a missing person case. I couldn't tell you the sorrow I felt as my gaze shifted back and forth between the photographs.

Finally, Marcel broke the silence. "I think I'm going to be sick."

"You and me both. So what happens now?" I asked him.

"Number one, we do not know if Elise is alive or dead. The picture of the severed foot depicts a foot that has been dirtied somehow, and the toenails are mangled as if perhaps they were dragged on some rough surface. Go with me here. I'm simply looking at what I see and trying to make sense of it. Number two, if Elise is still alive, then she is in terrible shape. Whoever took her foot off would have to have considerable medical knowledge to know how to keep her alive after that. I'm guessing that means a physician took off the foot. A physician such as our Jennifer Ipswich happens to be."

I could taste the bile in my throat. I heard what he was saying, but my mind was somewhere else racing along. All I could think to say was that we needed to find Elise immediately. She was going to need medical care—if she was still alive. Who could say what else Jennifer might have done to her? I shuddered to think.

Marcel spoke up. "If you could do whatever you wanted to find Elise, what would be your first step?"

"Really? I would grab Jennifer, and I would force her to tell me the truth."

"And how far would you go with forcing her?"

"As far as it took."

"What if I follow her twenty-four-seven instead? Reason I ask, if Elise is alive, at some point, Jennifer will go to her. That's all it will take. If Elise is dead, then Jennifer will not go to her. Then we'll know that, too. Either way, I'm guessing it wouldn't take any more than a week to prove my theory. What do you say, Boss?"

"I don't see any other way. If I had my druthers, I would take her out in the woods, make her strip off her clothes, and hang her from the nearest branch."

"Wow, rough, boss, rough. I'm going to play like you didn't say that."

"I'm going to tell you something, Marcel. If she doesn't lead you to her in the next seven days, then I'm going to grab her and take her to those woods. At that point, it's game over."

"Boss, I believe you. I believe that when you're pushed hard enough, you will do that exact thing. Lord only knows. I hope it isn't necessary. The guilt would kill you."

"The guilt of not doing it would kill me even faster, Marcel."

Chapter Fifty-Eight

MICHAEL

It couldn't wait. The photograph was so damning that I had to take action. I jumped into my car and drove to the hospital, where they had taken Jennifer for her gunshot. There was a chance she was still there, and I would prefer to confront her someplace away from her home and away from her work. The hospital seemed a natural choice.

I still had my voice-activated recorder tucked in my shirt pocket, ready to catch her confession when I confronted her.

I checked in at the nurses' station and got her room number. I went down to the end of the hall and entered the last door on the right. The curtain was drawn since it was a semi-private room. An older woman with an oxygen mask strapped to her face occupied the first bed just outside the curtain.

I called her name, "Jennifer."

"Is that you, Michael?" she responded.

I told her it was, and she invited me in through the curtain. I found the opening and entered.

Jennifer was lying on her back in her bed with her foot elevated by two pillows.

"I don't get out until tomorrow," she told me. "Which really pisses me off."

"How are you feeling?" I asked.

"I feel great. They've already had me up and around. I need to use a walker, but other than that, I feel fine. Maybe you can sweet-talk the doctor for me and help me get out of here later today."

I pulled the foot photograph out of my inside jacket pocket and passed it to her. "Please look at this. I want you to tell me why you took this picture."

Jennifer studied the picture, holding it near and then far. Then she tossed it onto the sheet and said, "I'm giving it back. It's a gruesome photograph, and I have no idea what it is about. Where did you get this, Michael?"

"This was found in your desk drawer on a SanDisk drive. It was the same drawer where you keep your camera. Beyond that, I'm not going to tell you how it was obtained. Please explain why you have this."

"I have no idea where this came from. Probably you should have asked Joe while he was still alive since that is his camera inside that desk drawer, not mine."

"Well, unfortunately, I never met Joe. So I'm asking you instead because it was your desk. The truth of the matter is, the picture was taken off of a SanDisk that had been erased. Someone was trying to get rid of the picture, and we were able to restore it from the drive."

"Well, you have the wrong person. That camera belonged to Joe, and I cannot explain what he was up to. I know that sometimes he had the camera with him when he went to France, but I assume he was using it in his work and never bothered to look at anything on it. I'm sorry, Michael, but you're talking to the wrong person."

"Do you recognize the foot in the photograph?"

"Absolutely not! Why would you even ask that?"

"It's a fair question. The photograph was found on a disk in your house. You've had sole ownership of the house and sole possession of the house ever since Joe's death. It's only natural you would be asked about the picture of a severed foot inside your desk."

"That desk is Joe's desk. My desk is in my bedroom."

For a moment, I lost the thread of what I was trying to accomplish. She was so smooth and so facile in her delivery that I found myself believing her. But then I snapped out of it. "Jennifer, the police have searched the lake where you said Elise threw the gun that shot you. So far, the police divers have found nothing like a gun. Did you actually see her throw the gun into the water?"

"Yes, I did. For your information, the police were here and asked me a world of questions, and I answered them truthfully. You can probably get my statement from them, being a lawyer and all." As she said this last part, she leaned back in her bed. As the sheet fell away from her upper body, I could see she was wearing a UCSD sweatshirt. The curtain parted at that moment, and Jennifer's nurse entered.

Ignoring me, the nurse said, "All right, Doctor Ipswich, the bathroom is empty now. Please sit up in bed and use your walker to stand. " Jennifer smiled at me and shrugged. I stood back to allow her to pass by once she was up and moving slowly with her walker. As she went by, I caught a glimpse of the back of her sweatshirt. It read, *Elise*.

When I saw the sweatshirt, it was all I could do not to cry out and accuse her of something terrible. So I kept it inside and, as coolly as I could, I watched her pass through the curtain.

I had come here to confront her about the photograph, and I had done that. She had sidestepped me by claiming that the camera and the pictures were the work of Joe. The problem was, at the time Joe died, Elise was still alive and still had both of her feet. So, blaming Joe was not going to work, but I decided to let her think it had worked and cease the confrontation.

When she returned to the room, I told her I had come by only because I was concerned about her and concerned about Joe's pictures. She again pleaded ignorance about the images and asked me what I was going to do with them. I told her I would do nothing, and maybe Joe had taken the pictures concerning some medical case he was working on. And I left it at that.

I excused myself, went out to the elevators, went out to my car, and left.

Now there was a foot to be found.

I dreaded the search.

Chapter Fifty-Nine

MICHAEL

Out of the blue the next day and ramming her walker through my door came Jennifer. She clutched a folder of papers. She hopped behind her walker over to my desk, looking enraged and out of control.

"I've been sued!" she cried out. "That no-good bitch sued me!"

"Whoa, whoa," I said and directed her to a chair. "Take a deep breath, and then we'll talk."

She pushed the papers across the desk at me. I did a cursory review of the four-page document she had handed me and realized that I was looking at the lawsuit Elise had filed against Jennifer earlier. Jennifer had taken the lawsuit and substituted dates to look like Elise was suing her yet again. Whether or not the signatures were genuine, I had no way of knowing. But my guess was they were probably forged. I looked up and asked Jennifer what happened.

"The sheriff came to my office and served me with these papers. This horrible person named Elise is suing me again!

Isn't there some way we can stop this and make her go away?"

I had no choice but to go along with this. "We can discuss filing a counterclaim against her for the same accounting and temporary support she is seeking from you."

The whole thing was ridiculous. The court had already modified the temporary support, and Judge Adamson had rendered an award. Moreover, Judge Adamson had already divided the property, and there would be no reason on earth Wilder or any other lawyer would fashion this lawsuit and file it again.

It was so bogus, yet I knew better than to challenge her at that moment. Instead, I would find out where this was going. It dawned on me that she made every effort to make me believe that Elise was alive and well and still pulling strings. The emails from "Elise," and the Elise lawsuit she had brought me, plus the change in makeup and the emails and the brick through the window—all done to make me believe Elise was alive and well and presenting Jennifer as someone I should be interested in romantically.

I pretended I was incensed at the lawsuit. "We can't let her get away with this! I'm going to go to Paris and take her deposition immediately! Then I'm going to file papers with the court and get this case dismissed. Please try to do your job at work, take care of your patients, and allow me to make this go away."

"I already checked with the courthouse. The case is actually on file there and has Elise's signature. I would know it anywhere."

"As I said, I will go to Paris and make her present herself at a deposition. I will demand that she explain why she is doing this again when the court has already decided the same case. It's preposterous. Please bear with me while I make this go away through the proper channels."

"Michael, I knew I could count on you. I can always count on you, can't I?"

"You can always count on me, Jennifer, for legal advice and legal help. Yes, I'm here to help you, one professional to another."

She actually had a look of relief on her face.

Once Jennifer had left my office, I immediately called Frank Wilder.

"Frank, I have to tell you that I'm distraught for Elise's welfare. Certain things have come to my attention that make me believe something bad has happened to Elise. I'm going to dummy up a deposition notice to take Elise's deposition in Paris. I don't expect you to be there unless you want to be. I believe that Jennifer will be there since I tried to force "Elise" to present herself at the deposition. I believe that Jennifer will somehow interfere or take steps to explain away the fact that Elise is not going to appear. Frank, I'm afraid something terrible has happened to your client."

"Michael, we've been bonkers over here, looking for Elise. Her mother knows nothing. The neighbors in her building know nothing, the family knows nothing, and her work knows nothing. Now and then, her mother receives emails from Elise's email account, telling her that she doesn't want to be in touch right now, but everything is good with her. She thanks her mother for looking after Çidde and then disappears again. We are sick with worry. Of course, I will go to Paris with you to find out what happens. Have you confronted Jennifer yet about any of this?"

"Not yet, but I have asked her about various things, and she always manages to sidestep me. I think this next action of going to Paris is going to bring it all to a head. And I have to say I'm happy you're going to be there. Maybe you can help me control what happens. I'm also going to be sending you a copy of the so-called lawsuit Jennifer is now claiming Elise has filed against her. You will see that it is the same lawsuit that you and Elise did, in fact, file against Jennifer. The dates have now been changed to make it look like a new lawsuit, but in all other respects, it's the same damned paperwork."

"To say I'm stunned is an understatement. But at least somebody is thinking and taking action that I certainly agree with. I will be there in Paris with you. Maybe we can talk again before then. In the meantime, if I hear anything, I will contact you. I would appreciate you do likewise."

"Of course."

We then hung up. So, all efforts to locate Elise had returned empty-handed.

I just felt awful and disheartened. I was afraid I knew what was coming, but I didn't want to think about it.

At least not yet.

Chapter Sixty

JENNIFER

Jennifer Ipswich had saved the voicemail recordings from Elise Ipswich when Joseph had become ill until he died. For the most part, the recordings were panicky, but the earlier ones contained messages regarding everything from their daughter's illness to Elise's work at LVP Partners.

In the quiet of the evening, Jennifer began playing Elise's messages and speaking along with them. After a dozen times through, she was starting to capture the voice. Ten times later, she felt she was doing an excellent job of mimicry. She was able to comment about things she expected might come up during Elise's deposition. Even up until the night before the deposition, Jennifer was practicing her voice.

Jennifer had taken over Elise's telephone and her email and Twitter accounts. Her parts were coming together and she was feeling stronger, more whole, by the day. She knew full well the items she would need to continue to impersonate Elise, her husband's other wife. Meanwhile, Joseph himself could rot in hell as far as Jennifer was concerned. He was the reason for the terrible things she had had to do.

"Elise" then sent an email to all parties that she could only attend the deposition by phone.

Chapter Sixty-One

MICHAEL

When I received an email from "Elise" saying that she couldn't be present for the deposition, I decided not to bother to fly to France. Elise wouldn't be there. It would all happen by long distance telephone—a land line in my office.

I was preparing for Elise's deposition when Frank Wilder called me.

"Michael," he said to me, "I have the number for Elise's phone in case you don't. Should we compare what we have?"

He then read off the number he had, which was the same number I had. "All right," I told him. "As far as I'm concerned, I'm ready for the depo. Frank, I'm counting on you to be the key player in determining whether or not we have the real Elise on the other end of the phone. It's just too damned bad she refused to do it by Zoom. More than anything, I want to get a look at the voice on the other end of the line. I don't know how clever Jennifer may be, but it wouldn't surprise me to hear her trying to impersonate

Elise. Most of all, I wish we had voice recognition technology, but Marcel has tried to obtain that service from Interpol, and they have refused because the case is not one they have ongoing, and they are facing an enormous backup in their lab. So, it's going to be up to you, Frank."

"Not to worry, Michael. I'd know that woman's voice anywhere. I think emulating a French person speaking English would be quite difficult under the best of circumstances. Yes, I'll be listening closely; you can count on that."

The next morning at six a.m., I had my court reporter seated in my small conference room, along with Marcel and myself, and I dialed Frank Wilder first, then dialed Elise's number to conference her in. I then centered the phone on the table between myself and the court reporter and waited for Elise to answer.

A female voice came on the phone almost immediately. She identified herself as Elise and asked Frank whether or not he had any last-minute instructions for her that they needed to discuss off-line. Frank told her there were not any, and she said, "Oh," in a voice that sounded like someone who didn't quite believe.

I then began the deposition. "Mrs. Ipswich, would you give us your full name, please?"

"My name is Elise Ipswich."

"Where do you live, Mrs. Ipswich?"

I live on rue Dumont in Paris, France."

"With whom do you live there?"

"I live with my daughter, Çidde, and no one else."

"How old is Çidde?"

"She is now six years old. She looks exactly like her father, I might add."

"Does anyone else live in your home with you?"

"No."

"Please tell us about your relationship with your mother."

"My relationship with my mother is very good. She loves me, and I love her very much."

"Have you been away from your home on rue Dumont the past month?"

"Yes, I have been living in the south of Spain while I recover from the death of my husband. My daughter has been with my mother during this period. I have been living like a hermit, unable to speak with anyone due to my grief. I'm sure you can understand."

"Yes, you must be very sad."

"I have a doctor here, and he has me on some strong vitamins and a sleep potion that I take at night. Without that, I'm unable to sleep. I toss and turn and think of Joseph and nothing else. Sometimes I can hear his voice calling to me. It makes me cry, and then I'm a wreck for the rest of the day."

"There has been some question on our end of the line whether we are talking to the real Elise Ipswich or not. Can you please give me Elise's driver's license number?"

"I cannot. My purse was stolen on the train down while I was sleeping. I have written to the French government and tried to replace all of my identification cards, but they have not arrived so far. I'm sorry I cannot help you here."

"Mrs. Ipswich, where did you go to college?"

"I attended university here in Paris and obtained my advanced degree in economics from the London School of Economics in London."

"And where do you work?"

"I work at LVP Partners in Paris. I'm an associate account manager, and I will soon be promoted to a full-fledged account manager. I have almost four years on the job and have one more examination to take, and then I will be promoted, and my salary will double."

"You've filed a lawsuit against my client seeking temporary support and equitable distribution of Joseph Ipswich's assets at the time of death. My question for you is, why have you filed this lawsuit when the court has already ruled on the same items?"

"Because I have not yet received that money. It got to the point where I was afraid that my lawyer, Mr. Wilder, was not working in my best interests. So I took matters into my own hands and filed a lawsuit again by myself. I have no regrets about doing this. I must receive the property my husband owned that I'm entitled to. My funds are limited, and right now, I'm living on my meager savings and a few personal items that I sold."

"How do we best know that you are, in fact, Elise Ipswich?"

"Perhaps you should ask Frank Wilder. He knows my voice as well as anybody I know, and he can tell you that this is Elise speaking. Do you have any other questions for me?"

"I'm going to halt this deposition at this point and reschedule it for a later date. It will be taken up as the case progresses. Please keep us advised of your address and your telephone number if they should change."

"I do not have an address. I'm staying with some friends of mine from my college days. My phone number you already have, and that will not be changing. It is my only true connection with the world at this point."

"All right, thank you for your time today, Mrs. Ipswich. This concludes your deposition."

I then disconnected my call from "Elise" and said to Frank Wilder, "Well?"

"I don't know, Michael. It sounds somewhat like her, but

I'm not convinced. I wish we could see the face, and it seems to me you fell down on not forcing her to make arrangements for us to have a Zoom call with her. I'm not going to conclude one without the other because I can't. Sorry, old man, but that's how we're going to have to leave it."

Chapter Sixty-Two

MICHAEL

I needed to be alone that day to think things over at my lunch hour. I left my building and walked down Michigan Avenue to Reser's restaurant and took a booth at the back. I ordered the beef stew and a large iced tea.

The waitress returned right away with the iced tea. I spread my *Chicago Tribune* on the table and began reading the front page. As usual, the news was soul-crushing, so I went to the sports page and began reading. I was engrossed in a story about the Chicago Bears when I heard a female voice say my name. I looked up, and there stood Jennifer Ipswich. She was smiling down at me and pointing at the chair across from me with a look of *May I?* on her face.

"Jennifer," I said with surprise. "What in the world are you doing here?"

She sat down in the chair and reached across the table. She put her right hand on my left hand. I immediately jerked away and pulled back from the table. "What the hell?" I exclaimed. I kept my voice low, not wanting to disturb other diners.

She smiled and said, "You know I want to be with you. We could walk down to the Sheraton and spend two hours together right now, and no one would ever know. Are you up to it?"

"Of course not! What in the world is wrong with you? You are not the same person I met last summer at the swimming pool. I cannot believe how you can change in the blink of an eye like this. For your information, I'm going to file to withdraw from your appeal and cut all ties with you. I've had it with your bullshit, and your crazy, and I'm not doing it anymore. Now, please get up and leave the restaurant. Leave me the hell alone, or I'm going to call the police. Which will it be?"

She pursed her lips and shook her head. Then she ignored what I had just said. "I hear you took Elise's deposition this morning. How did that go?"

"How did you know that? Nobody from my office told you a thing. Where are you getting your information? From Elise herself?"

"Yes, from Elise herself. We have become very close since she has gone to live in Spain, and we are together bemoaning our husband's loss. It's only natural that we would since we have both lost the same thing. I'm getting close to Elise, and I'm thinking of inviting her to come to Chicago and spend some time with me. I think it would be good for both of us. She could bring her daughter, and they could meet my children and get to know one another. What would you think of that, Michael?"

"It doesn't matter what I think. On top of that, I don't give a damn one way or the other. I want you to leave me alone and leave this restaurant right now. If you don't, I'm going to dial the police and get someone over here."

At that moment, she reached for my hand again, but I pulled away and began tapping 911 into my cell phone.

She purred while she watched me with my phone. "Michael, Verona is not that good for you. I know she's a nice woman, and I know you care for her very much. But the things I've heard about her—not good, Michael. As your best friend at this time, let me encourage you to get together with me and talk this over. I've seen how you look at me, and I know you want me. So please don't be shy."

"The police are on their way. I would recommend you seriously consider leaving before you wind up in handcuffs."

She stood from the table, slipped her arm through her purse, and adjusted it on her shoulder. She said, eyes wide, "Well? Are you coming, or am I going alone?"

"Get the hell out of my sight. Now!"

With that, she turned and scurried off, and the last I saw of her, she was at the front door, at which point she turned and blew me a kiss. It was all I could do not to get sick. The waitress arrived with my beef stew a few minutes later. I began eating but then had a strong urge to call Verona and tell her how much I loved her.

As I walked back to the office after my meal, that's exactly what I did. Verona could hear the neediness in my voice and was there for me. As we spoke, I began to realize she might not be safe. If Jennifer had done something with Elise, she would certainly not hesitate to do something with another person she saw as a roadblock to what she wanted. I made a note to myself to call a security service as soon as I got back to the office and arrange for security for my wife and children.

Back at the office, I did just that, then I called Marcel in and sent him out to my home in Evanston to await the security people and get them lined up for my family's protection.

He was off in a flash, and I turned my mind back to my law practice. Every so often, I would look up and shudder. She was growing quite fantastical in her illusions. Lord only knew what she might try. Suddenly, I could stand it no longer and left the office, telling my people that I would be back tomorrow and for them to tell no one where I was.

Especially Jennifer.

Chapter Sixty-Three

MICHAEL

Desperate people require desperate measures. It was time for us to act, time for us to get to the bottom of Elise's disappearance. Marcel got on the phone and contacted Visa and MasterCard. Within an hour, he had access to Jennifer's accounts. How again? I didn't ask. In particular, we were looking for charges she had made in Paris. It only made sense that she had gone to Paris and made Elise disappear from there. That was our best working guess.

Sure enough, Marcel came into my office, beaming. "Look at this," he said with great enthusiasm. He spread before me a series of charges from the account of Jennifer Ipswich. They were from Paris, and they began at the Ritz Hotel and the Bar Hemingway.

"All right," I said to the best investigator I'd ever known, "what comes next?"

"Next," he said, "yours truly is off to Paris. I'll report back within the next twenty-four hours after touchdown."

"Have a safe trip."

Chapter Sixty-Four

MARCEL

Marcel touched down three days later at Charles de Gaulle in Paris and took a taxi straight to the Ritz Hotel. He checked in, checked his room as was his habit, and went downstairs to look around. He found that the Hemingway bar didn't open until noon, so he returned to his room for a quick nap. He set the wake-up call for 11:30 and was immediately asleep.

At 11:45, he was up and dressed and riding the elevator down to the lobby. He stood outside the Bar Hemingway, and when the help inside saw him, early as he was, they let him in any way. "Would you like a table, the Hemingway booth, or would you like to sit at the bar, sir?"

"I'd like to sit at the bar, please."

The maître d' took him to the bar and told him he would have to wait until noon to order. He said that was fine and began looking around. At noon sharp, the bartender approached Marcel and asked him what he would like. Marcel motioned the bartender closer and told him he would like a look at the bar's video from 22 December. The bartender explained that would be available in the security office, which was the second door beyond the front desk. It was an unmarked door, and Marcel should rap five times with his knuckles. Marcel plunked down a €5, thanked the man, and headed for the security office.

The door to the security office was opened after Marcel knocked. "Sir?" said a young man that Marcel guessed was in his early thirties. He was wearing gold-rimmed spectacles and a white shirt with a vest.

"My name is Marcel Rainsford, and I'm from Chicago. I'm a licensed private investigator and a one-time employee of Interpol. I need some help with some video footage in a case that I'm working up that potentially involves a murder. The murder suspect and her victim were at the Bar Hemingway on 22 December. The time was 7:05 p.m. I need to see the bar's CCTV video for that time and thirty minutes before, until the two subjects leave the bar. Is this possible?"

"Do you have any identification, sir?"

"Marcel pulled out his private investigator's license and also his ID from Interpol, stamped *Retired* across the face. The young man studied the ID, studied Marcel's face, and handed both items back. "Please come in. Let's see what we can find."

When they played the video, the two women were easily spotted. Marcel watched the video for thirty minutes while the women talked back and forth, shook hands at one point, and then he watched as Elise got up from the table, shrugged into her winter coat, and left the bar.

"I need to see the video from just outside the hotel in the taxi area at seven-thirty-five p.m. Same day."

"One moment, sir. Allow me to insert the date and time in the exterior video system, and we'll have you going."

Sure enough, here came Elise walking outside the Bar Hemingway. She asked the red-coated attendant a question. When the man spoke back, his white breath hung in the air. He motioned one of the waiting taxis to pull forward. Marcel, holding a closeup keypad they had given him, clicked twice, and the license plate doubled in size. Now he was able to make out the license plate of the taxi. He went back and forth three times, each time writing up the next digit on the plate until he had the full number.

"All right," he said to the young man in the vest. "I'm done here, at least for now. I thank you very much."

Marcel then went outside and hailed a taxi. He told the driver in French that he needed to be taken to 1 Place du Châtelet. The driver looked at him in the rearview mirror and said, "That's where I pick up my cab. I can have you there in about eight minutes. Hang on, sir."

The name of the business was Paris Taxi. Marcel's driver pulled into the drive-through, and Marcel climbed out and paid the driver in euros. He then went inside and located the security office. "I need two GPS coordinates for one of your taxis on the night of 22 December. Here is the number of the taxi's license plate. At 7:35 p.m., your driver picked up a woman from the Ritz Hotel and took her for a ride. I need to know the address where she was taken. Can you help me?"

The security officer looked him over. He was a mid-fifties gentleman wearing khaki pants, a black shirt with a red tie, and a winter coat, waist length. He said in French, "May I ask what this is for?"

Marcel reached into his pocket and pulled out a $100 bill. "It's for this," he said with a smile.

"Yes, sir," the man said. "Give me five minutes, and I will have your address."

Marcel waited, checking his watch impatiently until the man returned.

"The address where your lady was taken was 11009 rue Dumont. She rode in our taxi number four-two-three-two. Will there be anything else, sir?"

"No, and thank you. Oh, yes, I need a taxi to take me to Nord Taxi."

Marcel was taken to Nord Taxi. His reason for going was twofold. First, he had seen Jennifer Ipswich follow Elise Ipswich out of the Ritz Hotel and take the next taxi in line after Elise's cab. Second, he was guessing they went to the same destination. At Nord taxi, he repeated the same exercise as he had at Paris taxi. He learned that Number 8897 also went to 11009 rue Dumont, waited two hours, and then returned the fare to the Ritz Hotel.

Marcel then caught a ride back to the Ritz Hotel. He went back upstairs to his room, called down for a pot of coffee, and sat himself down at a small table beside a window looking out on the street. He assessed where he was. First, he had Jennifer and Elise together in the bar until 7:35 p.m. They then left the bar in separate taxis and went to Elise's home address. He guessed that Elise was unaware she was being followed. Elise then went inside her home, and Jennifer was dropped at that same address. She presumably followed. Marcel could only guess, but he thought his guesstimate was pretty accurate. He could visualize Jennifer knocking on Elise's door and being allowed inside. That was on 22 December.

Enough guessing. He went downstairs and took a taxi to her house, and climbed out. "Wait here, please." It was an out-of-the-way lane, and he figured another cab wouldn't be along anytime soon.

He stopped outside her door and pulled on his rubber

gloves, then reached down and put paper surgical booties on over his shoes. Then he let himself inside with his picks.

Nothing out of the ordinary. The hum of electrical appliances running. Rain outside beginning to patter on the windows.

Into the bathroom. Blood stains in the tub as if it had been unsuccessfully rinsed out. He crossed the hallway into the bedroom, stopping just outside the door. It was the little girl's room. He entered and checked beneath the bed and in the closet, even knowing he would find it in the next room.

He checked the second bedroom. Elise's. A pile of clothing, loose hangers, and sweaters on hangers. Two khaki workshirts with stitching above the pockets that said *LVP*.

Then he went into the kitchen. A chest-type freezer. The next place to look, no doubt. He jerked and lifted the sizable lid. Four fifty-gallon garbage bags. Swollen and covered in frost. He brushed away the swirl of icy steam that arose, then unwrapped the plastic tie around bag 1.

Marcel had seen everything the world had to offer, so this horror was no surprise. He knew immediately what he had found.

Intestines, lower abdominal organs. He moved to the second bag. Limbs, arms, and legs hewn into pieces. Only one foot. Third bag, a mess of ribs and lungs, maybe the heart. He didn't open the fourth bag. No need. How had things been so neatly cut down?

And cut apart by what? He looked around the room.

Back to the bathroom. Behind the door. The culprit: an electric knife, the kind used to carve the turkey for grandpa. Except this one was covered in matted blood. Would it be enough to cut apart the humerus? The tibia? The spine? Then he looked beneath the sink. A hacksaw with a bent blade but still functional. Blood caked in the joints. Joe had been handy around the house. Marcel could only imagine. It had done its work even with a bent blade—the proof was in the bags.

He returned to the kitchen and checked the trash beneath the sink. It was there as he had guessed it would be, a delivery receipt for a brand new chest-type freezer—torn in long shreds and wadded up. He quickly pieced it back together. The credit card used to purchase the freezer: Jennifer Ipswich.

He returned to the freezer and opened the fourth bag, knowing already what he would find. The dissection was exquisite, accomplished only by a trained surgeon, someone skilled in anatomical dissection. He stuck his hand down inside and pulled aside the brain.

Below that, the head. He was sure it was her, but he could only guess by looking at the head because there were no identifying marks.

And the face was missing.

Chapter Sixty-Five

MARCEL

He returned to his hotel room. He called up Elise's call log from her cell phone records on that night on his laptop. He saw that no calls were listed but that a text had been made the next day. He went online, pulled up the records, and found the text.

Mother, I'm going to be leaving town today for several days. Please pick up Çidde from school. I'm very upset about Joseph's death, and I'm going off to mourn his death by myself. Please do not worry. I'm well and on my way to recovery. I just need time alone, and I will be out of touch for several days, maybe even a few weeks. I love you with all my heart and thank you for taking care of Çidde.
Love, Elise.

Marcel continued studying the cell phone's call records. He saw that an earlier transmission was an email from the phone to Frank Wilder. She wanted to discuss hiring him for her husband's death.

He kept reading. Here was an email from Frank Wilder to Elise.

Dear Mrs. Ipswich. I would be delighted to help you with your case. Is there any chance you will be coming to the United States anytime soon? I highly recommend that you do and plan on staying a few days while I get a lawsuit pulled together, signed by you, and filed. Usually in these cases, we can expect maybe 3 to 6 months before resolution. But in your case, I will be asking for temporary orders, meaning I will be asking for temporary child support and your own support out of the proceeds of your deceased husband's life insurance. Please call my office and confirm that you will be coming into Chicago in the next few days. This is very important, and I urge you to make your travel arrangements and then call me. Yours sincerely, Frank Wilder, Attorney and Counselor at Law.

Marcel had searched Elise's flat and knew that the cell phone was missing, knew there was no iPad or laptop, and he decided the only record he would probably be able to obtain from her electronic communications was what he was looking at online.

He saw a subsequent call to Chicago, and he was certain the number called would be Wilder's office.

He kept looking, but his search abruptly ended on 22 December when all electronic activity ceased for 48 hours before resuming again. He muttered to himself, "It doesn't take a rocket scientist to figure out who was manning the phone at this point. One sick cookie."

He next placed a call to Michael Gresham and updated him. Gresham was saddened to hear about the Elise Ipswich result. Marcel told Michael that he would call the Paris police and report his find. He would place the call from the Ritz Hotel lobby phone, so they wouldn't know his identity. Michael said he approved and told Marcel that he had several calls into the University of California at San Diego and some other contacts he had uncovered regarding Jennifer. Marcel would be updated upon his return.

Marcel hung up the phone, leaned forward in the chair, and placed his fingers on his closed eyes. He sighed and shook his head. He had seen similar, but he had never seen this. He was convinced an expert had performed the dissection.

An expert named Jennifer Ipswich.

He was now determined to place that carving knife in her hand.

It went without saying that Jennifer would have been wearing surgical gloves when she carved apart Elise Ipswich's body. Maybe even a rubber apron, and perhaps even clear goggles, because it would've been one hell of a mess, the body being fresh and very, very bloody.

In a ghoulish way, he had to admire the woman. There weren't many human beings that could dissect a person they had just murdered. Yes, it was a form of admiration that was very macabre, but it was also genuine. Marcel had killed close-up, blood up to his elbows, and he knew what it felt and smelled like.

This one was going to be a hard one to catch.

The experts always were.

Chapter Sixty-Six

MICHAEL

While Marcel was away in Paris, I was doing my own investigating by telephone. I called San Diego, looking for Jennifer's early boyfriend, David Goldman. He was the UCSD medical student she had been living with for a while. Goldman was the psych tech who had told Jennifer he had seen her rapid cycling. Because of his encouragement (Or threats to leave her. That was always unclear), she had gone to see her first psychiatrist. We knew the rest of the story from there, Marcel having obtained that doctor's records, and we knew that she had been medicated with antipsychotics. But what about Goldman? Just on the off chance, I wanted to know what had become of David Goldman, MD.

So, I set about searching.

First, I called the UCSD med school to obtain his current address. The California medical society maintained a public record of all physicians licensed in the state. Their professional address and phone number were included in the directory. However, there was no David Goldman among the thousands of names.

It puzzled me, yet I knew Goldman might have settled elsewhere and not even been practicing medicine in California, in which case his name would not be included in that directory.

What to do?

Just on a hunch, I went online and looked up the Health and Human Services Agency of the County of San Diego. Death certificates were available for public view. I began searching. I found his death certificate. Then I found a police report. Sure enough, my hunch paid off. David Goldman had died during a home invasion at his residence in Pacific Beach, San Diego County, California.

The strangest part of all?

The home invasion consisted of just one person entering.

A woman. Who escaped into the night by running along the beach into a waiting vehicle and roared away toward Los Angeles.

My pulse quickened. A little voice rose up in my mind.

We were on the right path in so many, many ways.

Chapter Sixty-Seven

MICHAEL

Following up on my work on David Goldman in California, I wrote my memo to the file. As I typed, I received an email. It was a forwarded email from Jennifer Ipswich. The original email being delivered by Jennifer was from my wife, Verona, to Jennifer. The email read:

Jennifer, I know that you are lonely and are looking to make contact with Michael. You must stop all of your efforts with my husband, or I will come after you. I have watched you come and go at your job and come and go at your home, and I know your habits. I also know about your children. I'm going to hunt you down, and I'm going to teach you a lesson. You can make this right by sending me the sum of $100,000 in care of my husband, Michael. You won't be safe from me until you send me this amount. I'm not kidding about this, and I'm not fooling around. Verona Gresham, wife of Michael Gresham.

For just one second, I was shocked. But in the next second, I saw right through the hoax. Nevertheless, I called her on the phone to make sure she was all right.

"Verona, I've just received a phony email that pretends to be sent by you to Jennifer Ipswich."

"Honey, I have no idea what you're talking about. I have not sent any emails to Jennifer Ipswich and never would. Let's talk about this when you get home tonight."

"Of course, you didn't. But I'm uneasy. I want you to keep an eye on the kids and maybe pick them up yourself rather than the bus."

"Will do. I can handle this. I'll see you tonight."

"I'll see you then. In the meantime, please keep the kids home until you and I have had a chance to talk. Goodbye."

I read the email again. I studied the metadata at the top of the email. It told me that the email came from an IP registered to Verona. Jennifer had opened an email account in my wife's name and had emailed herself and forwarded it to me.

I called the office number for Jennifer. I was told she was busy with patients. I was told she had also left specific instructions to interrupt her if I called. The receptionist said she would be on the line in just a few moments. So, I waited. Perhaps two minutes later, Jennifer answered my call.

"Michael, how sweet of you to call. I know you withdrew from my case, and I know that you're finished with me. So you must be calling about that email your wife sent to me. Have you spoken with her? Can you believe this? She's threatening me!"

"I know what you've done, Jennifer. And it's not going to work."

"Michael, I don't know what you're talking about. What is it you think I've done?"

"I know that you've opened an email account in my wife's name. In your own twisted way, you've sent an email from that phony account to yourself and have now forwarded that email to me. Well, it's not going to work. You've outdone yourself this time, thinking you know my wife that well. Verona would never write that email. I'm going to tell you this one time. If this continues, or if you ever send me another such email or text or correspondence pretending to be from my wife, I'm going to drag your ass into court and stomp all over it. Do we understand each other?"

"Michael, Darling, I know you're upset. You're just going to have to accept that your wife is not all you think she is. Please consider this and don't hesitate to call me if you want to talk. Thank you now, but I have patients to attend. Goodbye, Michael."

She hung up on me.

Chapter Sixty-Eight

MICHAEL

I went home that night with a heavy heart. Marcel had called me, so I knew what he had found at Elise's home. We were both distraught and sad. Marcel, who had once worked as a London police officer, had "worked" the scene at Elise's house. He had been unable to connect Jennifer to the hack job and the scene by any piece of evidence. The only exception might be fingerprints, but we both already knew she was too smart not to wear gloves. We were going to have to catch her in some other way. We didn't know how yet, but the hunt was just beginning to send her to prison.

Marcel had described to me in detail what he had found at Elise's home. I knew the foot was missing, which sickened me to think of, but we had seen the photographs and I was somewhat steeled against that.

But the face. Oh, my God, she had peeled away her face. My mind was racing, worried at what else she might have in mind. Marcel felt the same way. In the morning, we were going to talk about setting up a meeting with the French police and presenting our evidence about Jennifer

Ipswich. We had the connection of the foot photograph. We had the connection of the taxi evidence on the night of Elise's disappearance when Jennifer had followed Elise home. And we had the evidence of the facial dissection that only a skilled surgeon could perform. The face is very irregular in shape and would've been extremely difficult to dissect away from the skull. So, we had that, too. To my way of thinking, it was time to make our presentation to the Paris police and see where it went. I was convinced we had no other choice, but I still wanted to get Marcel's take on it.

When I arrived home, I was greeted by a very upset Verona. She was flailing about emotionally, and I knew something like this had never happened to her before. I was all about apologizing for the fact that my law practice had in its strange way of invading our home.

We went back over the brick through the window, and I took care not to tell her about Marcel's findings in Paris. There was no need for details. I talked around the edges of what was going on. Then we discussed the children's safety. We had already discussed the security efforts I'd made and the bodyguards that were now keeping their distance but following all family members at all times. I explained that each child had a bodyguard wherever they went. I explained that she did, too. "What about you?" she asked me. "Do you have a bodyguard, too?"

"Yes, I do. So does Marcel. If something does happen, we want someone there as a witness, if nothing else."

"Michael, the woman is in so much pain. Someone has got to stop her. I'm going to write her an email and tell her that I will not abide any threats against my children. I'm going to tell her that she is going to jeopardize her life if she does any such thing. I was so slow on the pick-up, too.

Totally blew right past me: she's your client, my patient. Slick."

"Please don't. You'll only incite her further."

"You know me, and you know my background. I'm Russian, and I cannot be bullied. She is making a huge mistake, using my name in a phony email. I'm not going to put up with that another second. Plus, I want to talk to her. I think I can help before this goes any further."

"Please, let me handle this. It's my problem, not yours. Everyone under our roof is safe. I'm going to keep it that way, and there's no need for you to inject yourself into this."

"I'm going to message her so that she knows I know. And I'm going to try to make an appointment to talk. Before she gets hurt."

"No, I'm telling you to stay away. You don't have the whole story, and she's dangerous."

I knew there was no sense in arguing with her further. Verona could be very headstrong when she got underway. She wasn't a person to be poked and prodded. She was the proverbial sleeping bear. Once awakened, she could be incredibly tough and aggressive. It just might be, I was thinking, that Jennifer Ipswich had crossed the line she never should've crossed. Or it might be Verona could save her from doing any more damage. She could be extremely persuasive.

More than ever, I was convinced it was time to take action in Paris. Something had to be done. Something had to be done to keep Verona out of this.

Time was of the essence.

Chapter Sixty-Nine

LAKESIDE

It was ten o'clock at night when the green and yellow taxi arrived in Evanston from O'Hare airport. The taxi took Lake Avenue down to Sheridan Road, right two blocks, and stopped in front of the address at the blond brick home that the passenger was looking for on East Germaine.

She paid the driver and climbed out with her backpack and rolling CPA case. Even though it was night, the stars were out, and she could see Lake Michigan between the houses just beyond Gilson Park.

She had studied the map and knew the area well. Like everything she did, her journey was planned out, and her surroundings memorized. She knew that off to her right and down about one mile was the Michigan Shores Club, where her husband and Jennifer would have enjoyed upscale dining and dancing. Off to her left were the CTA Purple Line, the Metra, and downtown Evanston shops and restaurants.

She felt a pang in her heart. There had been a time she would've died to live in such a place. But no longer. Now she only wanted to leave the United States, leave France, and sneak into Spain and fade into the shadows.

She climbed the steps to the front door and knocked. She had to smile. The two physicians referred to this place as their fishing camp, which had to be the biggest joke of all the fishing camp jokes, given that it had last sold for $3.6 million.

She was just about to repeat knocking when the door opened, and there stood Jennifer. She had not turned on the porch light, and the visitor's face could not be seen from the street or any of the surrounding homes. The visitor was ushered inside, and the door immediately shut behind her. The two women went into the kitchen, and Jennifer opened the refrigerator and handed a bottle of water to the newcomer. They then went into the dining room, where the newcomer dropped her bag, and Jennifer brought the CPA case.

"It's inside?" asked Jennifer.

"Safe and sound inside a safe. Fits perfectly inside."

Jennifer opened the CPA bag and withdrew the heavy safe. The newcomer spun the combination back and forth, opening the safe. Jennifer reached inside with both hands and lifted.

"My precious one," said Jennifer. She held the Qing vase up to the light. "Not a mark. Except for the missing dorsal fin. That's how I know it's mine."

"Then we're good?"

"We're good. The money is in my backpack. I'll give it to you,"

"Then I'm ready for Spain."

Jennifer nodded. She took a drink of her bottle of water and said, "You will change your name, your looks, and disappear with the money."

"Not good enough," said Elise. "How are we ever going to get rid of Michael and Marcel?"

"Michael, I think we can handle now. Marcel, we will wait until he comes to us. Which he will do once Michael is gone."

"Tell me about Michael. What are we to do?"

Jennifer smiled. "We are going to bring him here, and we are going to invite him into our web. Help me get Michael. Loving that Michael!"

"And how? Where will we do that?"

"Right here in my summer house. Specifically, in the basement. Have you ever been tied to a pole?"

"What are you saying?"

"I am saying that you are the cheese and Michael Gresham is the rat. A dear rat."

"You're bringing him here?"

"No, Verona is bringing him here."

"His wife, Verona?"

"Exactly. I sent a text message to her, and I'm sure she will react. It will bring her here with a great desire to speak to me. I have prepared her, and now I own her. Once I have her, I have Michael."

"And I will go away and leave you alone."

"That's all I've ever wanted—to be left alone. With Michael."

Elise was pawing through her bag but then looked up. "Are you on speed?"

"I'm on Michael!"

"Never mind about Michael. I'll be taking my money and going where no one will ever find me. Çidde and I will live a long and happy life together. No one will ever know."

"All I ask is that you help me with Michael first. Marcel, I'm not worried about. He will eventually come looking for

Michael, but there will be no Michael. There will be no Verona. There will be only me at my medical practice, doing my job with Michael."

"Stop that. You don't do your job with Michael."

"Watch me."

"Please."

Jennifer returned the vase to the small safe. She closed the door. "What is the combination to the safe?"

"Joe."

"What do you mean, Joe?"

"Count the letters in the alphabet to the J, count the letters in the alphabet to the O, count the letters in the alphabet to the E, and you have the combination. You can't go wrong."

"Very well. I'm going to make you a sandwich, and then I'm going to take you to the basement. Is there anything else first? Restroom? Coffee? Whiskey?"

"Restroom and a small glass of wine. Preferably, French."

"Can do. The restroom is right down that hall, and then we'll both have a glass of wine and make ready for Verona."

Chapter Seventy

VERONA

Late the following afternoon, Verona was alarmed by the email. She knew that her patient was acting out, and she also knew the patient was going through a traumatic time. She did not want to see Jennifer injure herself, and she knew that the email was a sign of psychosis.

She predicted that Jennifer thought she was Verona when she wrote the email and sent it to herself. It was a terrible game and a dangerous one. It pulled Verona along like any caring psychologist.

She went into her office and closed the door. She opened her file cabinet and withdrew Jennifer O'Connor's chart. What an actress, what mime, what a genius production, fooling me all that time.

She went back over her notes from the last three visits and saw how worried she'd been that Jennifer might be on the verge of doing something bad. It had been building and building, and now Jennifer was acting out. It was going to get worse, much worse than a simple email. She knew that she had to see her patient and try to talk her down. Not only that, but there was also more than merely caring for her patient. She was also afraid for the safety of Michael and the children. A sick mind could latch on to any of them and do extreme damage before anyone would even see it coming.

She placed a call to Jennifer's office, determined to set up a meeting with her.

But the office told her that Jennifer was busy with patients and was not taking any personal calls. Verona tried explaining that it was a professional call, not a personal call. Verona asked the front desk to talk to Jennifer a second time and plead with her to come to the phone. She said it was that urgent. The front desk person said she would, and Verona was put on hold, complete with some Kenny G sounds.

Minutes later, the front desk person returned and said that Jennifer had left for the day. Verona questioned her repeatedly, and when she hung up, she knew that Jennifer was avoiding her. She did not doubt that Jennifer was at her office and seeing patients. Verona decided she would go to Jennifer if Jennifer would not come to the phone.

Verona exited through her private entrance, never realizing she had ditched her bodyguard.

She went out to her Impala and drove east on Moser Road to its intersection with Western Avenue. She drove down two blocks and turned into the parking lot at Evanston Pediatrics and Adolescent Care. She pulled around back to where she had a clear view of the door marked *private*. Then she put the Impala in park but left the motor running. She sat back and peered through her sunglasses at the brown door. The time was 4:45 p.m., and people were beginning to leave the building.

Waiting in her car and studying each woman who came

out of the building, she read their faces out of habit. It was a professional trait, reading others by their faces and their body language. It was amazing how much she could learn just by doing that. It was something she did all day, and she didn't just set it aside when her professional day was over.

As she waited, thirty minutes went by, and they were still coming out. Then, at 5:30, Jennifer opened the door and walked outside. She had a book bag over one shoulder and a medical kit over the other. She stepped forward several steps and then paused, cupping her hand over her eyes and looking around the parking lot. Evidently, she had forgotten where she'd left her car. As bad luck would have it, Jennifer began walking right toward Verona. This wasn't what Verona wanted, so she looked away, trying to hide her face as Jennifer approached.

As it turned out, Jennifer was parked right beside Verona. Verona heard the car next to her start up, and she watched as it slowly pulled out of its slot. The car, a Volvo sedan, rolled around to the corner of the building and then went out of sight.

Verona followed out to Ringer Road, where she could see that Jennifer had made a right turn. Verona waited at the exit, allowing two cars to come between her and Jennifer's car. Then she pulled out and tightened up the distance from two cars back.

They journeyed along Ringer Road for several miles before making a left and heading toward Lake Michigan on the east side of town. When they made that left, no cars were separating them, but Verona kept her distance.

She poked along, casually falling back and then catching up somewhat.

After several blocks, Jennifer pulled into a strip mall and drove beneath the overhang of a drive-through dry cleaner.

Verona hung back, pulling into a parking slot 100 feet behind the woman.

She watched as the money was exchanged for the clothes, and then Verona made a shortcut across the lot and waited for Jennifer's car.

Within moments, Jennifer's car passed before her, moving right to left. Then she drove up to the exit and made a right turn. Verona followed from three cars back and, as they went along Tyler Street, the other intermediate cars began peeling off to the right and left. Finally, there was no other car between them, so Verona fell back. She allowed a motorcycle to zip out of a lot and pull up behind the Impala.

They drove in this configuration for another five minutes.

Then Jennifer made a left on Sheridan Road and pulled into the long driveway of a blond brick home on East Germaine. Verona passed on by and went down two more blocks before pulling over to the curb. Suddenly, she felt an urge. She whipped a U-turn and headed back up East Germaine Road.

She stopped and parked a hundred feet away in front of the neighbor's house. She then exited her car, thought better of it, and climbed back inside.

She studied the blond house where Jennifer had parked. Definitely three-million dollars at least—two stories, fully glassed-in front on the west and, Verona guessed, was fully glassed across the backside on the east as well. There was a two-car garage plus room for an RV. Deciding to be bold, Verona pulled in front of Jennifer's house. When she had stopped, she texted Michael:

Michael, I am at Jennifer Ipswich's house on East Germaine. Did you know she is my patient? She goes by the name of Jennifer O'Connor. I did not know she was your client. She fooled us both. Come check on me. I'm a little nervous.

She left the cell phone caught between the visor and the roof. She knew it could be located by triangulation. Michael had the software. Help would be on the way, but she doubted she would need it. She planned to have a healthy discussion with Jennifer. Hopefully, they would work through Jennifer's pain and arrive at a solution, just like they had done at the office many times before.

She then climbed out of her car and headed for the front door, where she rang the bell and waited. She was still wearing her blue windbreaker, slacks, and penny loafers.

A few minutes later, the door opened, and there stood Jennifer. She was wearing blue jeans, a T-shirt that said *Da Bears*, and a sweater open down the front. She held a spatula in one hand and looked like a genuine housewife getting dinner ready for the family. Verona smiled and lowered her hand from the doorbell.

"Verona! What in the world are you doing here?" She stepped back as if shocked to find her psychologist at her door. "Did you bring Michael? Well done, you!"

Verona didn't beat around the bush. "Jennifer, someone has taken my name and attached it to my email address, and now they're writing emails and pretending to be me. I know it's you, but I'm not going to be angry. But I do want it to stop. Could you invite me inside so we can talk?"

Jennifer smiled. She slapped the spatula against her open hand, threw back her head, and laughed. Real tears came into her eyes, and she wiped the sleeve of her sweater across her face. "Oh, one moment, please. My pot is boiling. Be right back."

Verona, caught by Jennifer's sudden departure, had no

idea what came next. On the one hand, she had delivered her message. On the other hand, she didn't want Jennifer to think she was a pushover. So she decided to wait and repeat her message if that was what it would take to get confirmation that the patient understood the game was over. It was a matter of helping her patient. Somebody had to step in and stop her from hurting herself or someone else.

Minutes later, Jennifer reappeared. This time, she held a silver pistol and came around the doorway, pointing it directly at Verona's chest. She smiled gleefully and said, "Come inside, Dr. Gresham. You and I have much to discuss." She laughed. "Not to worry, now. I'm prepared to pay for an hour of your time and get only fifty minutes again. You people!"

Verona was stunned. Her breath snapped in her throat, and she felt her knees buckle. A gun—that had never happened before, although she had had terrible times in Russia before leaving. But never anything like this where she was threatened with a gun. She didn't know what else to do except obey Jennifer's order and follow her inside.

Jennifer said, "All right, we're going to go into the kitchen, and we're going to sit down at the kitchen table and discuss this like two civilized human beings. Can we agree to do that?"

"All right," said Verona. "But you're going to have to put that gun away. I don't like being threatened, and I'm sure you wouldn't either."

Without lowering the pistol, Jennifer got behind Verona and prodded her with the barrel. She showed her where to sit at the kitchen table in a Captain's Chair. She reached inside the pantry and brought out two plastic handcuffs.

"Now, bring your hands together because I'm going to

tie you. Do you know why I'm tying you? So that you don't try to run off after our hour is up!"

Jennifer began zip-tying Verona to the chair, holding the gun beneath her arm while she cinched up the nylon. Verona struggled and cursed in Russian, but Jennifer stuck the muzzle of the gun inside her ear. "No, no, no, my dear little Russian! Stop moving or I'll have to shoot you!" Verona relaxed, then, and allowed herself to be fastened to the chair. Jennifer then went around the table and took a seat.

"Now, you were saying?" Jennifer smiled. The gun was laid upon the table. The muzzle pointed at Verona's chest.

Verona said bitterly, "I just want to know why you're bothering my family. We haven't done anything to you, and I want you to leave us alone. Is there anything so wrong with that?"

"You just don't get it, do you? Your husband Michael is hot for me and won't go away. I've told him to leave me alone, that he's married, but he says he's so charmed by me that he's not going to give up. It seems like we're going to have to send him a message."

Verona had collected herself somewhat. It was time to try reasoning with Jennifer. "I can see you really believe that, and I'm not going to argue it. But I do want us to agree to get some additional help today. Can we talk about that?"

Without answering, Jennifer then stood, went back to the closet, and selected a crescent wrench. She bent to her knees beside the stove and slipped the wrench behind it.

Verona saw her move her hand up and down and heard a grunt. Jennifer turned her head back around and spoke to Verona with her hand yet behind the stove.

"You didn't ask, but I'm loosening the nut that fastens

the gas pipe to the stove. Why? I'm sure you can figure that out, *doctor*."

"Please, I've delivered my message, and you don't want Michael to bother you. I'll make sure he never calls you or talks to you again. Just let me loose, and we'll be rid of each other. I promise."

Jennifer stood to her feet and smiled. "Women like you just don't get it. Men just can't leave me alone. Your husband fell, and he fell hard. The only way I'm going to get his attention and get him to leave me alone is to take you out of the picture and let him know I'm serious. I have to go to court in the morning, and I'm going to make sure you're well taken care of when I leave."

"What about the gas pipe?" said Verona. "You're going to blow this house up, leaving the pipe pulled off."

"Oh, I just loosened it. There's no gas escaping yet. But there will be when I go to court in the morning. In the meantime, you sit here and think about what you've done and try to get some rest. You're going to need to be rested up tomorrow when I leave. Promise you'll try to sleep some?"

"My husband is going to come looking. And the first thing he's going to think is that you've done something like this. I have no doubt he'll come here and find me. You're making a huge mistake because Michael can be very unforgiving. If he catches you like this, holding me hostage and threatening me, I wouldn't want to be you."

"Darling," said Jennifer with a lilt in her voice, "not a chance. You could never be me!"

Chapter Seventy-One

PARIS

Marcel wasted no time locating Elise's mother in Paris. He called her and made arrangements to come by and talk.

She lived on the outskirts of Paris, so it took Marcel's driver a full hour to get there in the heavy noon traffic. This part of the city was old and rundown. Soot covered the buildings, and smokestacks were billowing black smoke and reducing visibility as they drove along. The houses were built right up to the sidewalks, and they looked to be multi-family units. There were no yards in front, but there were trees everywhere, none of which looked healthy. The streets were heavily cracked, and the streetlights and street signs looked desolate and unmaintained. Finally, they arrived, and Marcel asked the driver to wait. The driver said he would.

Marcel went up the stoop to the front door and read the several names of residents inside. When he came to the bell marked Sarah Milam, he pushed the button. When a voice answered, Marcel identified himself. Then the door buzzed, and he went on inside. There was a stairway to his immediate right. He walked up two flights to number 306 at the top of the landing, knocked twice, and the door was immediately answered.

"My name is Marcel Rainsford. I know about your daughter, and I know she disappeared. I'm looking for her, not to bring trouble to her, but to help her. I would appreciate so much if you would talk to me for a few minutes and help me understand where I might find her."

Mademoiselle Milam looked Marcel up and down. She pursed her lips and turned her head to the side. "Çidde," she called. "Please run into your room, darling, as Nana needs to talk to a man."

She then had Marcel come inside and directed him to the couch, where he took a seat. She was nervous, and Marcel smiled to put her at ease.

He held out both hands, palms up, and said gently, "Please understand. I'm probably as worried about your daughter as you are. I come from Chicago, and I'm working with the lawyer who's trying to get money for your daughter. That's my sole reason for trying to find her. So far, it's been not easy, and we don't know how to pay her. Is there anything you might tell me about her whereabouts?"

The woman, sixty-ish with gray hair and blue-tinted spectacles, shook her head and clucked her tongue. "I can only tell you she has disappeared, and I hear from her rarely. I do have an address in Mallorca, Spain. I have it memorized. 11 San Luis, Mallorca, Spain."

Marcel nodded and committed the address to memory. Then he asked, "I'm sure you must miss her very much. Has she ever done anything like this before?"

"Please understand, Mr. Rainsford. Elise is nothing like this. She is as solid as the Eiffel Tower."

"If it's all right with you, I would like to confirm a few details about Elise."

"That would be fine, I'm sure."

"First, we have in our notes that Elise works for LVP Partners here in Paris. She's an assistant, correct?"

Mademoiselle Milam's face clouded over. She shifted her feet uncomfortably and arranged her dress across her knees. "I don't know about that. Elise is a turnstile guard at LVP. Has been for ten years. I've never heard of her being an associate as you mention."

Marcel lifted an eyebrow. His eyes swept around the room, taking in what might be his next question. He asked, "Did she by any chance live here with you?"

"She is going to. Since Joseph died, she hasn't had enough money to keep their condo. It's rented, you know."

"I've been told that she and Joseph owned their condo together. But that isn't the case? You say it's rented?"

"It's definitely rented. I signed the rental application with her. Plus, they wouldn't own together anyway. He didn't trust her with money."

"And what about Çidde, her daughter? As I understand it, she's very ill?"

"Ill? Çidde is as healthy as a horse. There's nothing wrong with her except occasional bouts with asthma. Her doctor says she will outgrow that. She goes to hospital now and then for breathing assistance, but that's all."

"Çidde doesn't have HIV?"

"Çidde definitely does not have HIV. The very thought is ridiculous."

"Çidde didn't contract HIV from a transfusion that happened?"

"Çidde definitely did not have a transfusion. I don't know why you even ask that."

"What about having her tonsils out? Did she have her tonsils out when she was younger?"

"She's never had her tonsils out, no. I would certainly know because I'm involved in her life every day when her mother goes to work. I'm the one who takes care of her. I would certainly know something like that."

"What about her medical needs? Did she require a thousand euros per week to pay for the drugs she requires?"

"Çidde doesn't take any medication. She has no medical needs whatsoever. I would certainly know, as I said. Çidde and I are very close. She might even be closer to me than she is to her mother. I know everything about that child. And she does not have any medical needs."

"Has Elise talked to you about Jennifer, Joseph's first wife?"

"I've never heard of anybody named Jennifer. Who is she?"

"Never mind. You are enormously helpful to me. May I continue?"

"Please do. Although I must say, you are asking questions about things I've never heard of."

"Has Elise been living on rue Dumont in Paris?"

"At one time, she lived there, yes. But now she has moved to Spain as I told you earlier. That address has been abandoned in Paris."

"Do you know if she is living with anyone in Spain?"

"Of course, Ignacio would be with her. Ignacio has been with her since forever. She always had him on the side. At least since high school."

"And who is Ignacio?"

"Ignacio was her first love. He was always with Elise when Joseph isn't around. I don't know exactly how it works, but I do know they're together now."

"What about university? Did Elise attend the university?"

"Of course not! She would not be working as a turnstile guard if she had attended the university. I begged her after senior school to go to the university, but she refused. Then she got pregnant and couldn't go anyway."

"You mean she got pregnant with Çidde?"

"No, she married Ignacio, and they had Wallenda. She's with them now in Spain."

"What about the London School of Economics? Did Elise attend there?"

"Of course not. I've never even heard of the London School of Economics. Why, did someone tell you she went there? Whoever told you that is full of it."

"Is there anything else about Elise that I should know that I haven't ask you?"

"You did not ask me about Justice Hall. I'm embarrassed to say, but you must know Elise was in prison for five years. Everyone knows that about her."

"Oh—tell me about prison, please."

"I don't think I want to go into that. You haven't asked about it, and it isn't pleasant for me. So please, let's talk about something else."

Marcel lifted his pen from the paper tablet and put it away in his pocket. He rested his head back on the couch cushion and shut his eyes for just a moment without speaking. Then he said, "Mademoiselle Milam, please excuse the indelicacy of my next question. But have you ever been treated for any form of mental condition, senility, or dementia?"

The woman reached to the coffee table and picked up a folded newspaper. She turned it over and displayed to Marcel a page with a crossword puzzle. Every square was filled in, and there were no mark-throughs. "You tell me. Do people with mental conditions match crossword puzzles like this one without so much as a dictionary?"

"That's a perfect point. And that answers my question. Thank you, Mademoiselle."

The woman swatted her hand through the air as if brushing flies away. She smiled and said, "It's nothing. You can come talk to me anytime you wish. You are a gentleman, and you have your questions, and I understand that. My only hope is that you are not the police and do not want my daughter for another crime. She has been doing her best to stay out of trouble and take care of her daughter. I don't think she has even missed one day of work in the last year. So please, be gentle, if you will."

"I can assure you I'm not the police. I'm only an investigator trying to get some money to her, as I told you before. And thank you again."

"It's nothing."

"Oh, but what was the crime? Why did she go to prison?"

The woman shook her head and scowled. "They said she hurt someone. That's all."

"Did she hurt someone?"

"Of course not. He was dying anyway."

"Was this someone she was married to?"

"She was twenties and he was forties, I guess. It was obvious what he wanted. Then he developed lung cancer—no one deserves lung cancer, not even a cradle robber. They said he was going to recover except for what Elise did. I thought he was going to die with or without her help. Water under the bridge."

"Thank you again."

Chapter Seventy-Two

MICHAEL

I left the courthouse and felt the beep of my phone. I knew I had a text, but it would just have to wait. I was too tired and still edgy about the court appearance that just finished.

Certain parties from the hearing just concluded had followed me outside, and eyes were still on me.

I walked to the end of the block and the streetlight. My car was located in attorneys' parking. I climbed in, pressed the button, and let it idle. My phone chirped again. Text waiting. It would have to wait.

I pulled through the lot and took California Avenue to the I-290 eastbound ramp. It was about three miles—ten minutes with traffic edging past a state trooper—to the Congress Parkway to South Dearborn street then north. I parked underground and went upstairs to my office—a five-minute walk to the Dirksen Building, the U.S. Federal Courthouse where I most often appeared.

Then I snuck back into the office and made the first evening coffee. It was now almost six p.m. I filled my silver travel container, leaving enough room for cream, then I fell onto my couch. Tired and upset with judges, I leaned back and closed my eyes. Marcel was returning from Paris, and Verona was probably home by now. I wanted to let the traffic thin out before I headed north to Evanston. It was then that I pulled out my cell phone and read the text.

Michael, I am at Jennifer Ipswich's house on East Germaine. Did you know she is my patient? She goes by the name of Jennifer O'Connor. I did not think she was your client. She fooled us both. Come check on me. I'm a little nervous.

The time of the text was 5:47. I checked my watch—almost 6:30.

In an instant, I was alert and moving. Verona was the queen of understatement. If she said, "a little nervous," I knew she was downright frightened. What was worse, she had neglected to include the address where she was.

But I had a triangulation app that could find a cell phone clear across the country to within six inches.

Then I was off.

Within minutes of climbing into my car, I had a complete map on my screen of her location. I pressed the accelerator and kicked up my speed as fast as I dared, heading for Verona's phone. As I drove along, I was planning what I was going to do when I got there.

But first, I couldn't believe my eyes when I read that Jennifer Ipswich had become my wife's patient under the name of Jennifer O'Connor. Why would she do that? What could she possibly get out of that?

I shuddered to think. I wasn't willing to admit she had somehow managed to involve my wife in her problems. But I knew she had done it on purpose, and I knew there had to be some ulterior motive in her mind. She was out of control by now and extremely dangerous. And, dammit, there was no Marcel. He was probably in the air on his way back from Paris. And last but not least, I didn't give a damn about the rest of it. I was going to save my wife and ask questions later.

Thirty minutes later, coming from Chicago, I was probably within a mile of Verona's phone.

As I drove, I became more and more pissed off that she hadn't given me a street address. I would much rather have a street address.

Several blocks away, I slowed almost to a crawl and began the final approach to what my cell phone app said was Verona's phone location. Then I saw her car down the block, and I decided to park this side of it on the wrong side of the street.

I parked and got out, and began approaching the blond house on foot.

As I crept along, I was saying a silent prayer that I wasn't being watched.

When I got even with Verona's car, I felt the hood. It was cold. Now I had a decision to make: should I go up on the porch and boldly knock on the door, or should I assume something was wrong and sneak around the house, trying to get a look inside?

I decided on the latter, and I slipped around to the side of the house where there were three windows. I crept up to the first window and looked inside. It appeared to be a bedroom, with the kind of afterthought furniture unused rooms often wind up with. Nothing was happening there, so I snuck up to the second window.

I looked inside, only to find an empty bathroom.

I then crept up to the third window and slowly moved my head to where I could look inside.

There, on the other side of a table, was Verona, zip-tied

to a chair. I sucked in a lungful of air as I swung around and placed my back against the wall, praying I hadn't been spotted. It was crazier than I had expected. I didn't trust Jennifer one inch. She was operating out of psychosis, and God only knew who she thought Verona was. I swung around and peered inside again.

Verona's head was lolled to the side as if she might be sleeping or unconscious. I fought down the urge to suddenly go smashing through the window and untie her. My adrenaline was firing. But I restrained myself because it looked like she was in no immediate harm. I forced myself to think.

Now what? I wished Marcel were there, but he wasn't. This one was on me.

Then something alerted me when I heard a garage door raising. It must be Jennifer, and she would see my car at any moment. There was no doubt in my mind she knew what I drove if she knew what color shirt I was wearing at home when I was watching TV. She was going to come flying back inside at any moment.

I bent over and crept past the window. I inched very slowly up to the corner and then peered around to find a large patio with a fire pit in the center and a zigzag path to the back door. The back door was sliders, which was a good thing because those doors are often made of an aluminum frame and give way easily.

Creeping around the corner of the house, I made it up to the sliding glass door as quietly as possible. Standing at the side, I used my fingers to tug at the door. It was locked.

I could see that I had no other option except to jimmy the door with my knife, which would be noisy and might result in injury to Verona or in me getting shot on the spot.

I pulled out my knife and slid the blade down to the locking mechanism. I then went past the bolt part of the lock, inserted my knife, and lifted it. Nothing gave, so I applied even more force. Finally, I felt the bolt of the lock lift and move back inside the frame.

Then I was inside.

Verona had heard me coming. She was alert now and watching me. She whispered, "Thank God you came. Jennifer unfastened the hose from behind the oven. I think she's letting gas into the kitchen, so for God's sake, don't make a spark."

I whispered back, asking where Jennifer was.

"I have no idea," Verona whispered. "Please, take off these plastic cuffs. My arms and legs are throbbing from no movement. And my butt is killing me."

That would have to wait for a moment. Right then, I needed a weapon because Jennifer was on her way inside. Frantic, I looked around.

Chapter Seventy-Three

MICHAEL

Seeing nothing that resembled a weapon, I crept into the front room and peered out the front door window. Sure enough, Jennifer's vehicle was roaring back up the driveway.

As soon as the car came to a halt, she leaped out and ran for the front door. As she was coming through, I stood to the side, my back scrunched against the wall. She was two steps inside when I took a breath and almost revealed myself, but she pulled back and didn't enter inside.

I could out-wait her because I knew she was impatient, and she was probably out of control. But then another thought came to mind: I had a relationship with her, and she had some feelings of trust toward me.

So, I decided to try to talk her down. I was going to try to get her to come to her senses and understand that I was not there to hurt her but only wanted to take my wife and leave. I would tell her that if she allowed that, I would not bother her anymore.

I pulled open the front door and stepped back. But as I

did, Jennifer came charging through, waving a gun, and immediately pointed it at me.

"So here we are," she said calmly. "You're everywhere at once, Michael. And now there are two of you. What's a girl to do?"

I raised my hands. The last thing I wanted to do was startle her, give her some reason to fire her gun. And I still believed I could talk to her.

"All I want to do is take my wife. I don't know what you're doing, Jennifer, but if you just let us go, I promise I will tell no one what happened here. You know you can trust me, and you know I'm a man of my word."

"I know that at one time I trusted you—as much as I ever trusted anybody. But no more. You broke into my house, and since you're here, and since you're trying to take away my shrink, I know for sure I don't trust you anymore."

She then swept the muzzle of the gun back and forth at me. "Into the kitchen. I'm going to tie you up with your wife. I don't trust you right now, Michael. Maybe once you're bound, we can talk."

When I moved toward the kitchen, I felt Jennifer fall in right behind me. It wasn't the right moment to act, so I kept moving. I knew about her and her diagnosis, and that went a long way with me. She was unstable and unpredictable and maybe much worse. I would not make any sudden moves or say anything other than "yes" and "no." But then I also knew I was *not* going to allow her to tie me up. She might get a shot off, and she might even hit me, but I was not going under the cuffs without a fight.

We went into the kitchen, where she directed me to sit down in a captain's chair at the table. She pulled out my chair while I remained standing with my hands in the air. As

I started to sit, I brought my elbow up suddenly and caught the side of her head.

The blow threw her backward, and she fell across the stove just long enough for me to turn and bring my fist around and connect with her chin. It was a satisfying blow, and she lost consciousness. I immediately wrenched the gun from her limp hand.

As she began to come to, she moaned and turned onto her side. I stepped back and slipped the gun into my jacket pocket. I pulled her off the floor and forced her into a chair. There were no plastic ties or rope, or I would have bound her up then and there, but she was still groggy, still incoherent, so I went to Verona and cut away the ties binding her to the chair. She stood and threw her arms around me and began weeping.

"Oh my God, oh my God, oh my God. Thank God you're here!"

I turned to Jennifer and shook my head. "What were you even thinking?"

She shook her head from side to side without speaking.

"I have a world of questions for you," I told Jennifer. "Are you going to talk to me?"

"We have nothing to talk about. But I am going to ask you to leave my house. I won't bother you again, and you'll never hear from me again."

"It's not that easy. I need to know what happened to Elise. I need that answer before I leave."

"Elise is in the basement, tied up," Verona said breathlessly. "Jennifer told me she was going to explode the house with Elise inside it, too. She unfastened the gas line behind the stove."

I walked around to where I could watch Jennifer's face.

Then I said to her, "What have you done to the back of the stove? Is the coupling back there unscrewed?"

She wasn't going to talk.

"Verona, take this gun and point it at Jennifer. If she tries to stand up, shoot her."

Verona did as she was told. She had her own Glock at home and was familiar with guns. We had been shooting dozens of times.

"It works just like your Glock at home. There's no safety. If you need to fire it, pull the trigger. I'll be right back."

She held it calmly and levelly pointed it at Jennifer. Jennifer didn't move.

I walked over to the stove and felt behind for the coupling. Sure enough, the nut was loose to any hard twisting. I finger tightened it and then looked around for a wrench. Finding none, I began opening drawers. The cupboard beside the sink contained what I was looking for—a crescent wrench. I headed back for the stove. I reached around and tightened the coupling until I was satisfied that it was cinched up. Then I came back around in front of Jennifer again.

"All right, tell me about Elise. She's really in the basement?"

Jennifer looked up at me. "You have everything I'm ever going to tell you, Michael." She sullenly tossed her head. "You hurt me, Michael! You can go to hell for all I care!"

Verona spoke up, "She fixed a plate of food and said it was for Elise." She warned me, "If you go down there, please be very careful, Michael."

"I know. I'm going to go down and see if there's someone in trouble down there. I want you to wait here with this gun and keep it on Jennifer."

"Pardon me if I shoot this bitch while you're away," Verona said, still raging.

"Is that a preferred method of psychiatric treatment?" I said with all manner of sarcasm.

I went out of the kitchen and located the basement door in the hallway between the kitchen and laundry room. I opened the door and found that it was utterly dark downstairs, so I felt around for the light switch, turned it on, and the basement was flooded in bright light. I started down the stairs.

Just as I got to the bottom, I heard whimpering off to my right and turned. There, wrapped in a rope harness and attached to a basement stanchion, was Elise. Her hair was matted and flattened against her face, and she was trembling. She had had a tough time of it down there, and my heart immediately went out to her.

I studied her before I approached. It appeared that she was, indeed, genuinely tied up against her will. So I walked over to her and lifted her chin so I could look into her eyes. She was squinting against the light and peered out at me through slits. "Mr. Gresham," she whispered. "Thank God you're here. That woman is crazy. Please do not turn your back on her. Please, take this terrible rope off of me."

Using my knife, I began to cut away the rope binding her to the stanchion.

Within moments, I had set her free, and she stood there, her head hung down and rubbing her wrists. She was unable to look me in the eyes, and I assumed she was in shock. And who wouldn't be?

"How long you been here?" I asked her.

She shook her head. "It feels like days. But maybe only two days. Honestly, I don't know because I haven't seen the sun since she brought me down here."

"How did she get you to her house? Did you come here on your own?"

"I fell for it again. She said that she had a check for me, and this time it was for real. I'm so desperate, Mr. Gresham, that I listened to her. I should never have. I will never listen to that horrible person again."

"Elise, I have a lot of questions for you. My investigator, Marcel, has been in Paris speaking with your mother. Much of what we know about you and what I have been told about you is contradicted by your mother. Plus, we know about the body in your condo."

"What body? I moved out of there weeks ago. I've been telling everyone I couldn't make the mortgage payments. It was the truth."

"Well, you might say that, but your mother contradicts your story."

"Mr. Gresham, my mother is in the early stages of dementia. She's not that bad yet that she can't watch my daughter. But the doctor says that in six more months, I won't be able to leave Çidde with her. It's sad, and I have no idea what she told you, but most of it shouldn't be believed. I'm sorry for what you've been through with her."

I didn't believe a word of it—just a gut feeling. But now, I wanted to get back to Verona and call the cops. At the very least, there had been an assault with a deadly weapon and maybe a kidnapping. It was time to get the authorities involved.

"Is it safe to go upstairs? I'm dying for a bottle of water."

"Yes, it is. Let's go."

Which is when I made the mistake of leading the way. I wanted to be the first one back to Verona, so I went first. I didn't see her do it, but I know that Elise immediately went for a gun tucked under the first step on the stairs and pulled it out. Suddenly, she cried out at me, "Stop!"

I heard the command and turned to see, and as I did, the gun roared. The next thing I knew, I was pitching forward and falling down the stairs. The last thing I remember was hitting my head against the first step, and I was immediately unconscious.

From what Verona has told me, she heard the gunshot and then immediately moved to the stairway door but didn't show herself. Instead, she stood at the side, her back flattened against the wall. Then she waited. At that moment, Jennifer called out, "Elise! Do not come up! The bitch has a gun and will shoot you!"

Upon hearing this, Elise halted on the stairs and rushed back down to the basement floor. She then got behind the water heater and waited.

After several minutes, Verona dared to look down the stairs, and she saw me lying at the bottom of the stairs, obviously unconscious. She said she knew I had been shot, and it was only a short time until I bled out. So she could not wait.

Now it was a standoff—Elise hiding in the basement behind the water heater and Verona at the top of the stairs. Both women had a gun. And I was at the bottom of the stairs, bleeding and unconscious.

Verona told me she went to Jennifer, placed the gun's muzzle against her head, and demanded her phone. Jennifer told her it was inside her purse on the table. Verona retrieved the phone and immediately dialed 911. The 911 operator said she was dispatching EMTs and police and that Verona should take no further action. Verona returned to the basement door and took up her place there.

But then Elise called up to her, "Come down and drop

your gun or I'm going to shoot your husband again. You have until the count of three. One—two—"

At that point, Verona cried out and told Elise to stop, that she was coming. She then made her way down the stairs, all the way to the bottom, and stood over me. She raised her gun and pointed it at the woman behind the water heater. "I'm not putting down my gun. You're going to have to shoot me before I leave my husband." Verona said she then knelt on the floor beside me and felt inside my shirt. I was soaked with blood where it was seeping out of my chest wound.

"I'm going to give you the chance to come out from behind that water heater, run upstairs with Jennifer, and flee before the police get here. But I'm not leaving this man's side, and I'm not going to let you shoot him again. If you doubt me, then try me. But I'm pretty good with this gun, and I promise you that I will get a piece of you before you kill me."

"How do I know you won't shoot me if I come out?"

"You have my word. My word is good. I have no reason to want to shoot you. I don't even know you. Come out now, go up the stairs, get your friend, and flee. That is the best thing that is going to happen to you today."

She said Elise stood and came around the water heater at that point, holding her gun and pointing it at Verona's chest. Verona kept her weapon trained on Elise and turned as Elise passed her by and headed up the stairs.

Verona, for probably the first time in her life, was not a woman of her word.

Taking careful aim, she trained her gun on Elise's back between her shoulder blades and pulled the trigger. Elise's arms flew out, and she fell backward down the stairs, coming to a rest on the third step. She didn't move, and

Verona said she knew she was dead. Verona then dropped to her knees and placed her hand solidly against the wound on my chest. She said she didn't move even when she heard the EMTs come charging in. She called to them, and they double-timed down the stairs. I was tended to and then transported to the hospital.

Jennifer, while Verona was occupied on the stairs, made her getaway.

She even took her backpack. And Elise's briefcase with its safe.

With the help of Elise's ID and passport, she made it to Europe.

There was a funeral to attend.

Chapter Seventy-Four

PARIS

The family and friends and believers were gathered together in the meetinghouse. All wore white, and all were prepared to hear the spiritual leader speak. There was no crying as crying was frowned upon. The deceased had been identified by her fingerprints and returned to her friends and family in Paris. The body parts had been collected up and wrapped in three sheets, as was the custom. The service began in a somber, dignified manner.

It was only when the service was underway that a figure dressed in black entered through the back of the meetinghouse and began walking to the room's front. Halfway there, the figure stopped and pulled down the veil in a very practiced manner. She then continued to the front of the room, on past the very front row until she had approached the body in its shroud. She then turned and faced the assembled mourners. She pulled aside her veil and, as one, they saw her face.

She touched the shrouded remains.

Several women stood and began screaming and

pointing their fingers at the lone figure. Two men rushed forward and seized her by the arms but had no idea what else to do with her and only stood there with her as the mourners turned away to avoid looking at her. Someone had the presence of mind to pull out their cell phone and call the police. She was restrained until the police came, and, as he walked up to her, one of the gendarmes choked up and vomited on the spot. With great apologies, he pulled out a handkerchief, wiped his mouth, and went ahead with his partner to seize the visitor in black.

The two gendarmes tugged and pulled the figure in black from the front of the meeting hall. They dragged her down the aisle and back outside to their waiting vehicle.

They put her in the back and began asking questions. Remarkably enough, she made no effort to disguise who she was or what she was doing there.

When they were done talking with her and writing out her full name, address, and all of her digits, they finally asked why she had done what she had done.

To which she replied, "I only came to say goodbye to my friends and family."

Then she began snipping stitches.

Chapter Seventy-Five

MICHAEL

Three months later, I was up and around and pretty much recovered from having a bullet pass through my lung. Breathing could be difficult at times of exertion, such as long runs, but I quickly recovered each time within four or five minutes.

Elise had died at the scene as soon as the bullet struck her. Her body was prepared and returned to Paris to be claimed by her mother. Her daughter, Çidde, had been placed with the grandmother by social services. It was just as well because Çidde had already spent long periods with her grandmother. Moreover, her grandmother was a young fifty and mentally fit according to social services with no deficits.

Jennifer, however, was yet to be dealt with. After Marcel met with the French authorities, Jennifer was indicted for the murder of Karrol, the Egyptian terrorist. The arrest and court followed very smoothly as the French government already had Jennifer snugged away in a psychiatric hospital just outside of Paris in a green valley surrounded with oak and sumac and fields of wheat. Her hosts said she was very happy there and was writing a book on childhood diseases from ticks. An amateurish oil painting of her Qing vase hung at her desk.

In France, the Court of Assize sat in France's departments with original and appellate jurisdiction over crimes or serious felonies. It was usually composed of three judges and nine jurors. The prosecutors were in touch with me and had informally requested that Marcel and I attend her trial and give testimony. Formally, they issued subpoenas to us, which could've been ignored, but which Marcel and I, of course, agreed to honor.

We arrived in France on a sweltering day in May. The traffic was unbearable, and the sweat rolled down your arms. We had each brought a summer-weight suit and non-wrinkle white shirts. The trial was scheduled to start Monday, and our arrival was two days prior, so the prosecutors met with us and sandpapered our testimony.

After preparing to testify, we were taken to the medical investigators' suite and introduced to Docteur Seurat, a master criminologist, and physician. He was a tidy man, elderly, carefully manicured nose and ear hairs. He was bald from the ears up but wore a goatee to prove he still had it but in a different measure than the rest of the choir. He ushered us right into his small workroom piled high with medical charts, radiologic films, miscellaneous skeletal parts, and coffee cups half full of black liquid and cigarette butts. He swept aside a place on his conference table and set a laptop computer in the center. He informed us we were about to be introduced to the mainstay of the prosecution's case.

In not very good English, he said to us, "The password

is green poo." He referred to the laptop computer, which he had now booted up and prepared for a demonstration.

I said, "Are you serious, 'green poo?'"

"Oui, Monsieur, she is a *docteur*, and she has told us she spent her days treating green poo in her infant patients."

"Whatever," I said.

Jennifer had been extradited for the murder of the Egyptian Karrol, plus she was charged with *Maltraitance d'un cadavre*—loosely translated to mean the mistreatment of a cadaver. I wasn't sure what they had in mind for that other than the bags of bones. Were they mistreated? After death, it gets rather semantic, no?

I was about to find out.

Docteur Seurat typed a few words on the keyboard of what turned out to be Jennifer's laptop. He then turned the screen almost to us but then delayed, telling us we must prepare our eyes for what we were about to see.

He said, "I've watched this woman testify. She hardens and resists certain questions like a stone—the questions that might send her to prison. She softens and welcomes certain questions like butter—the questions that illuminate the love she had for Joseph Ipswich, the man who died in her bed the night of their fifteenth anniversary. And notice that I refer to it as 'her' bed. This isn't accidental. Jennifer owns and inhabits every space of the marriage like it was made just for her to try on and wear as if Joseph—Joe—were a person she could wear. Still don't believe me? Let me show you the next picture and the next. Here is the first look."

He swung the laptop screen into view.

The picture was clear, and we studied it for several moments before looking up. "What in God's name?" Marcel muttered. "Next slide, please."

The *médecin* nodded but continued to allow us to examine the photograph.

When he made the picture full-screen, neither of us could take our eyes from it. Sitting against a wall was Jennifer with her arm around a dark woman whose head was tossed back and, where her face had been, there was a surgical field. You've seen a mound of beef liver at your butcher shop?

We studied the picture and realized that the object Jennifer was holding in her hand was a scalpel. On the other side of the woman—unbelievably—sat Elise with her back against the wall as well. Then we looked again and saw that Elise was holding a tattoo pen. She was holding it against the dark woman's ankle and grinning menacingly. Then I looked closer.

The foot was standing upright. It had been sawed away from the leg bone and was standing on its own.

"Marcel," I said slowly, "they were together. Maybe all along." It all came crashing down on me, and I saw the entire movie in my head. "It started the first time they met. They both wanted the Qing vase. So they set up the burglary. They didn't fight back and forth like they've told everyone. They were way down the road on that, way smarter than we gave them credit for. Out front, they fought and resisted, but then they had their night at the Hemingway in the Ritz Hotel. That was a celebration."

"Maybe, maybe not," said Marcel. "It might have also been an attempted murder. Remember, Jennifer wanted everything for herself, and there was insurance money Jennifer received for the vase's theft. It wouldn't surprise me if she went there to murder Elise instead of giving her the insurance money so they'd be even."

"And instead, they murdered the girl."

Docteur Seurat was quick to say, "The dead woman. She was long associated with a terrorist cell here in Paris. We believe she was after Elise for totally unrelated reasons. Or perhaps she was just in the wrong place at the wrong time. Either way, these two laid hands on her. Terrorism could take a lesson."

Marcel said, "Two women who loved their husband. I've seen lots of weird shit, but nothing like this. Wait, there was one in Africa—"

I broke in, "But why would they go to this length?" I still wasn't satisfied.

"This one-"—the doctor was indicating Jennifer—"does it because she can. I'll explain after the next photo."

"What about the face?" I asked the Frenchman. "Where is the face?"

The *médecin* nodded and went to the next picture. This time it was the same setup, but it wasn't. Jennifer was looking at the camera—same clothes, same blond hair as the last picture.

But the face.

The face would cause me to jerk upright in bed for many months after in a cold sweat, panting hard, for Jennifer was wearing the dead girl's face, the face of Karrol.

"That can't—"

"Oh, yes, but it is," said the *médecin*.

He enlarged the picture to show us. The face was sewn in place with stitches, the kind used to close a surgeon's incision. The eyes sagged sadly. The eyebrows looked to be in a constant rage as they compressed together with the facial tissue's loss of moisture. Where there were once teeth, now there were two more lips open and smiling. Smiling with Jennifer's teeth. And the living eyes—the eyes of a child needing approval. And I recalled the first time I had laid eyes upon her, there, at the swimming pool, the tiniest of white flecks encircling her face: scars. She had sewn herself before.

I jerked my eyes away and fought down nausea. Marcel clasped the back of my neck with his hand. "Easy."

Our guide, the docteur, continued with his talk.

"Assuming another's identity. That is part of her illness," said the gentleman. "She has cooperated with us, psychiatrists. It's gone on for a long time. She yearns to take on the life of other people. This is the heart of your subject. Incidentally, we caught her when she turned up at the funeral of her victim, Karrol. Jennifer was wearing the face to that occasion. Her excuse to the gendarmes was that she only wanted to say goodbye to her friends and family. She insisted she was Karrol come to her own funeral. Everyone there fled at the sight of her."

"Son of a b—" Marcel muttered. "No, no, not right."

I looked closer. "Wait. The wrist. Show me that closeup, please."

The picture quadrupled in size. "Now to the left," I requested.

The picture jumped to the left—Jennifer's wrist. Besides wearing the dead woman's face, Jennifer was wearing Verona's missing watch.

"My wife's wristwatch."

"Not surprising. She constructs her personality, a piece here, a part there, a wristwatch here, a face there. She demands to be whole."

"There must be a prayer to say." I was Catholic. It was all I had left in my tank.

"Part of the reason we wanted you to come here, Monsieur Gresham, was to see for yourself."

Marcel released the back of my neck.

He said, "I saw this one time before in Nigeria. A shaman wearing another man's face stitched to his own. It happens, Michael."

It happens. That was as good as I was going to get.

Marcel clapped his hands—I looked up. Anything to bring me along, away from the photographs.

Marcel asked, "But now Jennifer is about to meet her end here in Paris. Will your court send her to prison or a hospital?"

Marcel had changed the subject. For my benefit. Who had friends like that? I rejoined the living and listened to Docteur Seurat tell Jennifer's fortune.

"France is very quick to acknowledge mental disorders and excuse criminal liability. Likely, a hospital for our Doctor Ipswich. Wouldn't you say that's where a sick person belongs, gentlemen? Now, what about that wristwatch? I can probably get it back for you, eh?"

It was like coming up for air when we were back outside that building. I was undone, so Marcel made small talk, trying to calm me.

"What about supper?" he asked, totally out of sync with the world I now knew existed. "Duck à l'orange for yours truly. Wasn't it braised how you liked your bird? The *canard*?"

Then it all came up.

Chapter Seventy-Six

MICHAEL

Marcel and I testified at Jennifer's trial for the murder of Karrol. French law allowed testimony of prior bad acts. So my testimony consisted largely of recounting the testimony in Jennifer's criminal trial in Chicago for the murder of Joe. Much to the prosecution's chagrin, I was only able to say Jennifer was found not guilty.

"But did she do it?" the prosecutor asked me.

I could only repeat, "She was found not guilty.'"

"But what is your opinion? You do have an opinion?"

I thought hard about that. Then, "I have no opinion."

Marcel testified about his inspection of Elise's flat and discovering the body bags.

The prosecution for the death of Karrol, the Egyptian woman, proceeded to conclusion.

In the end, Jennifer's mental condition sent her to a hospital. If she were ever found to have recovered, she would go to prison. At the time of sentencing, Marcel and I had returned to Chicago and were back at work in my law practice.

On the plane ride home, I wondered, Did she do it? Did she murder Joe?

Chapter Seventy-Seven

MICHAEL

A week after our return, I was paid a visit by Amanda Siegfried, a Chicago PD detective assigned to an insurance fraud case instituted against the absent Jennifer.

"Mr. Gresham," she began, "we are preparing to go to trial against Jennifer Ipswich *in absentia*."

"And what are the charges to be brought against her in her absence?" I asked.

"Jennifer Ipswich has been charged with insurance fraud. We have proven from a very thorough examination of the scene of the theft of the Qing Dynasty vase that Elise Ipswich had committed that burglary. We placed her there by a pair of blue nitrile gloves found in the hallway outside the medical offices, stuffed in a trash container. The gloves were turned inside out, and fingerprints lifted and compared to the fingerprints of Elise Ipswich. We also have CCTV of a woman wearing a face mask and a hoodie with a tiny icon on the back that matches the icon used in its advertising by LVP Partners."

"But how do you connect Jennifer to that theft?"

"You might not believe this, but the Qing Dynasty vase was found at Jennifer's hotel room in Paris the day she went to the funeral. It was inside a small locked safe simple to open. Along with one million dollars in cash."

"She said the vase was stolen, but now she had it back?"

"Yes, Jennifer had the vase in her possession after the insurance claim had been made for its theft."

"She let Elise steal her vase, got the insurance money, and gave Elise the insurance money. Now they're even."

"Nicely summed up. Exactly so. Except Elise never got the money. Jennifer took it with her when she fled to Europe after the shootout."

I said, "To say that I am amazed would be a gross understatement. But then, I'm sure you also know about the conspiracy to commit murder Jennifer faced in Paris. The two women had worked as one."

"Quite so. It also seems they had settled their differences about the property left behind by Joseph Ipswich."

"How so?"

"Jennifer's cell phone provider turned over to us a series of text messages, in French, between Jennifer and Elise in which it was established Elise would consider her one half paid to her upon receipt of the Qing Dynasty insurance money. All was well between them at the time they murdered the Egyptian girl. Quite a client you had, Mr. Gresham."

"Yes, indeed." Now I understood completely. It was all about the Qing Dynasty vase. Jennifer just wouldn't let it go. A woman—albeit not a very nice one—had died over that vase.

"And how is your wife doing by now? I assume she came through this well?"

"Yes, except now she requires official photo IDs from new patients."

Chapter Seventy-Eight

MICHAEL

I received notice Jennifer's house was being sold Friday at an auction sale. I asked Marcel, did he want to attend? Maybe drop in and find what the cops had missed?

A look crossed his face just as I said that. A look that said everything and nothing. Then he clicked through the police report on his laptop, found the name he was after, and dialed a number. "Police department," he said, his hand over the ringing phone. Then it was answered. He asked for Officer Bryant James of the third shift. Minutes later, a voice said hello. Marcel introduced himself. "You're the officer who helped search the Doctor Jennifer Ipswich home. You remember that?" Pause. "You do? All right. Please tell me about the search. What did you do in the living room?" Reply barely heard by me. "What about the bedrooms?" Again, a long reply. "What about the kitchen?" More words, not as long this time. "And the appliances? The refrigerator? Everything opened? All right, Officer James, thank you so much."

"What?" I didn't expect that he had found anything. Not in that time.

"Oh, Sweet Jesus," he said. "Be back in one hour, Boss!"

Sure enough, one hour later, he returned to my office.

He told me he went to her house, "let myself in." He gained entry and went directly to the refrigerator. He held his breath as he opened the refrigerator freezer.

The ice cubes were still there.

He dished them into a plastic bag from a kitchen drawer.

Then he snuck back outside and hopped into his truck, and headed back south to Chicago.

Along the way, he stopped at Chicago Forensic Laboratory, a collection of ingenious chemists, botanists, serologists, and others just like them, all under one roof, all offering their professional services to industry and legal cases. Marcel pulled into their lot and found Inder Singh, a gentleman from India who sometimes did our work. He was both an organic chemist and biologist and knew everything there was to know about how to kill with substances. Marcel transferred his ice cubes to him.

"And this house where the ice came from? Its address, please?"

Marcel gave him the address of Jennifer's house.

A week later, Dr. Singh's report arrived, and Marcel came dashing into my office with it, a splash of yellow highlighter over these words:

Delphinium species are found throughout the United States and

Canada, where they are also grown as ornamentals. They produce aconite.

Aconitum plants grow to 3 to 4 feet. The leaves are palmately divided into five lobes, which are divided into narrow segments. Flowers, which are dark blue to purple or purple and white, are composed of five petal-like sepals, one of which covers the flower's top. The latter forms a hoodlike structure over the flower, hence the name. These plants, although perennial, dry up and appear dead soon after the onset of summer heat.

All parts of Aconitum plants are toxic, with toxicity greatest in roots and decreasing through flowers, leaves, and the lowest toxicity in stems.

FINDINGS:
The delphinium plant was found growing all along the subject's slump block fence in the rear of the house. The plants were exactly as I have described. Photographs available.
The ice cubes: positive for aconite.

"She was almost perfect," Marcel said almost in a whisper. "But she forgot the ice cubes."

"So, she has the means of killing. Did she ever give Joe any of those ice cubes?"

He slyly smiled and slumped further down in the client chair he occupied on the other side of my desk.

"That," he said, "we'll never know. Because he—"

"—Because he was cremated by the widow."

There was a long, thoughtful pause. I knew where this was going. We both reached the same conclusion at about the same moment: I had set a killer free to kill again.

"I'm out for the rest of the day," said my friend.

"Yeah. I guess me too."

We went our separate ways and never spoke of it again.

Chapter Seventy-Nine

MICHAEL

Following a trial *in absentia*, Jennifer was found guilty of insurance fraud after thirty minutes of jury deliberation.

The finding of guilt and the sentence of five years imprisonment was meaningless given the hold the French had on Jennifer. But now, the insurance company that had paid the $2.3 million loss was entitled to reimbursement by *its* insurance company, Great Reef Reinsurance Company of Australia. No doubt both insurance companies now had losses to be written off on their tax returns. Such was the nature of big business. Hey, I knew better than to ever worry about insurance companies.

Amanda Siegfried sent me a clipping a few weeks later. The vase had been sold in New York for an undisclosed amount to an anonymous buyer. The seller? Great Reef Reinsurance Company of Australia. Amanda had written on the clipping, *Happy?*

Happy? Happy the insurance company got its money back? Didn't they always?

The whole business had exhausted me. Jennifer's

medical partners came to me about dissolving the medical partnership. I was unable to help them with that because I no longer represented Jennifer. The Illinois Medical Society interviewed me. They pulled her license. Finally, after all of that, I thought I was done with the Jennifer Ipswich case. Now I could move ahead, having done what I could for a very sick woman. It was a welcome relief to put her in the rearview mirror and say farewell.

But then, one evening, I was sitting in front of my TV watching Brian Williams's news show on MSNBC when the cell phone in my pocket chimed. A text message had arrived. I pulled out the cell phone and read:

Love you, Hunk. Your Verona.

Did I dare show the screen to Verona, who was sitting right beside me, doing a crossword puzzle and half-listening to the news? Her cell phone was over on the kitchen counter in its charging cradle.

I decided not. She had been through enough over all this.

I turned my cell phone off. Tomorrow I would change the number.

It bothered me the rest of that night, however. And at one point, I got up and went and closed the curtains.

"I felt a chill," I explained to Verona. "Just a small chill."

Next in the Michael Gresham Legal Thrillers Series

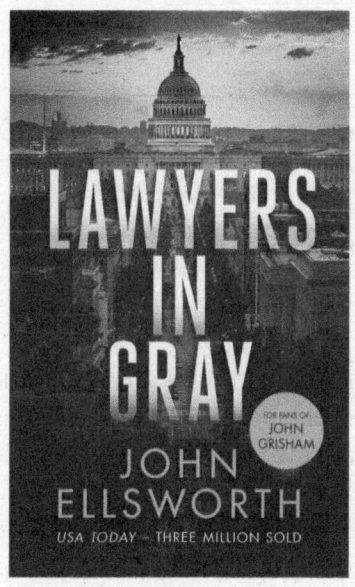

vinci-books.com/lawyersingray

Betrayal runs deep. The hunt is on.

When American oil secrets are sold to the Russians, Michael Gresham sets a trap to expose the traitors. But with a deadly assassin closing in, he must outmaneuver spies, corruption, and a ticking clock—before he becomes the next target.

Turn the page for a free preview…

Lawyers in Gray: Chapter One

FRANK HEMET

On Monday morning, Frank Hemet drove down 6th Street to Indiana Avenue and the Gray law building in Washington, DC. He had made it in plenty of time for his interview at Gray, Soledad, Wilmar, and Bendix.

After circling the block twice, Hemet spotted an opening, cut the car sharply right, and slid into a parking spot on Indiana Avenue NW. He stepped from his Porsche into ankle-deep snow and began the trudge. Up the curb at the corner, then four doors down.

Upstairs, the Hiring Committee was taking a final look at his application. Printed crisply on linen paper, his resume made him out to be the kind of lawyer they were looking for: University of Michigan law, number two in his class, a clerkship in the Seventh Circuit for a year, a mother who'd recently gone into assisted living in Arlington and now her devoted son was returning to DC to look after her. A family man and that meant everything to a law firm that prided itself on its family values. It all looked good.

Except Frank Hemet's resume was a lie.

They had thoroughly prepared him. His leather Lauren topcoat shed the gently falling snow, while underneath, his two-button Dior suit of navy virgin wool looked rich and capable. They knew that the hiring committee would ask him about federal trials, so he'd been rigorously prepared. He'd watched several trials in US District Court while his assigned federal prosecutor explained what was happening and how Hemet might copy and use it when the time came. They quizzed him every day. They were dead serious about federal trial practice.

He adjusted his half-Windsor in the plate glass door, stood up a little straighter, and approached building security just inside.

"Frank Hemet here for Gray, Soledad, Wilmar, and Bendix."

The older man scanned his screen. "Here you are, Mr. Hemet. Take the visitors' tag and the middle elevator to seven. Get off and go right to reception. They're expecting you in five minutes."

"Thank you, Mr. Duncan."

He did as told, appearing nervous when the elevator doors whooshed open on seven—the more anxious, the more realistic.

They greeted him with an outer office silent as the moon and a staff-free zone at the cherry reception desk. He gave it several minutes, thinking someone must have just stepped away and would be right back. But then the clock turned over, and it was 8:04. What the hell?

He walked beyond reception and peered down the hallway. A small knot of suits gathered at a corner office. He headed straight for them.

It was an anxious group outside the office, and nobody bothered to ask who he was. An older woman whispered to

Hemet that Tommy Gray wouldn't answer his home phone, his mobile phone went to mail, and his office phone kicked over to after-hours routing, even though it was after eight o'clock in the morning. Everyone knew that he never arrived after seven for work. His arrival time was mythical, as constant as the sunrise.

Lanny Jones from Security produced a keyring. He pushed through the crowd.

"It damn sure isn't like him," said Jones as the key turned. The door opened in, and Hemet let the flow of lawyers carry him inside. The next part was a startling death scene.

Sprawled back in his blue leather executive chair was Tommy Gray. Hemet's stomach spasmed: half of Gray's head was pasted to the wall behind him. The 12-gauge shotgun lay on the floor to Gray's right.

A blond man with a transparent lock of hair centered on his scalp entered the room, spun around, taking it all in, and exclaimed, "I have dibs on this office."

"Arnie, give it a rest," said a woman who looked older than the others—Hemet's quick assessment after looking into the most intelligent eyes he'd ever come across. She wore a pencil skirt and a yellow silk blouse. He memorized how her fingers were perfectly manicured, and her eyes were of Elizabeth Taylor violet.

She continued castigating Arnie. "Law firm by-laws hand out office suites. Not your dumb-ass dibs. Who even does dibs anymore?"

When he heard Arnie's claim on the office, Hemet's face tightened, and he said, "Show some respect! He's still warm!"

Arnie responded by touching the dead man's arm. He shook his head. "Not warm at all. Cool as a Safeway ham."

Hemet was upset beyond just the man's idiocy. When he had met with Tommy Gray last Friday at headquarters, Gray had made the offer, and Hemet had accepted. But what happened now that the Chairman was dead?

Two men came forward and had a look. Others turned away in tears, while some tried to remain strong, betrayed by faces that spelled shock. As for Hemet, he had seen so many death scenes he felt nothing either way. But with Gray dead, he knew he needed to improvise, starting right then if he would be hired. He thought he saw an opening in his favor with this group: they needed him. He immediately became indispensable.

He jumped forward and restrained Arnie as he was about to compromise the crime scene by moving the shotgun. "It's a potential crime scene," he said as Arnie twisted violently away from him. "Don't touch or move a thing unless you want your fingerprints on the evidence the police will be examining. And you don't want your fingerprints on that 12-gauge you're about to move."

"Well, look at this, everyone," said Arnie sarcastically. "This has got to be the new criminal lawyer we haven't hired yet." he stuck out his hand and smiled a porcelain smile. "Arnie Truckee, Frank. See? I already know your name. My old man always said never forget a man's name. It's his most important possession. Is your name your best asset, Frank?"

Hemet ignored Truckee. "Listen, everyone, touch nothing. We might be standing inside a crime scene, and that's how we should treat it for the moment. We should all leave the office and wait for the police elsewhere. Has someone called them?"

Inga Kopovsky, the lawyer with the intelligent eyes, held

her phone out to Hemet. "Done, dialed 911 as soon as we came through the door."

"Well done," he said. "All right, everyone, let's go into the main conference room. Inga has the police on the way. We want to present a calm front ready to cooperate without a hair out of place. Inga, please lead the way."

"Hey, I like this take-charge guy," Arnie cried. "I feel innocent already!"

They made their way into the firm's swank meet-and-greet room—cut from the same pattern as 10,000 others in Washington, DC—and painted in the same Pantone gray as the building's exterior.

The partners gathered around, selected chairs, poured water out of crystal pitchers into crystal glasses, and made anxious chatter. Once everyone was seated, Hemet spoke up again. "Let me just suggest that we try to figure out who spoke last to Mr. Gray. The police will want to know who was last with him, so let's work that out before they get here. We don't need any slip-ups in the story we're going to tell them."

Tissues were balled up and sent to the trash, and handkerchiefs folded and put away—no more tears, time for strategy—precisely what lawyers love best.

Said the partner Hemet would learn was Mergers and Acquisitions, "He spoke with me last night about eight o'clock as I passed his office as I was leaving for home. He called me, and I stuck my head in the door. He wanted to know how many new cases I'd opened this month."

"Typical," snorted Truckee. "I'd expect nothing less from the money-grubbing senior."

"Arnie! For fuck's sake!" Inga drew a deep breath and stopped. "Pardon me."

"It sounds like he was compos mentis," offered Sylvester

Clemens, the partner heading up the Trusts and Estates practice, where every case asked the same questions about mental competency. "Asking about new business—that's a good sign he was all there," Clemens continued with a knowing smile and pointed at his head.

"I was in Tommy's office, using the en suite bathroom when Alfred passed by," said Inga, giving a name to the M and A man. "I could hear Tommy call to him."

"You were?" asked Truckee suspiciously. "In his office doing what?"

Inga sniffed and tossed her head. "That, dear Arnie, will be a confidential matter between the detectives and me. That's all I have to say about it to you."

"So you were the last one to see him alive?" guessed Truckee. "This is getting a little funky. Everyone knows he had an eye for you. Are you listed in his last will and testament by any chance?"

Inga ignored the comment. "It looks like our board of directors is all here. I'm calling an emergency meeting. I think we need to appoint Frank Hemet here as our representative with the police. And we need to hire him to do that. Not how we usually do things, but this could blow up in our faces. All in favor?"

Six hands went up. Arnie played tricks, raising then lowering his hand several times. Inga said, "Motion passed. Frank Hemet, welcome to Gray. Can we take it you have accepted our offer?"

"What is the offer?"

Roman Challis, who had automatically become Gray's next Chairman and managing partner, spoke up. "Here's the offer: two-fifty a year guaranteed against actual earnings. Retirement fully funded, health and dental 100%, Wizards tickets, and biannual bonuses. What say you?"

"Yes, I accept the offer. Why don't we move beyond that quickly, and let's plan our meeting with the police? I want to talk to them as the firm rep for openers."

"Question," said Arnie, raising his hand to be called upon. "The police will want to speak with all of us. Should we have our separate lawyers with us? That would get expensive fast."

"That's an excellent question, Arnie," Hemet replied. "For safety's sake, if you were around the office between four p.m. yesterday and seven a.m. this morning, it would be advisable to have an attorney. We're talking about deniability here and the ability to prove your innocence."

"What about me?" said Mergers and Acquisitions.

"Yes, sir?" he said. "What is your name?"

"Alfred Falsgraf. I do M and A. I was with Tommy Gray last night about five-thirty and again at eight as we talked about the firm's most vital M and A case. We were together for maybe fifteen minutes. Do I need counsel?"

"I think you do," Hemet said without hesitation. "Incidentally," he tacked on, "Does anybody know whether Mr. Gray was right- or left-handed?"

"Left-handed," Inga immediately said.

"Left," said Falsgraf. "He always sat beside me at Thursday lunch. It was an effort banging elbows as we ate. I'm right-handed. We fought it out every week," he added with a sad smile. "God, I miss Tommy already."

"Well," Frank said, "his being left-handed is interesting. I say this because the gun in his office is beneath his right hand. If he shot himself, he did it using his right hand."

"Jesus!" said Arnie. "Man, I'm so glad you're on our side, Hemet."

Hemet looked from face to face. "Any ideas about that?"

"Strange," they all agreed. "Unexplainable. Makes little sense."

Inga pursed her lips and blew a stream of air. "Wow."

Hemet said, "It wouldn't be unheard of for someone to shoot themself with their weak hand, but it would be awkward. People who commit suicide almost always make double sure they don't survive and go to extra lengths to make sure the manner of death is foolproof. That's why it bothers me he used his weak hand to shoot himself. We'll leave that one for the police to figure out."

"Now, I want my own lawyer," Arnie said. "Mr. Hemet, you can go home now. You just earned your salary for a year."

"You're suggesting there's a killer loose among us?" Falsgraf said with a slight lisp. "I dislike this, period. Was I the last one with him last night? Oh, my God."

"Don't panic," Hemet said. "My observation is probably easily explained away. Maybe he ate left-handed and did other things with his right. It happens."

Falsgraf said to Arnie, "I'm with you. I'm lawyering up. Wait, Mr. Hemet—"

"—Frank, please."

"Frank, please answer this. Why can't you act as the criminal lawyer for everyone in the firm? Wouldn't that work?"

"No," Hemet said. "There will be conflicts among you all."

"And a lawyer cannot represent clients with conflicting interests. Got it."

"Three bonus points for you," Arnie said with a yawn he did not cover. "You're a lawyer, Falstaff—"—purposely calling him by the name of a once-popular beer. "You should know these things without stopping to think about it."

"Given the right hand, left-hand question," Hemet said, "it would likely be a good idea for us all to return to our offices and start calling criminal lawyers—just to be safe. And Mr. Challis, leave the building. Go somewhere they can't locate you because I don't want you giving a statement just yet. You're a political representative of Gray, and whatever you say will impact the firm's contract with DOJ. So you disappear. Inga and I will hunt down the lead detective and give an official firm statement. They'll be after that any minute, anyway. So the rest of you should head on out. Now."

Inga Kopovsky stood aside while the group rose and headed for the door with Roman Challis in the lead. When they were gone, and it was just the two of them, she sat down. They could hear the police calling to each other in the hallway outside. He held a finger to his lips. She crossed her legs and pulled a cigarette out of her jacket pocket. She lit up and blew smoke at the wall and said in a whisper, "If they swab his penis," she said slowly and judiciously, "they'll find my DNA on him."

"So, you were lovers."

"Sometimes yes, sometimes no. We fought like cats and dogs."

"Who all knows you fought?"

She took a deep drag and held it down. Then, in a long exhale, she said, smoke creeping out from beneath her shiny white teeth, "Our computers know. We fought by email."

"They'll have his computer locked away already," Hemet said, picturing the police he knew were already at work in Gray's office.

"I know. I'm sunk."

"Without giving me details, when was the last time you fought?"

"Last night. When I left him, I was in a fury, and so was he. 'You deserve to have someone just step up and shoot you,' were my parting words to him. Jesus, Joseph, and Mary."

"Indeed. Not good at all because it's on the CCTV video. What did you fight about?"

"Top-secret documents."

"What about them?"

"I was afraid they were going to be disclosed."

"Disclosed? By Tommy?"

"That's right."

Hemet moved on without following up. There was more, but he didn't want to know it just then. "When was the last email you received from Gray?"

"Midnight. Tommy said he should just shoot himself if I felt that way. Something to that effect."

"Oh. Not good, Inga."

"You will be my lawyer."

"I will?"

"I'm speaking as the second chairman. You now represent me. Don't worry. I'll pay your usual fee."

"Let's talk about it."

She shook her head and tapped ash into her cupped hand. "No need to talk. You're my guy."

Hemet had to ask. "Inga, if I may, how old are you?"

"Fifty-two. I practice tax law and have for nearly thirty years."

"And Tommy Gray was seventy?"

"Yes. Just."

She cocked her head and looked at him. Then a smile crossed her face. "Oh, come on, say it."

"What? No, I wasn't—"

"Yes, you were. What are two old coots thinking, doing it on the desk at fifty-two and seventy."

"I wasn't thinking exactly that," Hemet said, and he felt somewhat outsmarted, for she had got the truth out of him. That couldn't happen again, he thought, with a newfound respect for Inga Kopovsky.

"We had makeup sex, if you must know."

"When?"

She smiled and stubbed her cigarette out in a cut crystal glass.

"This morning at five in his office. Yes, he was as alive as he ever got when we screwed. I can attest to that."

"What happened after that?"

"I went home to change for work."

"And you came back, and he was dead?"

"Pretty much. Does that make me a suspect?"

Hemet's forehead furrowed as he gave it his best thinking.

"Maybe the strongest suspect." He at last said.

"So, what do I do?"

"Get yourself a real lawyer and don't talk to the police. Ever."

"I said you were my lawyer."

"You don't want me. I'm not that kind of lawyer."

"What kind are you then?"

"Not that kind."

There was a knock on the door. Hemet answered and found himself face to face with two suited-up detectives, badge lanyards around their necks, notepads at the ready. Hemet blocked the door.

"We've got a problem right outta the gate," said the deeply tanned detective just returned from Cabo. "The serial number on the Mossberg shotgun is filed off. So we're looking for a metal file with filings to match the gun's metal. Where do we start?"

Hemet said, "I suggest you start with a search warrant. After you have probable cause, which you don't."

The detectives traded a look. "So that's how you wanna play this?" said the detective with no tan.

"Is there any other way?" stated Hemet. He smiled at the detectives. "You are on notice that I represent all attorneys and staff in this law firm. You are on notice you are not to speak to any of them outside my presence. Now leave our building and don't come back without a search warrant," he finished and shut the door on them.

"You lied," said Inga, "you *are* that kind of lawyer."

"Suppose you show me to my new office."

Lawyers in Gray: Chapter Two

MILES STANDISH

My name is Miles Standish, and I was once the managing partner at Frank Hemet's new employer, Gray law. Top secret documents had walked out of Gray while I headed up the 700-lawyer firm. The papers had surfaced inside the files of our adversary, a group of Russians who were fracking American oil and gas deposits.

The mess was blamed on me, as it happened on my watch. I had no idea who the guilty party was, and I had no idea how to catch them. I wasn't a spy and didn't know the first thing about spying. That was all about to change.

I was fired, and Tommy Gray took over until his death. His time at the helm was about three months, give or take. During that time, I fumed and fought back feelings that threatened to load my gun and send me back to the law firm and start shooting. As an Afghanistan combat veteran, I was pretty capable of gunning down those who had voted me out.

The week after Tommy's death, the US Attorney hit me with a grand jury subpoena. So I waited for my day, then drove downtown and parked in witness parking at the US District Court building on Constitution Avenue.

The time was 8:57 when I arrived outside the grand jury room. I was escorted inside by an overweight US Marshal who kept his hand on his gun the whole time he steered me to the witness chair as if I were incapable of finding it on my own. I was sure the grand jury noticed.

The Assistant US Attorney with the shaved head drank down his cold coffee and wiped his mouth on his navy coat sleeve. His name was Llewelyn Jewel, and he projected the unbelieving voice all feds were taught to use, and said to me, "Your name is Miles Standish?"

"Correct," I answered, steadying my voice.

"Narrowing down, now. While you were the managing partner at Gray law, top-secret government documents entrusted to your firm wound up in Russian hands, is that correct?"

"Correct."

"Suppose you tell the grand jury how that happened."

"I don't know how it happened."

"Suppose you tell the grand jury how you sold those documents to the Russians."

"I did not."

"I believe you're lying. Let me tell you why."

"Well, that's fair-minded," I said sarcastically. I was there for target practice, I realized.

He dropped his cheaters over his gray eyes. "I have examined your 2018 tax return, Mr. Standish. The return includes what the IRS calls a LUQ—a large, unexplained, questionable deposit. Your deposit is November 17, 2018, for $225,000. Does that ring a bell?"

"It does."

"What is that deposit about?"

"I did off-site work for a client."

"Off-site?"

"On my own time. Gray law allowed us 100 hours of off-site work a year. What we earned, we kept."

"Client name?"

"Privileged. I can't tell you that."

"Would it be Western Energy Reserves?" That was the Russian fracking group using a common American-style name.

"Same answer."

"Could it have been payment for top-secret documents you sold?" He looked at the jury, telling them here came the key point.

"No."

"Isn't it true you were fired from Gray law because you were thought to be guilty of selling documents?"

"I've heard that rumor. But I don't know the exact reason I was let go."

"Come now. Are we sure about that?"

"Yes."

"A little background into your job at Gray law. Tell the jury your version of the Russian invasion, as you've been known to call it, Mr. Standish. The jury wants to hear more about the Russians."

"Well, Russian wildcatters came to the US in 2014. They were a flood of locusts. They managed to toxify an Oklahoma lake and my firm was hired by the DOJ to help stop them. We received Top Secret government records. Long story short, these records turned up in the Russian files. We had leaked."

"So you admit they came from your law firm, Mr. Standish. Would I be right?"

"So it would seem."

"And what did DHS do when it found out its documents were leaked? What did the EPA do?"

"The EPA panicked over the leak. They called me in and told me they would sever all ties with Gray law unless the firm took significant security measures. I returned to Gray and called an emergency board meeting. The board's immediate response was it needed to take decisive action to show the EPA we were cleaning up our law firm. They decided I would be the burnt offering and voted me out 3-2. Then they voted in Tommy Gray as the new Chairman. Tommy had served ten years in Army Intelligence in Iraq. The board rallied around Tommy, the son of the founder of Gray law. The board could trust Tommy to turn the ship around. The irony was, so could I."

"How close were they to exposing you? Isn't it true you were the one selling documents?"

"No."

"Did you have any off-shore bank accounts in 2018?"

"None."

"Have you had any since?"

"None."

"I'm ready to eat lunch. We're going to lunch now. You're excused now, Mr. Standish. We will contact you for fingerprinting and DNA samples and a mug shot."

"Am I being arrested?"

"I can't say. Have a nice lunch."

Just like that, the grand jury had departed, and Llewelyn Jewel turned away, leaving me sitting in the witness chair, looking half guilty just because I was a lawyer. I was a target, a person who might be indicted at any minute.

I gathered my things and thought back to the day I was

let go from Gray law. It was pretty damn demeaning. The memory is painful, but it came to mind whenever I was trying to switch gears and think about something pleasant, like my greenhouse plants.

After they fired me, my secretary loaded my junk drawer and ego wall in a cardboard box that said *Amazon* on the side. We hugged goodbye. She cried and told me I'd be back. Then, I was climbing into my Mercedes in the basement. I pressed the starter button on the dashboard and let out a long sigh. 'Well, this sucks,' I said. I was forty-four, unemployed, and in a marriage that was dying a slow death.

I headed home.

I was days away from becoming a spy but I had no clue.

Lawyers in Gray: Chapter Three

BENJI

I left the courthouse feeling sick to my stomach and confused about how I'd come across. Did I look like the ordinary spy trading US secrets for Russian rubles? How did the grand jury perceive me? They must have noticed my trembling hands and fluttery voice—which would make me look guilty as hell.

Driving along Constitution Avenue, I switched on my blinker for Pennsylvania Avenue when my phone chimed. A new text. Ordinarily, I would never have looked at it while I was driving, but there was always the off-chance it was Benji, so I tapped the screen for text messages.

Sure enough, a message from Benji. He was my ten-year-old Little Brother, and his texts and calls got top priority. Especially since Immanuel Rayito had moved back into Benji's house. He was a thug Benji's mother kept around for God only knows what. Big Brother Big Sisters had existed in DC since I was a young lawyer learning how to patty-cake. A community mentoring program matched kids from low-income, single-parent households with adult volunteer mentors. Most mentors were in their twenties. I had stuck around longer than that because there were never enough Big Brother men to go around and because Deonna couldn't have kids, so I got my fathering with Big Brother. But the real reason: I'd once had a Big Brother, and he'd changed my life.

So I pulled over and texted Benji back. Do you want to meet? I asked him. Almost immediately, the text came back, "roger." We had a spot near his low-income housing, our special meeting place. We never varied. We always went to Smitty's Cafe.

His home was Carver Terrace on Maryland NE. Twenty minutes later, I pulled into the lot at Smitty's, parked, and went inside. Smells of fried, fatty hamburger, scalded coffee, Lysol, and greasy menus. I would have to send the clothes I wore to the cleaners after the visit, for they wouldn't be fit to wear again.

It didn't take me long to find him standing slumped on his right hip at the jukebox, feeding quarters (where was he getting quarters?), bringing up Kanye and Jay-Z and Snoop. Hey, it was his quarter, so why would I tell him his sounds sucked? I came up behind him and grabbed his shoulders. He turned his head and smiled. "You came."

"I always come. One of these years, you'll get that. There's a table by the kitchen door. Let's grab it."

We did, and soon we had coffee, pie, and cherry Cokes on the way. I gave him space, letting him talk about his text when he was ready. First, we did the Wizards. I followed them religiously for Benji. Then we decided on the next movie we'd catch. Then a long discussion about why he couldn't put on weight and try out for football in September. He was very undersized for his age group (50th percentile) but determined he'd be 90th by August. His regimen consisted of protein shakes, malts, and weight-lifting to build muscle. But those things cost money, and he had none. I looked at his undersized frame and was filled with despair and a great tenderness for my boy. He just didn't get it. He had suffered malnutrition at a younger age, and his growth had stopped. I'd already had him to a nutritionist and a physical therapist for guidance in athletic training. But his damaged body just wouldn't jump back into the growth spurts enjoyed by healthy ten-year-olds. So we kept searching for answers.

"So, Immanuel kicked my ass last night." He looked away, maybe to avoid the rise he knew this would get. His mahogany skin, short braids, and flawless face made him look even younger than his ten years. It was all I could do to keep myself from swooping him up and taking him away from his worthless mother, and raising him myself. He needed it. Maybe I did, too.

"Did he break anything? Are you pissing blood? Do we need to go to the ER?"

"It wasn't like that. He used his belt." Benji turned in the booth and pulled up his shirt, showing me his back. Long, angry striations ran vertically and horizontally on his skin. Someone had played tic-tac-toe on my boy's back. I was instantly enraged. The soldier inside of me, the one who'd done two combat tours in Afghanistan, boiled up. I would kill the stepfather who came and went in Benji's household.

"Get up. We're going to talk to him."

"No, bro, he'll kill me for telling you."

"No, he won't. I'm going to put the fear in him."

"Like what, dude?"

"Like a gun up his ass."

"Wow. Now I want to be there."

"Drink up your Coke, and let's go."

I stood and tossed a twenty on the table and headed for the door. Benji caught up. We climbed into my Mercedes and headed off for the Carver Terrace on Maryland Avenue.

We didn't talk as we weaved in and out of rush hour traffic. Finally, we pulled into the parking lot for the paper-bag-brown Carver Towers and parked. Benji reached over and touched my arm. "You really carrying?"

"No."

"Immanuel be carrying a razor. He'll cut you, Mr. Standish."

"We'll see about that." I went around my car, popped the trunk, and grabbed the tire iron. "We'll see about him and his razor. Take me to your number."

We climbed concrete and steel stairs up to the fourth floor—the elevators had been out for weeks. Benji slipped his key in the knob, and in we went.

Sure enough, Immanuel was lying back on the couch reading the sports page and listening to ESPN. He was no sports enthusiast. He was a gambler—betting twenties on sporting events.

He turned his head. "What's this, Ben? You bring the man wit choo?"

"I'm not the man. I'm the Big Brother. And if you ever touch this boy again, I'm coming back, and I'm going to bash your fucking head in. You feel me?"

"I feel you, dog, but that's fucked up." He climbed up from the couch and came around to get in my space. My hand tightened on my tire iron. Just try it, I thought. Come on, come on.

He flicked his wrist, and an eight-inch switchblade flashed between us. "So. You got the tire tool. I got the blade. Who goes first, honky?"

"That would be me. I'm going to hit you once and knock your fucking brains out of your ugly fucking head, so you never touch Benji again. Get it?"

He leaned away when he saw my anger. "It not like that, dog. The boy had it coming."

"Why did a ten-year-old boy have an assault and battery coming from a prick like you?"

"He lifted five dollar out my wallet."

"Like hell he did. Benji's no petty thief like you."

"Watch that mouth, honky."

"Do something. Do anything. Come on." I was so ready to beat him bloody. Just come on! My mind was screaming. I raised the tire iron, and he stepped back two steps.

"You crazy, nigger."

"I am crazy. I love this kid, and I hate child abusers. Next time, I bring a gun, and you're going down. That's a promise, dog."

"Try me, dude."

"When I leave, if I ever hear again you've touched Benji —or his mother, I'm coming back for you, and I'm going to hurt you, fuckhead. Now get out of my sight."

He was caught between wanting to attack me and wanting me to go away. So he stepped back and went back to his newspaper."

I headed for the entrance, where I stopped and shook hands with Benji. We always shook hands now. He'd let me know when we'd outgrown hugs over a year ago. Now it was handshakes and a look into the other guy's eyes, just like I taught him.

"Call me," was all I said.

"Good on you, bro," he whispered back.

"Call me."

I went home and made some calls. For one, I had my

investigator from my old firm take on the investigation of Philomena Rashad, Benji's mother. I told him I wanted her watched for a month. All the time she spent at home; all the time she spent away or flat didn't come home at night. Photos of everyone coming and going, especially men. Track her at her work. Does she have a real job? Is she someone who's leaving for work in the morning but diverting to the underworld, the world of hard women and even harder drugs? Why was I doing all this? Because I wanted Benji, and the time would come when I'd need this information about her.

Two hours later, I called Benji's cell.

"How's it going over there?"

"I'm trying to do my math problems. Immanuel left right after you. He didn't say where he was going."

"Do you have food?"

"Not really. There are some spaghetti noodles. I eat those with salt and ketchup sometimes."

"Jesus. I'm on my way. I'll text you when I'm downstairs."

"Where we going?"

"We're going to get you something to eat. I'm thinking Safeway, and I'm thinking of a week of food. Stuff you can prepare."

"I don't know if I can wait that long, honest, Mr. Standish."

"Miles, Benji. I'm Miles to you. And if you can't wait, we'll hit a drive-through and get whatever you like. Then the grocery store. Then we can take a look at your math problems."

"Wow. Okay."

"Have you heard from mama?"

"Not since last Wednesday. Over a week ago. I'm shitting bricks they're gonna come tell me she's dead. Every time I hear someone out in the hallway, I say a prayer. The same prayer every time, and so far it's working."

"Do you think we should call children's social services? I'm leaning that way."

"No! They'll put me in foster care that's worse than here. You promised you'd never do that to me. Don't forget."

"I did make that promise. But I'm wondering if we should reconsider."

"That sounds like lawyer talk, Miles, that reconsider. A deal's a deal. There is no reconsider to real people."

"You're right, Benji. So I'm at Rochester and Grand. I'll be at your place in ten minutes. Look for a text and come right down."

I didn't tell him I hated his neighborhood at night, that it scared me. But he probably already had that figured out-- Benji was wise way beyond his years.

"I'll come right down. Goodbye."

We shopped Giant that night, then hit Jack in the Box and picked up ten tacos and drinks, then back to Benji's, where we escaped the porch sitters and made it upstairs. The math book took up the rest of our time that night. I left for home at ten.

Benji was admiring his stuffed cabinets in the kitchen as I closed the door behind me.

Good for him.

Grab your copy…
vinci-books.com/lawyersingray

About the Author

John Ellsworth is a attorney turned author. His legal thrillers have sold more than three million copies, achieving bestseller status.

He lives on the west coast of the United States, where he continues to thrill readers with his edge-of-your seat courtroom dramas.